Contents

CHAPTER ONE

The Windy City

ALONE AND IN THE DARK, Ernie pressed his back against the building. It was windier than he'd expected and he could see his breath in the swirling snow. A storm was coming. The narrow ledge was caked with ice and the cold seeped through his sneakers. Six stories below, snow carpeted the alley. Even the garbage cans looked like soft sculptures. Shivering, he zipped his jacket to his chin, then inched along the ledge. The snow shushed with each step, while his fingers, stiff with cold, struggled to grip the crevices between the bricks. He blew into his hands, warming them, then pivoted carefully and grabbed hold of a drainpipe. Wrapping his legs around the pipe, he shinnied up the icy pole to the top of the tenement.

He hurried across the rooftop, his feet disappearing in the snow. No matter how many times he made the jump, it still scared him, and tonight the roof was slick and the wind gusting. He picked up speed, sprinting toward the edge of the building, then he was in the air, pumping his legs across the fifteen-foot chasm. He landed hard on the roof of the adjacent building, tumbling in the snow, then he was running again. He didn't stop until he reached the abandoned water tank.

This was the place he came to get away from Mrs. McGinty and her rules and regulations—the place that kept him from going crazy. From here, he could see the downtown skyscrapers, the lights from O'Hare Airport and, only a few blocks away, Wrigley Field, now dark and dormant.

Ernie pried back a rusted corner of sheet metal and crawled into his hideaway. The roof was missing, but the tank shielded him from the wind. He retrieved a blanket and scrap of carpet he'd stashed and shook off the snow. Wrapping the blanket around his shoulders, he stretched out on the carpet and looked up at the stars. There was something familiar and comforting about gazing at the constellations, like looking into the faces of old friends. It made him feel a part of something bigger.

Ernie pulled two Christmas cookies from his pocket and ate them slowly, savoring every bite. He wondered why he was still stuck at the Lakeside Home for Boys. Other kids left for foster homes, some were adopted, and a few even got to return to their real moms and dads. But not him. He'd been there ten years, and Mrs. McGinty said he had no one to blame but himself. According to her, they'd tried many times to find him a home, but no one had wanted him. Now he was considered a "lifer," a permanent ward of the state. Ernie felt like his mother was the city of Chicago and his father the state of Illinois.

It started to snow again and he tried to catch a flake on his tongue. He thought about running away while everyone was asleep. *Where would I go?* He'd already run away more times than he could count. The first time he was only six. The police found him in a little park on the south side, sitting in a muddy puddle, crying. They'd brought him back to Lakeside. They always brought him back to Lakeside. Mrs. McGinty told him he was born with a restless soul, and left it at that.

Ernie stood up and shook off the snow, stowed his blanket, then crawled out of his hideaway. The first light of day was reaching across the rooftops of Chicago. To the east, he could see Lake Michigan, a lake so big it seemed to go on forever. He wondered if his mother and father were out there, somewhere. He didn't understand why they'd given him away, but he figured it was something he must have done.

With a deep sigh, he hurried back across the roof.

Feeling like a cat burglar, Ernie slipped through the window into the sixth-floor dormitory. He tiptoed across the room past twenty-five sleeping boys. He was quick and steady and secret. When he reached his bed, he kicked off his sneakers, then wriggled out of his damp jeans, T-shirt, and sweater. His hand-me-down clothes never quite fit, and his disheveled hair was forever in need of a cut. He had hazel eyes that seemed to change color, depending on the light. When he smiled, which wasn't often, his whole face lit up.

Shivering, Ernie slipped beneath the covers, then glanced at the boy sleeping in the adjacent bed. Nate yawned and looked at him with sleepy eyes. "Where'd you go?" he whispered.

Ernie pointed toward the ceiling.

"You're crazy, it must be freezing up there."

Nate LeCroix was a skinny African American kid from St. Louis with a runny nose and an easy smile. He was the only other person in the whole world who knew about Ernie's secret place, even though he'd never actually gone there. He said he wasn't about to jump across any buildings, no matter how great it was.

Nate's parents had died in a car accident shortly after moving to Chicago, and the court had placed him at Lakeside in September. He'd been assigned the bed next to Ernie and they'd become friends. Nate liked to talk and Ernie liked to listen. Ernie especially loved to hear him talk about his mother and father and growing up by the Mississippi River.

Ernie stared at a crack in the ceiling. "I had that dream again."

"The one with the humongous tree all lit up like Christmas?"

He nodded. "And there was a big face in the rock and she talked to me again. And there was water. Water everywhere."

Outside, a snow sweeper rattled past. Ernie pulled the covers tight, trying to get warm.

"Hey, Ernie," Nate whispered. "Merry Christmas. And happy birthday."

"Oh, yeah. Thanks."

But Christmas wasn't really his birthday, and Ernie wasn't even his real name.

Twelve Years, Nine Months,
and Five Days Earlier . . .

CHAPTER TWO

The Crystal Acorn

T HE TROUBLE ALL STARTED up in the woods on the plateau overlooking the Warbling River. It was the first night of spring, a night when the wind rustled through the treetops as if mother earth were whispering a secret she could no longer keep. The stars seemed so close it felt like the Big Dipper wanted to scoop the river with its glittering pan. But something was very peculiar—even though there wasn't a single cloud in the sky, it was raining.

It wasn't a harsh rain, but a gentle one that pattered the canopy of the forest ridge. Deep inside that forest was an old oak tree, its trunk so wide that even ten people stretching their arms couldn't reach around its waist. At the foot of the tree, nestled between two gnarly roots, was a puddle. Waves rippled outward from its center. And that was another peculiar thing, because there wasn't a trace of a breeze on the forest floor.

Then, in the blink of an eye, two tiny creatures jumped feetfirst out of the puddle, landing softly on the mossy ground. Clutching the short ends of a forked stick, they shook themselves like two puppies after a bath, then stretched on their tiptoes to full height, which was barely eleven inches tall. Their faces were kindly, with sparkling turquoise eyes, their skin an earthy brown, their chestnut hair long and wild. A translucent webbing stretched between their sturdy fingers and toes, and the soles of their feet were like the pads on a dog's paw. They wore patchwork shirts made from water lilies, duckweed, and marsh fern, and leggings of redtop and yellow foxtail. Around their waists were tree-bark belts with curious tools and pouches. The Puddlejumpers jabbered anxiously in a language unfamiliar to the human ear, but even in the hubbub you could hear that she called him "Root," and he called her "Runnel."

The forked stick suddenly took on a life of its own, lifting to the sky and vibrating with a deep resonant hum. With both Jumpers hanging on for their lives, it wove back and forth across the dome of stars, searching for a destination. Wedged between the two short ends of the Y-shaped stick was an acorn. It wasn't an ordinary acorn, brown with a snug cap—this was an ice-blue crystal acorn.

When the stick finally locked on to the Big Dipper, the Acorn shimmered with a piercing white light. Root and Runnel shared a frightened look just before the stick lurched across the forest floor, dragging them behind, their toes barely skimming the ground. The bright glow of the Acorn helped light the way as they galloped headlong through the oak and pine, sending rabbits and field mice scurrying in their wake.

The Acorn stick led the Puddlejumpers out of the forest and down the slope of a muddy field. They slipped and slid over a crop of newly sprouted wheat, then skittered past a corral, barn, and silo nestled in a copse of elm and willow trees. They spun to a stop in front of a one-story farmhouse, its porch brushed silver in the moonlight. All was quiet, except for the pattering rain and a cow mooing from the barn, until a woman's piercing cry shattered the night. The Jumpers wanted to flee back to the sanctuary of their puddle, but knew they couldn't.

Pitch, the old black-and-white border collie asleep on the porch, lifted her nose to sniff, but the Puddlejumpers were already around back, jumping up and down trying to see through a lit window. Root caught hold of the sill and clambered onto the ledge. He offered Runnel his hand, and quicker than a twinkling, she was beside him.

Breathing hard, they pressed their noses against the windowpane, fogging the glass. They had to wipe away their breath before they could see inside. In that moment they knew the Crystal Acorn had delivered them at the perfectly perfect time. Before their eyes a miracle was taking place. A human baby was being born. A boy.

A cloud burst and the rain began to fall in torrents. Blinking back tears, Root and Runnel warbled so joyfully that animals in the neighboring fields paused to listen.

The Puddlejumpers had found their Rainmaker.

CHAPTER THREE

The Prophecy

OLD DOC THORPE, lanky with dark eyes in a long, thin face, knew the mother was in trouble. He gave the newborn to Clara Bonnell, the chubby midwife who'd delivered almost as many babies as he had. The baby was wet and kicking and crying with life, but his mother lay still as stone. Dolores had lost too much blood giving birth, and now Doc Thorpe saw that she was slipping away. Clara made the call to 911, but the ambulance in West Branch would take close to an hour to reach the house. Doc felt for her pulse. There was none, so he started CPR, filling Dolores' lungs with air, then pushing on her chest multiple times. Russ Frazier, lean and ruggedly handsome, his face tanned from a life spent working in his fields, watched from the foot of the bed in shocked silence. Doc did every-thing he could to bring her back, but knew in his heart she was already gone. He just didn't know how to stop trying.

After several minutes, Doc and Clara shared a look of sorrow as Russ sank to his knees beside the bed. He gazed in disbelief at his beloved wife, her expression peaceful. He gently brushed the damp hair from her forehead, then took her hand and pressed it to his lips. And although he could hear Doc Thorpe's voice behind him—"I'm so sorry, Russ"—he couldn't answer, as if time itself had stopped.

In Russ' mind, it was that blustery autumn afternoon when he and Dolores walked along the Warbling River. She was thirteen and he was fifteen. He told her that he was going to marry her someday. She laughed, but let him hold her hand.

The memory made his heart ache from the inside out, and now the tears came.

An hour later, Russ felt Doc's hand on his shoulder.

"I have to be getting on, Russ," said Doc. "Agnes Goetz has come down with pneumonia and I've got to look in on her."

Doc didn't expect Russ to get up, but he did. They'd been good friends for many years, despite their age dif-ference. In fact, Doc was the very man who'd brought

Russ into the world thirty-one years before.

Russ led Doc through the kitchen to the back porch, where they embraced. "I'll call Floyd and make the arrangements," said Doc somberly. "He should be here within the hour. Clara, she'll stay the night."

Numb to the world, Russ nodded, barely hearing the baby's wail from the bedroom. Doc opened the screen door. What they saw next surprised both men. Dangling from the eaves was a curious mobile: seven handcrafted wooden elves surrounding a finely cut, ice-blue crystal acorn. The carvings were precise and vivid, each face alive with expression. The Acorn itself was cradled in a woolen harness decorated with an oak tree insignia.

Doc gently tugged the harness and the elves began to dance around the Acorn. The men were so mesmerized, neither one noticed that the baby had stopped crying. It was quiet again, except for the rain and Doc's subdued voice. "Looks like Charlie Woodruff's work. God bless him, he carved a beaut for your little one." The Acorn refracted the porch light into a million tiny rainbows that swirled across their faces. "I knew he was carving, but nothing like this," said Doc. "What's that acorn—crystal?"

"Looks to be," said Russ.

Doc tapped it with a finger. "Hard as a diamond."

Blinking back tears, Russ unfastened the mobile from its perch. The elder man squeezed his friend's shoulder. "I'll stop by in the morning."

Russ watched Doc open his umbrella and, dodging puddles, hustle to his old sedan. Pitch was chasing in circles as if she'd caught a scent, but when she saw Doc she gave up her search and went over to lick his hand. He gave the dog a scratch behind the ears. "Hey, girl—you take care of Russ now, hear me?"

Pitch wagged her tail and started back to the porch. Doc settled into his car, then, with a last wave to Russ, motored up the drive.

Russ watched the sedan's taillights disappear in the rain. Normally he loved the rain. To a farmer, rain meant nourishment, growth, even life itself. But not tonight. Tonight it was only dark and wet and dreary.

Russ called to Pitch, "C'mon, girl, let's go." He wanted her inside tonight. He thought he might find some comfort hearing her familiar breathing as she slept at the foot of his bed. He held the mobile up to the light and felt over-whelmed. *Dolores would have loved a gift like this.* Brushing away tears, he carried it into the house.

Near the corral, beyond the reach of the porch light, Root and Runnel sighed with relief. They'd accomplished every-thing they'd set out to do. The Crystal Acorn was exactly where it belonged—inside, with the human baby.

When the porch light went out, they climbed to the

top of a fence post and stared at the house, burdened by the enormous task before them. As a rule, Puddlejumpers stayed away from humans, and Root and Runnel were no exception. In fact, if you asked them, they would tell you that they were just two very ordinary and unremarkable Puddlejumpers who were now faced with the awesome responsibility of watching over the Rainmaker.

Now everything was up to them, for the ancient prophecy had begun.

On the first night of spring he will take his first breath,
beneath the Big Dipper, finding life where there's death.
We will call him Wawaywo, our Rainmaker son,
and keep him with us till the last battle is won.

CHAPTER FOUR

Keeping Watch

T HE WHOLE NEXT MORNING, Root and Runnel
spied through a knothole in the side of the barn. They were
deathly afraid of the humans and terrified of being caught.
Just when they finally made the decision to cross the yard,
humans with sad faces began to arrive with platters of food.

"*Wataka mala-ki, Wawaywo,*" said Root.

"*Mabaa-way,*" agreed Runnel. They needed to get to the
baby.

The Jumpers spent the rest of the day discussing their
predicament under a big black-and-white cow. The more
they talked, the more nervous they got. The more nervous
they got, the more milk they drank. Before long, they were
fast asleep in the hay.

In the evening, after everyone had left, the Puddlejumpers finally stirred from their nest and made their way across the yard. They climbed the trellis to the roof and settled inside the rain gutter. Peering down, they could see the father at the kitchen table with the baby in his arms. He was laughing and crying at the same time, which seemed strange to them, even for a human. They watched intently as the chubby one came into the room, took the baby, and disappeared down the hall.

They scampered up the shingles to the crest of the roof, then down to another window, but the curtains were drawn and they couldn't see a thing. When the Rainmaker started to cry, they knew they'd have to go inside.

It was probably a good thing that Russ had the baby to look after, otherwise he might have just given up. All he did was sit in the rocker by the crib, give the baby his bottle, and rock him when he cried. It was a painful sight for anybody who knew him. Russ Frazier was a man of contagious laughter and boundless optimism. If you needed help, he was the first person you called. If you were feeling down, he'd sit at your kitchen table till you felt better. When your glass was half empty, he was the one who filled it.

Now he was the one in need, and neighbors came streaming over with food and clothes and diapers and toys. The baby lacked for nothing, except what he needed most, his mother.

Betty Woodruff was a quiet comfort to Russ. She and her husband, Charlie, lived one farm over from the Fraziers', and the families had been close all through the years. In fact, Betty and Russ had gone through high school together. Now she was pregnant, but that didn't stop her from bringing over a home-cooked meal just about every night.

The Goetz family did most of the farm chores. Emil and Elsie, with the help of their son Neal, irrigated the wheat, milked the cows, collected the eggs, and took care of the pigs and horses. Together, they helped keep the farm on its feet. That's how it was in Circle, people helping each other without expecting any favors in return.

Three weeks passed, and people up and down the Warbling River plateau were concerned that Russ, lost in his grief, still hadn't named the baby. Betty stopped over with strawberries and fresh cream, but her real purpose was to discuss the matter of the nameless baby. This indecision was so unlike him. Growing up, Russ had been the first at everything—first to drive a tractor, first to win a blue ribbon at the county fair, he was even the first boy in their class to kiss a girl. She knew that because she was the one he'd surprised with a smooch when they were in the second grade.

Betty was mustering her courage to speak up when the wall ironing board swung down and plunked Russ on the head. It startled them both and they couldn't help but laugh. When the screen door mysteriously banged open and shut, they laughed even harder. It was a glimpse of the old Russ and she knew right then that he was going to be okay. They spent a fun afternoon trying out names. In the end, Russ decided to name the baby Francis, after his father.

But before going to sleep that night, Russ came upon the book Dolores had last been reading. Paging through it, he found a slip of paper with a list of names in her handwriting, one of which was circled.

Shawn.

It was as if Dolores were touching his shoulder and whispering the name in his ear. That was the last time he cried, thankful that he could fulfill her final wish.

The next morning, Russ bundled up baby Shawn and walked out behind the barn, where the elm and willow trees announced themselves, their buds a brilliant newborn green. Feeling the warmth of the sun on his face, Russ told Shawn about his mother as he gathered some flowers from Dolores' garden: wild violets, the first of the sweet peas, a few daffodils, and her favorite, the tulips. When his bouquet was complete, he buckled Shawn into the pickup, then traveled the road along the Warbling River into town.

Circle, Illinois, was a thriving place and well loved by its inhabitants. Located on State Highway 99, there were two churches, an elementary school, a Handy Hardware, and a bar called the Willow Lounge. The post office was on the corner next to a little dress shop, All Dressed Up, that Ginny Hawkins kept open when she could. The only restaurant was the Turkey Roost, known for its Thanksgiving dinners all year round, complete with live turkeys in the pen out back.

At the far end of town, Russ gassed up at the Sinclair station, where Roy told a knock-knock joke while cleaning the windshield. Russ returned the favor by narrating a diaper-changing adventure that soon had his friend bent over in laughter. Afterward, Russ went across the street to the Trading Post for groceries. Although it had only been a few weeks since he'd been in town, it felt like a lot longer. His friends, relieved to see him up and about, fawned over the new baby and did their best to act like nothing else had changed.

At the little cemetery just outside of town, Russ placed the spring bouquet on his wife's grave. He kissed his son on the top of his head and tried to be thankful for all that was good in his life. "Let's get home, little one."

On the way back, Russ decided to do something he should have done weeks before. As he pulled into the Woodruffs' drive, Betty and Charlie came out to greet him. Betty rocked Shawn on the porch swing, while Russ and Charlie settled on the steps with muffins and fresh cups of coffee.

"Shawn and I have been wanting to thank you for that beautiful mobile you carved," said Russ.

"Mobile?" asked Charlie, puzzled.

"Yeah, the one you left on my porch—little elves around an acorn. It's a work of art."

"I'd like to see it, but I sure didn't carve it."

"Well, if you didn't, who did?"

"Beats me," said Charlie as he got up and went into the kitchen. "But we do have a little gift for Shawn." He returned with a wooden rattle decorated with fanciful farm animals in pink and blue. "I carved it and Betty did the painting."

"It's from that cherry tree Emil lost in the tornado last year," added Betty.

Russ gave it a playful shake. "The tree lives on!"

Betty laughed. "If he breaks it, you can plant a new one—those are cherry seeds inside." She kept Shawn busy with the rattle while Russ and Charlie continued to speculate about who else might have made the mobile, but the identity of the carver remained a mystery.

When Russ got home, he rigged the mobile to the crib rail. He jiggled it, and Shawn watched the elfin figures dance around the Crystal Acorn, just above his head. Russ was having so much fun playing with his son that he barely heard the knock. He went to the back door, where he found Betty holding up a small Snow White lamp. "Look what I found in my attic—a young lady on the lookout for seven little elves. Seen any hanging around?" she joked.

Russ laughed, welcoming her into the kitchen. "Now that you mention it, I have noticed some characters that fit the description. C'mon, let's introduce everybody."

They whistled the chorus to "Whistle While You Work" while Russ clamped Snow White onto the crib next to the elves. The paint was a little tarnished, but when Betty popped in two double AAs and turned on the lamp, the bulb under Snow White's skirt cast a warm glow on Shawn's face and the soft red quilt his mother had made.

Now that he was a single dad with a newborn son, Russ found that working the farm was a lot more complicated. He usually tried to keep Shawn with him, toting him in a baby carrier on his back. On the days he couldn't, he left him with Betty. Each night, after the work was finished, Russ spent the whole evening with Shawn and soon learned to decipher every giggle, gurgle, and grunt. But even with Betty's contributions, raising a baby was more work than he could have imagined. Little did he know he was getting some help on the side.

Root and Runnel had become expert at secreting themselves under beds, inside closets and cupboards, atop curtain rods, behind furniture, and just about any other place an eleven-inch-tall Puddlejumper could think to hide. Whenever Russ was busy or distracted or asleep in the chair next to the crib, they were there to rock the baby to sleep or give him a fresh bottle, burp him, and even change his diapers.

Shawn's eyes always sparkled when they arrived. He loved the warmth of their tiny webbed hands, their earthy smell, and the melodic sound of their voices. Root and Runnel were part of his life, like his red quilt, toy tractor, and the mobile on his crib—and as much a part of his family as his dad.

Everything was going according to Puddlejumper plan, until the morning the baby inexplicably began to cry . . . and cry, and cry . . . that whole day and all through the night. Something was very wrong.

After a thorough examination, Doc Thorpe diagnosed colic. The gripe water he prescribed to settle the baby's tummy had no effect. Nor did any of the home remedies Betty suggested. Not knowing what else to do, Russ tried to comfort Shawn by gently rubbing his belly and singing old nursery rhymes. He spent hours carrying the baby around the house. Still he cried.

When the exhausted father finally passed out on the living room couch, Root and Runnel climbed to the peak of the house. Root pulled an acorn cap from a pouch on his belt and, forming a V with his thumbs, blew an urgent whistle to the horizon. Shawn's wail resounded from the nursery as they sat atop the old weather vane, and waited.

CHAPTER FIVE

Night Visitors

P AV ARRIVED just after midnight. She had a shock of white hair and piercing green eyes and, at fifteen inches, towered over Root and Runnel. She was the only Puddlejumper ever born without webbed hands and feet, and rarely swam because she couldn't keep up with the others. Instead she spent a lot of time in the Up Above collecting plants, roots, bark, and minerals. Whenever a Jumper was hurt or sick, she always knew the right combination of elements to make a curative salve or a restorative soak. She was like a spring-fed lake, calm on the surface with waters that ran clear and deep.

Pav immediately went to work inspecting the baby. He cried as she prodded and poked, peeled back his lids and read his irises, blew in his ears and looked up his nose and tweaked the joints of his fingers and toes. Cooing softly, she pinched precise portions of pollens and herbs from pouches on her belt. She added shavings of water moccasin skin and a mosquito stinger, then mixed everything in her chestnut urn. After dissolving the concoction in an acorn cap of milk, she used a hollow reed to blow the medicine down the baby's throat.

Before departing, Pav gave Runnel a poison oak balm for his diaper rash and an otter-milk formula for his daily feeding.

In the morning, Russ found the baby in his crib with a big smile on his face. The change in his demeanor was like night to day. Russ wondered if Shawn had a guardian angel or if Dolores were helping them from the other side. He was so relieved that he lifted Shawn above his head and waltzed around the room, singing, "Oh what a beautiful morning, oh what a beautiful day, I've got a wonderful feeling, Shawn's tears have all gone away." As usual, there was an audience of two hidden behind the changing table. Root and Runnel had never seen him so happy.

Shawn's sudden cure from the colic was a mystery, but then there were other strange occurrences for which Russ had no explanation. For several weeks he hadn't been getting as much milk from his cows. He regularly gave extra milk to the Woodruffs, but now there was barely enough for his cereal. For the first time in years, he had to buy the store-bought variety in town. Sometimes he found the cartons sitting empty in the refrigerator. One night he came upon a puddle of milk near the open fridge door. There was just no explaining it.

There was also no explaining the toys that somehow found their way back into the baby's hands after he'd put them away. Or the voices he sometimes heard coming from the nursery, as if Shawn were in a conversation with someone. Or the puddles he'd found in different places around the farm. They appeared out of nowhere and seemed to persist day after day, even without a drop of rain. There was one near the corral and another one behind the barn, and it hadn't rained in a week.

When Doc Thorpe stopped by to check on Shawn, he and Russ visited the puddles together. "Could they be seeping up from an underground spring?" wondered Doc.

"I doubt it," said Russ. "It's not just one spot. They're here, there, and everywhere."

They went inside to play a game of chess. Pitch stayed behind, staring at the corral puddle. When Doc left an hour later, the dog was still there, sticking her nose in and out of the water like she was bobbing for apples. Both men shared a good laugh over that one.

When Shawn was three months old, another Puddlejumper came to the Up Above. His name was Cully. He was a scout who'd traveled farther from the Kingdom than any other living Jumper and was famous for telling stories that lasted whole days. He was agile and quick, which surprised everyone, because he was built like a stump. He loved to eat and drink, and his big belly shook when he laughed.

It was the night of the full moon when Cully made his first visit. He'd come to initiate Shawn into the ways of the Puddlejumper tribe. Perched on either side of Snow White, Root and Runnel could hear Pitch wagging her tail at the foot of the crib and Russ' snores from the other room. Cully gripped the baby's finger and began to whisper, his voice rippling like a quiet stream past Shawn's ear, "Wawaywo, listen, I've come to tell you about the Beginning. We were pebbles at the bottom of the ocean when a blue whale took us in her belly and brought us to MotherEarth. There we lived a thousand years, until we plunged down the great waterfall, where we were born rolling and tumbling all the way to the river."

Root and Runnel listened intently from the crib rail. Like all Puddlejumpers, they loved to hear their tribal lore. Though they knew the baby couldn't yet understand their language, they were convinced the meaning would find a way into his heart and soul.

"Wawaywo, I want to tell you about the rain, the rain that feeds us and brightens our spirits with its lively patter and sweet smell. Rain fills the streams and rivers, every lake and well. It washes everything clean and brings the earth to life." Shawn listened, entranced by Cully's soothing voice. "But there are those who hate what we love most."

Root and Runnel shuddered.

"Troggs," he whispered. "Troggs are big—bigger than anything you've ever seen. They crush and kill everything in their path. As sure as the acorn drops from the tree, they will come to find us. Nothing can stop them, except the rain. When it rains, Troggs bury themselves in the ground and howl and curse. Thunder scares them and lightning blinds their eyes. They hate the rain, they hate even water itself, every drop, and because we are the caretakers of the water, they hate us most of all."

Shawn began to fidget, almost as if he could understand.

"A day is coming when you will journey to the Most Dark, a terrible Trogg wasteland where sap never runs and water never flows and the fires burn hot and forever. Wawaywo—you will lead us in battle against the Troggs. You are the Rainmaker."

When the baby started to cry, Cully fell silent.

In the nights to come, he would tell other stories, happier ones, but tonight the truth needed to be told. As the sun came up, ending the first night of Shawn Frazier's education, Cully did his best to make the baby laugh. When funny faces didn't work, he stood on his head and spit acorns. Shawn giggled for the first time and Root and Runnel laughed so hard they fell right off the rail.

Fixing a bottle in the kitchen, a sleepy Russ heard something hit the floor in the nursery. He hurried in, but all he found was Shawn in his crib fingering an acorn. Mystified, he took it away before the baby could swallow it, then noticed three more right next to him. *How on earth did acorns end up in Shawn's crib?*

After a week of temperatures nearing one hundred degrees, a warm rain drenched the Warbling River plateau. Root went out to collect fresh rainwater for Shawn's bath from the puddle behind the barn. Glad to be out of the house and in the rain, he was catching droplets on his tongue when another Puddlejumper suddenly burst through the puddle. Root ducked, barely avoiding the Jumper's landing.

It was Chop. At nine inches, he was the smallest Puddlejumper. He was also the most irrepressible, and now he was speaking so fast that Root couldn't understand him. Root made him take a breath and slow down.

"*Ma bata-pa, Wawaywo,*" he declared emphatically. Chop wanted to see the Rainmaker. Root knew he'd left the Kingdom without permission and had jumped against explicit instructions, but he also knew he'd be impossible to turn away. He decided to allow him a glimpse of the baby, but only if he agreed to return immediately afterward to the Underneath.

As this was Chop's first experience with humans, Root expected him to be as cautious as he'd been. Instead, he made a beeline for the house, racing ahead through the rain. Root caught him just before he barged into the kitchen, where Russ was making breakfast. He made Chop dry his feet so he wouldn't track mud across the floor. When Russ opened the fridge, they scampered past him and down the hall.

Runnel rarely lost her temper, but when she saw Chop, she spun like a top, leapt into the air, somersaulted, and landed on his chest, pinning him to the carpet. She was steaming mad—if they were discovered, the human might take the baby away. When Root explained that he'd already agreed to let Chop see Wawaywo, she reluctantly stepped aside. She knew that Root wouldn't go back on his word.

Chop zipped up the leg of the crib, where he stared wide-eyed, almost forgetting to breathe. When Shawn reached out and grabbed his hand, Chop nearly fainted. Runnel, quick to forgive, offered Root a knowing smile, remembering their first encounter with the Rainmaker.

At the sound of Russ' approaching footsteps, the Puddle-jumpers scattered. Camouflaged among some stuffed animals, Root and Runnel watched, horrified, as Chop made the mistake of hiding in the diaper pail. They remained perfectly still while Russ changed Shawn's diaper, but could barely look when he opened the bucket's lid with a foot pedal and dropped the messy diaper inside. It landed with a squishy thud.

Later, after Root and Runnel finally got him cleaned up, they escorted Chop back to the puddle to make sure he returned to the Underneath.

Toward the end of summer, Root and Runnel confronted a new problem. Unfortunately, Chop had bragged to anyone who would listen about his encounter with Wawaywo, and now Puddlejumpers from near and far were jumping puddles to get their own glimpse of the baby. There were even a few who pilfered a sock, bootie, toy, or teething ring as souvenirs. Root and Runnel ran themselves ragged trying to keep everyone out of the house.

That's when the notorious Buck arrived and quickly put an end to the commotion. He was a chief scout, like Cully, and the only Puddlejumper ever to escape the Most Dark. He had a jagged scar on his right cheek and a nasty claw mark that ran the length of his back, which few Puddlejumpers had actually seen, but all knew about. Upon his unlikely return from the Most Dark, he told about the many captive Jumpers he'd seen there, suffering, enslaved by the Troggs. But Buck didn't tell about something else he'd seen in that place of darkness—something even more horrible than any Trogg. The secret was a terrible burden for one Puddlejumper to bear, but he didn't want to frighten the others any more than they already were.

Buck rounded up the perpetrators in the hayloft, where he reminded them that the very future of the Kingdom was at risk. He promised consequences for any further trespassing, then sent the chagrined Jumpers skidding back to the Underneath. After that, he used clay, pinesap, and sundew mucilage from pouches on his belt to seal every puddle on the Frazier farm. In a few days' time they would evaporate without a trace.

Buck immediately went to work. His first task was deciding how they would transport the Rainmaker. In a grove of oak, he and Cully selected a solitary maple tree. After beavers took it down, the Jumpers built three wagons sturdy enough to carry a human baby and all of his things.

Next, Buck chose six raccoons strong enough to pull their precious cargo. Jumpers had a long history of enlisting raccoons, beavers, foxes, and deer, even birds and insects, to help them in their work. Despite Buck's fierce nature, he was the most skilled and patient when it came to working with other creatures.

After acquainting the raccoons with the harness, he

trained them to pull in tandem, running through the forest and along the plateau, building endurance. As they gained experience, he added more stones to the wagons to simulate the weight of the baby. During practice runs, the wagons crashed more than once, and Buck's crew needed to repair them several times. His final hurdle was teaching the coons how to jump a puddle. It took long hours of practice. One raccoon broke his leg and had to be replaced. But they finally got it right.

After mapping an escape route from the farm to a puddle deep in the timber, Buck walked the terrain to make sure there would be no surprises. And it wasn't just planning how they would do it, but when. On clear nights, he rode the back of the farm's great horned owl to the top of the tallest pine, where he could see the full panorama of the starry sky. Swaying in the wind, he studied the rotation of the planets to determine the optimal time.

While Buck prepared during the long hot summer, Root and Runnel continued to watch over their Rainmaker. Cully never ran out of nighttime stories, while Pav treated pinkeye and fended off a nasty case of cradle cap.

Those who spent time with Shawn were getting impatient because, in their minds, the baby was already theirs. But it wasn't just them. The entire Kingdom was waiting for the homecoming, waiting until all things were right and ready.

The moment finally came on the day of the autumn harvest.

CHAPTER SIX

Kidnapped

RUSS AND SHAWN were up before daybreak. Russ made a big breakfast of scrambled eggs with garden vegetables, strong black coffee, and toast slathered in Betty Woodruff's homemade rhubarb jam. For Shawn, he made pureed vegetables to eat with applesauce and milk.

Shawn was turning six months old that day and Russ was already in a celebratory mood. For him, the day of the autumn harvest was the most important day of the year, and surely the happiest. It was the day when his hard work came to fruition. He kissed his son on the crown of his head and said, "Time to get to work, little man."

In the first light, Russ ran across the yard holding Shawn above his head, pretending he was an airplane.

Making a loud sputtering sound, he spun him around and headed toward the barn. "This crazy pilot is flying backward!" he shouted playfully. Shawn, who was facing the house, squealed when he saw Root and Runnel bounding out the dog door. For them, today was a special day, too. It was the day they would harvest their Rainmaker.

In the barn, Russ nestled Shawn in the hay, covered him with his red quilt, then focused on his old John Deere tractor, its green paint chipped and faded. It was on its last legs, and he hoped it would get him through another season. He fetched his toolbox and prepared to battle the quarrelsome engine one more time. He tweaked the timing with a screwdriver, then fiddled with the carburetor, adjusting the flow of gas. When he looked up from his work, Shawn had kicked off the quilt.

Afraid his son might get a chill, Russ set his tools aside and went over to cover him, but when he got there, the quilt had been neatly retucked right to Shawn's chin. Mystified, he was staring at his giggling son when he heard what sounded like a tiny sneeze. Unnerved, he saw two pair of turquoise eyes looking up at him from inside the hay. There was a possum family living in the barn, but possums didn't have eyes like that. He grabbed a pitchfork to shoo away whatever it was, when, behind him, the tractor sputtered to life. Russ rarely cursed, but this time he did. "Godzilla!"

Spooked, Russ went over and turned off the engine,

but when he returned to the hay, the eyes had disappeared. He gathered up Shawn and buckled him into his special homemade seat atop the tractor, which adjoined his, but faced backward. He climbed aboard, not noticing that Root and Runnel, with hay still stuck in their hair, were now concealed under the fender. Shifting into gear, he steered the noisy tractor out of the barn and headed for the north slope. He looked back at his son with a resigned smile. "They don't call 'em Johnny Putt-Putts for nothing."

In the empty barn, the toolbox creaked open and a nine-inch, grease-stained Puddlejumper emerged. Chop wasn't going to miss the big day, no matter what he'd been told. He convinced himself it was a good thing he'd come. After all, he'd just saved the day by starting the tractor. To reward himself, he feasted on milk from the big black-and-white cows.

Once Russ lowered the cutter and began to harvest, he felt again the simple pleasure of knowing he'd found his place in life. He admired the trees along the boundary fence, especially the oaks and maples dressed in their fall colors. He took a deep breath. There was a sweet crispness in the air that promised winter but remembered summer.

The hours passed quickly as the tractor made its way back and forth across the field. Russ sang and told Shawn stories, his own versions of Jack and the Beanstalk and Pinocchio. At the top of the knoll, he pointed to the woods beyond the boundary fence. "Paul Bunyan himself asked me about cutting down that timber. He was riding Babe, his big blue ox," said Russ. "But I told him, 'Not on your life, Mr. Bunyan, I'm saving those woods for Shawn.' When you get a little older, we'll go up there and I'll show you all my favorite spots."

Shawn giggled and Russ laughed. He was sure his son was responding to what he'd said, but Shawn wasn't even listening. He was watching a tiny Puddlejumper skittering across the field, staying close. Russ turned to check on his baby just as Chop vanished under the mown wheat. The only thing he saw was how much Shawn seemed to be enjoying the harvest.

In near darkness, a score of Puddlejumpers watched from their roost along the rafters of the barn as an exhausted Russ, with Shawn in his backpack, fed and watered his cows, pigs, and horses.

When he was finished, Russ closed the barn door and started across the yard. A brisk wind stung his cheek and rain began to patter the ground. "Looks like we might see some big rain tonight," he said, hustling toward the house as dark clouds gathered in the twilight.

Russ prepared a bottle, then, humming a lullaby, laid Shawn in his crib. He flicked on the Snow White lamp, illuminating the elfin mobile dangling just above the baby's head. He washed his son with a warm moist cloth, then blew his lips in a noisy sputter against the baby's belly, which made Shawn giggle.

Outside, a steady rain was falling.

"If this rain ever quits, we'll get the rest of our wheat in—what do you say?" asked Russ, knowing that the long-grain wheat in the field south of the barn still needed another week in the ground. He shook a few drops of milk from the baby bottle onto his wrist to make sure it was the right temperature. Shawn babbled as if trying to talk with his dad.

"No, you cannot run the tractor," Russ teased. "Maybe next year if you walk the straight and narrow." He kissed his baby, then gave him the bottle. "Okay, my little farmer, go for it."

A sharp knocking rattled the kitchen door.

"Coming," he called, then snugged the quilt around his baby boy. A persistent *RAT-A-TAT-TAT* echoed from the kitchen. Russ tapped the mobile, which sent the carved figures dancing chaotically around the Crystal Acorn. Shawn pumped his legs and squealed with delight. "You sure like those little guys, don't you?"

As soon as his father left the room, Shawn dropped his bottle and reached for the dancing elves.

Annoyed by the persistent knocking, Russ hollered,

"All right, already," as he hurried through the kitchen. When he opened the door, no one was there, but his cows and pigs were wandering around the rain-swept yard. Pitch snapped at their heels, trying to herd them back into the barn. One of his horses was trotting up the muddy drive toward the highway.

"God-zilla!" cursed Russ as he dashed out into the storm.

In the nursery, Shawn giggled as Root and Runnel pattered along the railing. Runnel jumped into the crib and stuffed a teething ring into the baby's mouth to keep him quiet. Root drew a sharpened stone from his belt and slashed the Crystal Acorn from the mobile, then held it up to signal the others.

Pandemonium ensued as Buck and Cully pried open the window and led a gaggle of Puddlejumpers into the room. Dashing every which way, they stuffed a burlap sack with toys, teething rings, bottles, clothes, and the Snow White lamp, setting the loot aglow.

At the window, Chop pulled his chin up to the sill and peeked inside, his eyes wide with excitement. Convinced he could help, he vaulted into the room and joined the fray, but he was one too many Jumpers thrashing through the bureau. It tilted off its axis, wobbling dangerously back and forth.

Outside, Russ was returning his horse to the barn when a crashing sound from the house snapped him to attention. Abandoning the animal, he sprinted for the porch and hurdled the steps in a single leap. He raced through the kitchen, down the hall, and banged open the door. His baby's room was in complete disarray—the bureau toppled and clothes strewn across the floor. The window was open and the curtains, wet with rain, billowed inward. What he saw next was more terrible than any nightmare.

The crib was empty.

"Oh God, please no!" he prayed. The Crystal Acorn was gone, too. Only the dancing elves remained.

Backing away from the crib, Russ stepped on something under the rug. It was Chop, the only Jumper who hadn't made it out. His shrill cry sent Russ' heart to his throat and he stumbled into the wall, barely glimpsing a shadow leaping out the window. He rushed to the sill and peered into the dark. Just beneath him, Chop pressed against the house, shivering in fear. Thunder boomed and lightning streaked the sky. Russ saw a glowing bundle disappear into the wheat and heard a chorus of high-pitched hooting. "*Hooty-hoo! Hooty-hoo! Hooty-hoo!*" It sounded like a cross between an owl's eerie call and a loon's mournful cry. It was a sound he'd never heard before.

Russ leapt out the window and bolted across the yard. "No!" he screamed. "Shawn!"

But the Puddlejumpers had no intention of getting

caught as they careened through the wheat aboard the wagons drawn by their raccoons. Squinting into the hard rain, Buck commanded the first wagon with a skittle of Puddlejumpers crammed in the back. They hung on tightly as their wagon bounced over the muddy furrows and up the slope. Root steered the second one, Runnel riding behind with the baby. She did her utmost to keep Shawn comfortable, but he kicked and screamed, testing her already frayed nerves. Cully piloted the third wagon, hauling the sack of glowing loot.

At the top of the ridge, where Russ' farm ended and the woods began, Buck shouted a warning and the Jumpers ducked as their wagon shot under the split-rail fence. Root reached back to make sure that Runnel stayed low. Cully ducked, too, but his wagon slammed to a halt. He somersaulted over his coons and landed hard on his back. The overstuffed sack had wedged against the lower rail.

Buck and Root dashed back to help Cully to his feet. He stumbled groggily, but Russ' shouts and Pitch's barks from the other side of the rise quickly revived him. The Jumpers pulled and pushed and squeezed the sack in a frantic effort to get it under the rail. Finally Root yanked out the quilt and the wagon barely cleared the fence. Unwilling to leave anything behind, he dragged it back to his wagon and they were off, the quilt flapping like a flag in a tempestuous wind.

The Puddlejumpers raced desperately through the

trees, searching for the hatchway. Glancing behind, Buck saw the dog bounding over the fence and charging after them. Pitch was closing in fast when Buck finally spotted the puddle beneath a giant oak. He smacked into the water like a falling star, straight and true. Root ramped off one of the tree's exposed roots, tipping so steeply that he lost hold of the quilt before he could recover his wagon and make the passage. Cully's wagon jumped right behind, disappearing down the puddle's black hole into the earth.

Just as fast as it opened, the hatchway closed. Raindrops pattered the puddle's surface as if nothing had happened.

Russ jumped the fence and entered the woods at a full run. Under the dark forest canopy, he stumbled and fell, scraping his chin. *How can this be happening? Who would do it?* He picked himself up and continued on. *Why would they do it? Why?!*

Up ahead, Pitch was circling a puddle beneath one of the big oak trees. When Russ caught up, he saw that she had something between her teeth. *Shawn's quilt.* He stifled a sob, his body shivering in the rain. "Drop it," he said quietly. She obediently let Russ take it. "Good dog." Breathing hard, he crouched to scratch her behind the ears. She whined and prodded him with her nose. "What is it, girl?" He scanned the woods, hoping to glimpse the light flitting through the trees. He put the quilt to his dog's nose. "Okay, let's go—you find him, you find our boy." He started off, but the dog didn't budge, barking and pawing the water. "Pitch, come!" Russ commanded.

The dog barked a final time at the puddle, then joined her master running through the dark. But with the glowing light no longer ahead, there was nothing left to pursue. Russ ran anyway, shouting his son's name, wishing the trees could answer.

CHAPTER SEVEN

The Water Kingdom

J UST BENEATH the forest floor, the Puddlejumpers listened as the father's shouts drifted farther and farther away. Once it was quiet, Pav and other Puddlejumpers waiting at the rendezvous offered hushed congratulations while making sure that everyone was all right. Although the babynappers had tumbled through the puddle hatch onto beds of thick fleece, it had been a rough landing. The sack had split open, and toys, teething rings, bottles, and clothes lay scattered across the cobblestone tunnel. Shawn was so startled by it all that he stopped crying, and Runnel could finally uncover his mouth.

The Puddlejumpers nestled the baby into a birch-bark canoe moored in a nearby stream. Runnel held him close as Pav fed him a gourd of milk spiked with pollens and spices. Buck freed the raccoons from their harnesses while Cully supervised the loading of Shawn's belongings into other canoes. They were about to set off when a muddy and disheveled Chop came tumbling through the puddle. Staring wide-eyed at the startled Jumpers, he blurted, *"Na-kwe-lay kazinga,"* which, roughly translated, meant, "Well, I made it."

Relieved, everyone pressed around him, pushing and prodding and pinching in playful reproach.

As the Puddlejumpers launched downstream, they couldn't help but hoot with anticipation.

They were almost home.

Lanterns embedded in the walls brightened the otherwise dark passage as seven birch canoes navigated the tumultuous watercourse. A thick green moss blanketed the walls and roof of the tunnel. Here and there tangled roots poked through the dirt. There was a clean and loamy fragrance in the air. Buck paddled the lead canoe with Chop perched at the prow. Cully and Root oared the second canoe, where Pav and Runnel tended the baby.

Spurred along by the turbulent water, the birch canoes wound deeper and deeper into the earth. After descending the four major rapids—Wapata, Bootenay,

Sisbaba, and finally Tittabuwasi—the water flattened out and the Puddlejumpers floated down a deep river. Soon they came upon a veil of lush ivy draped like a curtain across the water. One by one, the canoes threaded through a break in the greenery.

On the other side, the river opened into a cobalt-blue lake. This was their home, the Cavern of Pools, an underground hollow that sparkled like a radiant jewel. At the center of the lake stood Grandfather Oak, an ancient giant that reached three hundred feet to the ceiling of the cavern. A thousand ice-blue crystal acorns shimmering on its branches bathed the cavern in the ethereal light of dawn. From the oak's every leaf, twig, and branch, water poured down, a perpetual rain that pattered the surface of the lake. All around the cavern, waterfalls tumbled from the upper elevations. These waterfalls formed streams, which flowed down the gentle slopes of moss and clover, past hundreds of small shining pools dotting the meadows. The pools reflected the dome of the cavern, where rainbow-colored stalactites sparkled like generous constellations.

To signal their return, Buck shouted a victorious "*Hooty-hoo!*" Chop emulated the great scout with his own excited cry. Buck gave him a helpful shove into the water, but Chop didn't mind. He swam at the prow like a dolphin romping at sea.

In the meadows, hundreds of Puddlejumpers vaulted out of the pools, jumping from their homes just below the puddle hatchways. With cacophonous hooting, they sprinted down the green slope, then dove into the lake and swam out to greet their Rainmaker.

One Puddlejumper catapulted into the canoe and stood dripping wet next to Shawn. It was Greystone, the tribe's Ancient Guide. Though blind, he had deep-set amber eyes that seemed to look right through you, but his big ears compensated for the lack of sight. They were so keen he could even hear when it was raining in the Up Above. His beard, which he sometimes wore in a swirl on top of his head, was now braided and nearly touched his toes. The Puddlejumpers watched in awe as he used his skilled hands to see Shawn's face. Finally he kissed the crown of the baby's head and whispered, "Wawaywo," then leapt to the bow and proclaimed his name to the Kingdom.

In jubilation, each and every Jumper echoed his call, "Wawaywo!"

The seven canoes continued toward Grandfather Oak's umbrella of rain. Their grandfather seemed to bow his leafy head as the canoes began to spin, drawn by a swirling undertow. Runnel and Pav secured the baby, and the Jumpers braced themselves just before the rushing water sucked their canoes into a hollow at the base of the trunk, plunging them down a steep gorge. They threaded the gnarled roots of the oak in a swooping, rollicking white-water ride that took everyone's breath.

The canoes splashed down in the sapphire waters of

the Laughing Grotto. A resplendent rainbow arched from one side of the cave to the other and a refreshing mist filled the air. Water trickled down the onyx walls veined with gemstones and silver, tinkling like a thousand wind chimes in a gentle breeze. The Puddlejumpers placed Shawn on a stretcher of woven wheat and carried him across a white sand beach to a threshold in the rock.

Greystone led the way across the portal, then down a spiral stairway into their sacred Deep Down. Buck and Cully each carried a tiny lantern, casting giant shadows that danced along the wall. Like every other place in the Kingdom, there was water—water cascading all around them—water flowing ever deeper into the earth.

At the bottom of the stair, they reached an oak platform suspended by ropes of woven hemp. Heads bowed, the little ones teetered with their precious treasure onto the platform. It swung like a pendulum over a bottomless chasm. But the Puddlejumpers weren't looking down into the darkness. They were looking at the most magnificent sight in the Kingdom.

It was MotherEarth, an immense stone being within the canyon wall. Only her face was visible. If the Puddlejumpers stood on each other's shoulders, like a living totem pole, it would take thirty of them to reach the top of her moss-covered head. Her skin was smooth, caressed by the eternal veil of water streaming across her benevolent face. Every time she breathed, the rock rippled back and forth.

Each and every drop of water journeyed down Grandfather Oak to touch the face of MotherEarth. Now the Puddlejumpers had taken Shawn Frazier on that same journey, and it was time for him to begin his new life.

Root and Runnel proudly presented the human baby to MotherEarth. Her emerald eyes sparkled as Pav leaned out over the fathomless depths and collected water flowing off her lips. The tribe's healer trickled the water over Shawn's eyes, ears, nose, and mouth, then rubbed the rest down the back of his neck and spine. Shawn shivered and squealed in surprise. MotherEarth laughed and the rocks shook all around them.

Greystone uncapped Shawn's Crystal Acorn and caught a droplet from MotherEarth's chin. He snugged the cap and fastened it around the baby's neck on a loop of milkweed fiber. This Acorn, harvested from Grandfather Oak, was Shawn's birthright as the Rainmaker, his talisman, and the weapon he would one day use in the last great battle.

As the little ones pressed close to touch the baby's Crystal Acorn, MotherEarth intoned a chant that resonated throughout the Deep Down like the call of some primordial whale.

CHAPTER EIGHT

The Spiral Tattoo

AFTER MOTHEREARTH'S blessing, the Puddle-jumpers returned to the Cavern of Pools, where they celebrated as only Puddlejumpers can. Oak barrels were filled to the brim with milk and feast pots overflowed with their favorite foods, including fresh berries and cream, nuts of all shapes and sizes, rolled wheat pasta with dandelion sauce, and even an acorn taffy that poured like sweet butter from the churn.

Under Greystone's direction, scouts carried Shawn on the wheat stretcher down the meadow to the lake. Every Puddlejumper followed and lined up along the shore. The tribe watched with anticipation as Buck and Cully launched the six-month-old into the water. Shawn promptly sank.

Holding their collective breath, the Jumpers leaned forward, all wanting to help the baby, but Greystone made them wait, saying simply, "He looks like a human being, but he's a Puddlejumper now." A few bubbles percolated to the surface. Seconds felt like hours. Runnel, alarmed, waded into the water just as Shawn popped to the surface and gulped a deep breath.

The tribe shouted, *"Kadudee, matadie ra!"* and slapped the water with their webbed hands. Shawn struggled onto his back, but seemed to calm as he looked up into the radiant branches of Grandfather Oak. Runnel swam in a circle around the baby as Greystone spoke, "Wawaywo is big—bigger than us—but he'll be biggest when he grows small."

The Jumpers laughed and slapped the water again. As Greystone told of the wonders that were yet to come, they listened spellbound, lifted by his every word like an ocean swelling with the tide. Suddenly he dove under the water and didn't surface until he reached Grandfather Oak, where he climbed onto the trunk above the hollow. As the water roared beneath him, he shouted, *"Walagadooroo!"*

A great excitement filled the cavern as Puddlejumpers scrambled to find a partner. "Crown the Oak" was their favorite game. The object was to place a golden hoop at the top of Grandfather Oak. To begin, all the teams lined the shore around the lake. When Greystone tossed the hoop into the water, the players dove to the bottom to recover it. Swimming in the depths of the lake and on the surface, they worked in tandem, maneuvering their way onto the sprawling oak. The duo possessing the hoop played against everyone else. Once on the tree, Puddlejumpers sprinted up the trunk and along the branches in a wild scramble to reach the summit first. Some Puddlejumpers got knocked off into the lake and, if they weren't quick enough, were swept all the way down to the Laughing Grotto. There was lots of wrestling and tumbling and tackling and dunking. The hoop could be thrown through air or skipped on water or rolled on branches. Finally, a determined Puddlejumper placed the golden hoop on the uppermost branch and declared their team the winner.

By long tradition the game was always played with something at stake. On this special day, the Puddlejumpers cheered Root and Runnel as oak champions for the second time. Six months earlier, they'd earned the right to run beneath the stars and live among the human beings and keep the Rainmaker safe. Now, standing at the crown of Grandfather Oak, Root and Runnel humbly bowed their heads as the cavern resounded with hoots. There were others quicker, more agile and stronger, but no two Jumpers played the game with more heart.

Shouting *"Hooty-hoo!"* Root and Runnel dove from the summit with a backward twist and double flip before entering the lake like a pair of whispers. Greystone waited until they surfaced before sprinting up a cobblestone pathway toward the top of the meadow. He didn't stop until he reached a stone shelter known as the Well. It was the Puddlejumper gathering place overlooking the great lake and Grandfather Oak. Standing on the threshold, he drew a snail's shell from his belt and blew a deep, sonorous summons.

Every Puddlejumper rushed to the Well. They flooded inside, splashing through shallow water that bubbled up from a spring and flowed across the floor. Little geysers occasionally erupted, showering some and goosing others. The Jumpers crammed into every nook and cranny, window and ledge, anticipating the moment they'd heard about all their lives but never thought they'd see.

A hush descended on the Well as a covey of Puddlejumpers labored to carry the baby across the threshold. Shawn reached up to brush his hand through a mobile that covered the entire ceiling. The wooden figures knocked together in a melodic drumbeat. This was the tribe's treasured memorial—hundreds of carvings representing every inhabitant who'd been taken by the Troggs. It was their way of remembering them.

The Puddlejumpers laid the baby on a bed of wheat at the center of the Well. Greystone chanted one of the old songs as Pav crumbled a petrified wheat stalk over Shawn, ensuring nimble hands and a brave heart. Dipping into her chestnut thimble, she rinsed his eyes with morning dew, then sprinkled them with ground bat guano, ensuring great vision. There was a murmur of surprise when Greystone offered Root and Runnel a stiff pine needle and a thread of woven catfish whiskers but, as oak champions, they had earned the great honor.

While Pav gently pressed the top of the baby's spine so he wouldn't feel any pain, Runnel stitched a spiral into the ball of Shawn's right foot. After she pulled the final stitch, Root snipped the thread and held the baby's foot aloft for all to see. Everyone craned their necks to get a glimpse of the Spiral Tattoo, the same tattoo that was on the sole of every Puddlejumper. A few overzealous ones even tumbled from the rafters.

Unable to wait another second, Chop brought his acorn whistle to his lips and blew a rich, musical sound, which triggered a joyous trumpeting of whistles that filled the Well and echoed all the way down to the lake. The Puddlejumpers hugged and hooted and hollered.

To commemorate the occasion, Greystone gave the baby a cedar chest. On the vaulted lid was an impeccably carved likeness of Wawaywo's face. When he opened the chest, a galaxy of dried dandelions floated upward like a thousand good wishes. The Jumpers spent the rest of the day trying to catch them.

Now he was one of them, a Puddlejumper. And the Spiral Tattoo, the key which enabled the Jumpers to jump back and forth between the Underneath and the Up Above, would forever be on the sole of little Shawn Frazier.

CHAPTER NINE

Alone Together

SHAWN WONDERED where his father had gone. He missed his face, the low rumble of his voice, his familiar smell. He missed the airplane rides in the yard, and playing in the wheat, and the warmth of his dad's arms in the rocking chair. Where was his house and barn? What had happened to the sun and stars?

Root and Runnel had fixed up a comfy crib room in their den by the lake. It was quiet inside, except for the faint sound of waterfalls. The light from the crystal acorns on Grandfather Oak filtered through the ceiling puddle and cast a soft glow throughout the four round rooms. A mossy carpet covered the floor and the furniture was hand-crafted or borrowed from nature, like the bird's-eye maple table and the mushroom stools. The earthen walls were covered with birch bark and decorated with items found in the Up Above. There were eyeglasses and keys, somebody's driver's license, a fork, a crushed Pepsi can, a hubcap, and a tarnished brass doorknob.

The Puddlejumpers did their best to make the baby's room feel familiar. Root clamped the Snow White lamp to his crib and attached a mobile he'd carved featuring the animals Shawn knew from the barn. But all of their hard work didn't seem to matter, because he just wouldn't stop crying. Bawling, he crawled round and round the den, as if searching for a way out.

Cully came by in the morning and did everything he could to calm Shawn, but even standing on his head and spitting acorns didn't work. The Puddlejumpers told one another the baby was worn out from his encounter with MotherEarth and the sewing of his Spiral Tattoo.

When the tears didn't stop, Greystone brought Pav to the den to find out what was wrong. By then the whole tribe had gathered in clusters up and down the mossy meadows and along the lake, whispering anxiously. The baby's wail was as constant as the plunging waterfalls. It filled the Cavern of Pools with an overwhelming sadness.

After Pav examined the baby, she could only offer a shake of her head. She knew of nothing that could mend a broken heart. They felt sad for him, but there was nothing they could do.

The Rainmaker was essential to the Kingdom.

CHAPTER TEN

The Only Clue

THE NIGHT RUSS FRAZIER lost his son, his world might as well have come to an end. When he was alone in the weeks that followed, he cried and cried until there were no tears left. Every muscle, every fiber of his body, ached with the loss of his baby boy. Sometimes he thought he didn't have the strength to take even one more breath. But somehow he did.

Russ never finished harvesting the long-grain wheat along the south slope. Instead he spent every waking moment looking for his son. He traveled from town to town, handing out pictures and questioning anyone and everyone. He worked with the local sheriff, the Illinois State Police, and even the FBI, but no one ever uncovered another clue that might lead to the kidnapper. The single shred of evidence was the red quilt Pitch had found up in the woods. Whoever took the baby, it was as if they'd vanished off the very face of the earth.

The kidnapping had captured the attention of the entire state. The papers, TV commentators, townspeople, and even the police began to refer to Shawn Frazier as "the Quilt Baby." For a while it was all anybody could talk about, but as winter approached and there was nothing new to report, people gradually returned to the business of their own lives. The Quilt Baby was forgotten.

As the winter snows began to melt, Russ finally stopped pestering the authorities and returned to his empty house. Everything on the farm soon fell into disrepair and neglect, except for Shawn's room, which Russ kept just the way it was before he was taken. The baby pictures remained on the wall next to a photograph Betty had taken of Russ with Shawn on his back, shaking his rattle. A stuffed teddy bear sat on top of the dresser next to a candy-red tractor. And the mobile's wooden elves kept their silent vigil over the red quilt. It lay clean and folded in the empty crib.

With old Pitch sleeping by his feet, a gaunt and bearded Russ spent long days on his porch gazing into the fields, praying that somehow, by some miracle, his son would return.

With the coming of spring, he got ready to plant his fields. He had to. It was all he knew.

CHAPTER ELEVEN

Puddlejumping

AT THE SPRING EQUINOX, the Kingdom celebrated Shawn's third birthday. The Rainmaker had gradually acclimated to life in the cavern and was happy among the Puddlejumpers, but he was growing faster than Pav had predicted.

Greystone summoned Root and Runnel to the Well to discuss Shawn's future. Now that he was three, they decided it was time to begin his Puddlejumper training. While other scouts roamed the borderlands, keeping watch for Troggs, the two chief scouts, Buck and Cully, would start to prepare him for the day when he would fulfill his destiny.

Greystone made three hard-and-fast rules. First, they

should always inform him of their destination. Second, they should never use the same puddle for the coming and going. And last, they should never go near the Frazier farm, or for that matter, anywhere they might encounter human beings.

The next morning Root and Runnel bundled Shawn aboard a log raft, custom-built to accommodate someone three times their height and five times their weight. Shawn's eyes sparkled. *"Ta wayo!"* he squealed, which meant "I like me!" and Root and Runnel smiled at each other, then corrected him. He'd wanted to say *"La wayo"*—"I like it!"

A flotilla of seven canoes towed them against the current back toward the surface while Shawn continued to pepper them with questions, not all of them making sense. He'd grown to love his Puddlejumper parents and felt safe with them. They moored under the hatchway at Tittabuwasi, where Buck and Cully rigged a harness. A dozen Puddlejumpers hoisted a giggling Shawn up and through the puddle hatch.

But in the Up Above, Shawn had a difficult time. The sun was too bright for his eyes, the pollen made him sneeze, and the bustle of insects and birds distracted him. Clouds scared him. Root and Runnel did their best to reassure Shawn, but it wasn't easy.

It didn't get any better the next day when Buck initiated him to the dangers lurking in the Up Above. He pointed out poisonous snakes, poisonous spiders, poison ivy, poison oak, poison sumac, poison hemlock, tar pits, toad-stools, and snapping turtles. Shawn could hardly believe such a world existed. His head was spinning.

Buck's next task was teaching Shawn how to orient himself to the four directions—north, south, east, and west. "*Kee?*" complained Shawn, which meant "why," a question the Puddlejumpers often heard. Buck patiently explained that if he didn't know the directions, he could lose his way and have a hard time getting back to the Underneath. If a Trogg was nearby, he might never get back. Shawn listened intently, but he still felt a little confused about which way was which.

In the deep timber, they encountered a fierce mother bear and her two cubs. Buck held her gaze and whispered calmly, speaking in bear grunts until he could stroke her long, black nose. After a while, he was able to charm her enough that she even allowed Shawn to wrestle with her cubs. When it got dark, the five of them bedded down in their cave with Shawn nestled between the bundles of black fur. Buck was anxious about keeping the Rainmaker out all night, as Troggs were more active after dark, but he thought it important for him to learn that animals could provide a place to hide in times of crisis. That night Shawn dreamed about bears who could talk and walk on two feet and carry him wherever he wanted to go.

Buck woke Shawn so early the next morning the stars were still out. On the way home, he showed him how to find the North Star. That way, even in the dark, he would never lose his way.

When Cully took Shawn to the Up Above, he made the jump at Warble Creek. He spent the morning under a chestnut tree teaching Shawn how to do sleight of hand, which Puddlejumpers sometimes used to distract a Trogg. First Cully showed him a chestnut, then waved one hand in front of the other and the chestnut disappeared. Shawn's eyes darted in every direction. "*Meta lo galo?*" he squealed. After pretending to search everywhere, Cully pulled the chestnut from under Shawn's armpit. Mesmerized, Shawn yelled, "*Eta, eta!*"—"Again, again!"

Cully's big appetite made him an expert in knowing what to eat in an emergency. He pointed out persimmons, pine nuts, pokeweed, sassafras, and spatterdock. After considerable prodding, Shawn tried munching the stalks of young cattails, sucking honey out of honeysuckle, and crunching brittle reindeer moss from the north side of trees. The whole time Cully never stopped talking about ways to survive if lost or in trouble.

On the way home, Cully brought Shawn to an overlook known as Owl Perch, just in time to witness majestic thunderclouds rushing up the valley. When the rain began to fall in a ferocious downpour, Shawn was so excited he shouted, *"Hooty-hoo!"* Surprised by the outburst, Cully shook with a big belly laugh. They sat with their legs dangling over the edge of the cliff, exhilarated, as the thunder and lightning echoed all around them.

Later that evening, after Shawn was tucked safely in his stump bed, the Puddlejumpers gathered in the Well to hear Cully tell the story of the Rainmaker's first "Hooty-hoo."

After each foray to the Up Above, Shawn went swimming with Chop. Root and Runnel had taught him to swim even before he could walk, and now Shawn slipped into the lake without hesitation. He paddled fiercely toward Grandfather Oak while Chop ferried around him. As the undertow took hold, Shawn rolled onto his back and shot feet-first into the hollow of the tree. Tucking his arms and pointing his toes, he plunged down the steep gorge. He and Chop screamed during the plummet, but as soon as they splashed into the Laughing Grotto, they popped to the surface hooting. After their swim, they sat on the sandy beach and practiced whistling with an acorn cap. Chop showed him how to form his thumbs in the shape of a V to make the shrill sound.

One day Chop tried to teach him how to skitter across a stream in the cavern, but Shawn didn't have webbed feet and sank to the bottom, cutting his foot on a sharp rock.

Shawn didn't cry, but when Chop saw the blood, he tried not to panic and rushed him to Pav.

This wasn't Shawn's first visit. He was a human being learning to be a Puddlejumper and had earned lots of cuts, scrapes, twists, and bruises. While Chop anxiously watched Pav clean the cut on Shawn's foot, he noticed a dark cloud cross her face.

"What's wrong?" he asked.

"Nothing," she answered.

After they left, Pav brooded about the disturbing break she'd seen in the Rainmaker's lifeline. She was skilled at reading the fleshy webbing of a Puddlejumper's foot, but not a sole belonging to a human. She found Greystone at the Well and told him about it. Disturbed, he hurried to Root and Runnel's den.

While Shawn slept, the Ancient Guide delicately traced his lifeline. His fingers hovered at the break. Pav, Root, and Runnel pressed close, awaiting his word. After a time of contemplation, he simply said, *"Matuba ka-lo-lo."* Matuba was the potion that would transform Shawn into a Puddlejumper. It was a powerful concoction that required strong bones and a conscious mind. To be safe, they'd decided to wait until he was five before allowing him to "sip the acorn."

"Once he grows small, we'll study his foot again," Greystone promised. But even while reassuring them, he knew that whatever was inscribed on Shawn's sole, there was nothing they could do to change it. Like the river, he would find his own path.

Unsettled by what he'd seen, Greystone advanced the timetable—Shawn needed to learn to puddlejump immediately. The sooner he could get in and out of the Underneath on his own, the safer he would be. He chose Root and Runnel for the task, which surprised them. They thought the honor should go to Cully or Buck, who were both experts in the art of jumping.

The very next morning, Root and Runnel brought Shawn to a puddle deep in the timber. They began by showing him how to plant his Spiral Tattoo flush on the face of the puddle, but that was as far as they got. Each time he ran up to the puddle, he would stop short or miss his plant or skid onto his rear. Puddlejumping came naturally to Puddlejumpers, but for Shawn it seemed impossible. Root and Runnel tried to be patient. After all, he was only human.

Shawn plopped down in the puddle. "I can't do it," he muttered, his lower lip starting to tremble.

"Keep your eye on the puddle," reminded Runnel.

Root scaled a stump to climb onto his back. "I'll jump with you this time," he said.

Buoyed by their encouragement, Shawn rose slowly to his feet and returned to his starting position. Straddling his neck, Root got a good grip on Shawn's ears. "We are the water," he whispered. "And so are you."

With a running start, Shawn sprinted toward the puddle. When Root yanked his ears, Shawn lifted off the ground, tucked his arms, hit the puddle flush, and passed through straight as an arrow. Root somersaulted off just before Shawn tumbled into a pile of leaves that had been gathered to soften his landing. He couldn't wait to go again.

For the rest of the day, Root and Runnel coached him on various techniques of jumping puddles, from the running leap to the skidding slide to the spiral plunge. That was just the beginning, as there were some Puddlejumpers who knew a hundred ways to jump a puddle.

Under their tutelage, Shawn made his first solo jump the next morning. Of course Greystone, Buck, and Cully were there to congratulate him. They wanted to put him on their shoulders, but knew they couldn't lift him.

That night Root and Runnel brought Shawn to the Well, where all the Puddlejumpers witnessed the gifting of his first Puddlejumper belt. When Greystone buckled it around his waist, the Jumpers hooted and blew their acorn whistles. After all the difficulties, Shawn had taken to life in the Kingdom as a Puddlejumper takes to water.

In the midst of the celebration, Greystone called for quiet. Everyone fell silent. If they kept absolutely still, they could hear the song of their MotherEarth rippling from the depths of the Deep Down.

CHAPTER TWELVE

Something Unspeakable

AT THE END OF SUMMER, the Puddlejumpers watched anxiously as large flocks of crows wreaked havoc on the wheat fields, despite the best efforts of the human beings to stop them. The big black birds were more aggressive and more brazen than ever before. Even the owls, their natural enemy, had disappeared, and Puddlejumpers feared the worst.

As autumn turned chilly, then cold, something unspeakable was whispered in the wind. Day after day, the sky hung low and flat. The air was bitter and lifeless. The trees lost their colors and their bare branches turned a deep black. The scouts reported that animals all across the plateau had retreated into their dens and the songbirds were nowhere to be found. The entire tribe was on high alert. At each hatchway, Jumpers kept watch morning, noon, and night.

When it finally happened, it was the dead of winter. Chop, now a full-fledged scout, was patrolling in deep snow on the north rim of the plateau when he caught the first telltale whiff. It was a putrid mixture of dead fish, hog puke, and skunk farts. Holding his breath against the stench, he pressed his trembling hand against his brow and peered toward the horizon. *Could it be?* He shuddered as the eight-foot beasts lumbered into view on the far ridge.

Troggs!

Even from a distance, Chop could see their bloodshot eyes, scaly faces with puss-filled warts, and coarse hair covering their misshapen bodies. They were so ugly that as he stared at them, his eyes started to burn. He splashed his face with water from the gourd on his belt to lessen the sting, then put his finger in the air and knew he was in trouble. The wind was out of the south and it wouldn't be long before they had his scent. Troggs had ten-foot-long tails with a big hairy nostril at the tip, enabling them to smell Puddlejumpers from a great distance. Suddenly the creatures lurched in his direction, their serpentine tails arched overhead, wet nostrils sniffing and snorting. He sprinted through the timber as fast as his legs would churn. He didn't look back, not once.

Although Chop could have jumped at several different

puddle hatchways, he wanted to reach the waterfall at Red Moss Point. He dove through the freezing wall of water and disappeared down a whirlpool hidden in the rocks. A tunnel led to the convergence of the Seven Streams, where a large den served as the main scout headquarters.

Chop burst inside and, just as he'd hoped, found Buck and Cully. They were in the midst of planning where to locate emergency escape tunnels. Shivering, he uttered the word they hoped never to hear.

"Troggs!"

Before he could say another thing, Buck and Cully vaulted through a hatch to a secret stable, where a dozen scouts awaited orders. Dispatched to the Up Above, those Puddlejumpers rode sleek red foxes across the plateau to the far reaches of the Kingdom, alerting all to the terror. In the Underneath, swimmers were sent up the Seven Streams, and to the Cavern of Pools, and all the way to the Deep Down. The Kingdom was in complete disarray.

Although it had been a long time since anyone had last encountered a Trogg, any Puddlejumper could tell you about them. The terrifying memory was seared into their minds, a scar that never healed. Two generations before, Troggs destroyed their Great Hollow in the Smoky Mountains, wreaking a swath of destruction. The human beings thought tornadoes had uprooted the trees, but the Puddlejumpers knew better. The next attack occurred on the shores of Lake Erie. In Greystone's time, the Troggs had savaged the Tumbling Falls near the headspring of the Mississippi, pillaging their homeland and enslaving half their number. Devastated, they fled to the sanctuary of the Warbling River plateau. Here the exiles lived in peace, but Troggs never stopped looking for Puddlejumpers. They needed them.

The Rainmaker was in grave danger, as were they all. If the Troggs caught them, they would be enslaved forever in the fiery wasteland of the Most Dark. But worst of all, the Puddlejumpers knew that if the Troggs killed their chosen one, all hope would vanish and their MotherEarth would wither and die.

The Well was bursting with Puddlejumpers, yet it was eerily quiet. As Chop reported the details of his sighting, a wave of fear overwhelmed the mind of every Jumper, and there were angry voices and a growing hysteria. When Greystone's voice rose above the others, the Well again fell silent.

"*Matalala, Wawaywo,*" he said.

The Jumpers dispersed without another word.

In their den, Root went from room to room frantically packing their keepsakes, while Runnel sat with Shawn. "We're going to visit our relatives on a faraway hill," she explained. "Maybe we'll come back in the spring." She said it mainly to reassure herself and Root, but no amount of assurances could diminish their fears.

When everything was ready, and the raft was packed with foodstuffs and warm clothes and all the necessary things for winter, the Puddlejumpers gathered at the lake's edge, bathed in the fragile light of Grandfather Oak. Shawn didn't fully understand the implications of his departure. He smiled at his friends' somber faces as those nearest touched their hearts before reaching up to touch his. It was the Puddlejumper way of keeping him in their lives, and they, in turn, in his. When Greystone placed his hand on Shawn's heart, he kept it there a very long time.

The Rainmaker was lifted into the air by dozens of little hands and passed from one to another until he was deposited next to Pav waiting on the raft. Last aboard, Runnel and Root lugged the cedar chest filled with his Puddlejumper keepsakes. As Greystone and other Jumpers pushed the raft away from the bank, Shawn finally realized that he was leaving and broke into tears. The heartsick tribe waved from shore as Root and Runnel grimly poled against the currents into a dark tunnel.

They spent the night at Red Moss Point, where Cully met them to provide maps for the unknown territories. He showed Root several different trails in case they ran into trouble, while Pav and Runnel were busy tending Shawn.

They rubbed a balm over his entire body to protect him from the cold, then Pav brewed a willow-bark tea that would warm him from the inside out. That night, the Puddlejumpers barely slept.

The next morning, everyone boarded the raft and set out for the far end of the Underneath. They hadn't floated very long when Runnel realized they'd forgotten Shawn's cedar chest at Red Moss Point. She wanted to return, but Cully insisted there was no turning back.

Far beyond Turtle Head Rock, a flashing lantern summoned the raft to the bank. It was Chop and he told them the dreadful news. While Greystone was sealing the hatchway in the woods near the Frazier farm, Troggs had clawed their way into the puddle and snatched him away. Devastated by the loss of their Ancient Guide, the Puddlejumpers dove deep under the water and didn't want to surface, but Cully pleaded, "*Mataki, mataki-lo.*" They needed to keep going.

Wiping his tears, Cully scrambled up the notched wall and swung upside-down to plant his Spiral Tattoo. He broke through a sheet of ice into the Up Above, where Buck, armed with a double-barreled cattail plunger carried in a birch-bark quiver on his back, was waiting with three sleds drawn by teams of harnessed raccoons. One sled was bigger than the others and had four raccoons instead of two. The other Jumpers jumped the puddle *rat-a-tat-tat*, landing softly in the snow between Buck and Cully. In their grief, the Puddlejumpers could see only one thing— the water symbols Greystone had carved on the sleds to protect them on their journey. If only they had been able to protect him.

As snow began to flurry, the Jumpers bundled themselves in wool against the freezing cold, then packed the supplies. Buck lashed a hornet's nest to Root's sled, wrapping it in wheat straw while giving him urgent instructions to use it only as a last resort. Chop gave last sips of water to the raccoons and Cully bundled Shawn into the big sled, pretending it was all just another adventure. "Pay attention and remember everything you see," he advised, then reached behind Shawn's ear and produced a roasted chestnut, ready for eating. He tucked it into Shawn's eager hands. "We'll be home soon, and I'm expecting you to tell us a great story in the Well."

"*Kayko*," responded Shawn, munching the nut.

When the loads were secured, Pav stood quietly beside Shawn's sled. He seemed to know it was time to say goodbye. In the Puddlejumper way, Shawn touched his heart, then hers. Overcome by a feeling that she would never see him again, Pav pulled a sharp stone from her belt and cut off her beautiful white hair. The others watched stunned as she wove it into a bracelet around Shawn's wrist.

Her voice quavered as she said, "This will protect you on your journey."

Everyone pressed gently around her, touching her frayed hair, but Pav urged them on, "*Tookla, tookla!*"

Runnel squeezed her hand and settled behind Shawn. Root, Buck, and Cully jumped on their sleds, snapped the reins and were off. Riding at the back of the last sled, Chop feathered the snow with a pine bough to cover their trail.

Waving farewell, Pav watched them disappear into the snow as the sky threatened and the wind began to howl.

CHAPTER THIRTEEN

The Great Divide

THE SCOUTS TRAVERSED the crest of the plateau, a difficult windblown route that avoided the farms in the valley below. When the snow began to drift over their heads, Buck stopped the caravan to rest the raccoons in a grove of pines. While Shawn hungrily ate a wheat cake and sipped Pav's tea, Cully climbed to the top of a towering pine to scan the horizon. He squinted into the snow as the treetop swayed in the icy wind. A shrill caw startled him. In the next tree, there was a big black crow staring right at him. He shivered. Crows were never a good omen. Scavengers, they often fed off the carnage left behind by Troggs. The bird dismissively flapped its wings and took to the air. Cully watched its flight into the valley with a feeling of dread. That's when he saw them: four hulking brutes were slogging through the snow, with tails arched rigidly over their heads like riflescopes, scanning, searching for a scent. He could hear the muffled cries of three Puddlejumpers that a Trogg had stuffed into its fleshy stomach pouch. Like a Venus flytrap, once a Jumper was captive inside the pouch, with its spiky bristles, there was no way out.

Cully tumbled out of the tree, snapping branches and jabbering all the way down, *"Jo waba konibi wa!"*

The Jumpers scrambled aboard their sleds and frantically drove the raccoons hard along the ridge. Runnel bundled Shawn in flight and the look on his face frightened her. Chirping fiercely to one another, the scouts veered off through the trees in separate directions, hoping to draw the Troggs away from the Rainmaker.

Root and Runnel escaped along a deer trail while the Troggs charged after Cully and Chop. Glancing back in the blinding snow, Cully could see the monstrous shapes ripping through the brush and hear their awful grunts. Chop heaved supplies overboard as Cully threaded between the trees, driving the coons at breakneck speed. Suddenly their sled launched off a snowbank and crashed in a frozen marsh. The raccoons scurried away as the Jumpers slipped under the broken ice into the frigid water. They swam underneath as the Troggs stomped across the marsh in a furious attempt to crush them.

At the far shore, Cully and Chop tunneled into an otter den, seeking refuge, but a Trogg tail snaked in right behind, its hairy nostril sniffing noisily. The otters circled around the terrorized Jumpers, protecting them with their scent. The confused tail grabbed the smallest otter, shook it, then tossed it aside in frustration. As the tail slithered out, a grateful Cully and Chop curled up with the animals and listened to the departing howls of the Troggs.

On the next ridge, Buck shuddered at the spine-chilling sound. Trusting that Cully and Chop could take care of themselves, he returned to the grove of pines, where he picked up the imprint of Root's sled in the freshly fallen snow. He tracked their route until it was obliterated by a tail print that cut a huge swath in the snow. One of the Troggs had caught the scent of the Rainmaker.

As the forest darkened, the only sounds Root could hear were the panting of his raccoons and the wind in his ears. His face was crusted with snow and his whole body ached. He'd been standing for hours reining the coons, struggling to stay ahead of the Troggs. Shivering in back, Runnel tucked a woolen fleece around Shawn. He was pale and his teeth were chattering. Suddenly the sled swerved and side-swiped a tree.

"Root," she called. He turned around and their eyes met. "We have to stop. He's hungry and cold and you're falling asleep at the reins."

"*Mataki, mataki-lo.*"

"Please—we need rest, too, and so do the raccoons."

Root knew she was right. In the last mile, the coons had begun to falter. Though reluctant to stop, he found a ravine where he hoped it would be safe to rest for a few hours.

Halfway down the slope, Root and Runnel dug a cave in the snow big enough to enclose the sled and raccoons, then dusted it with fox dander to cover their scent. They made a nest amid the animals' warm fur and snuggled there with Shawn, who quickly fell asleep. After the tumult of the day, the quiet of the woods wrapped them in a kind embrace. The storm had subsided, and through a small opening at the front of their shelter, they could see the Big Dipper. They shared a smile, each knowing the other was thinking about the night of Shawn's birth.

But their remembrance was broken by the telltale crush of snow. *Crunch. Crunch. Crunch.* Footsteps. Big footsteps. Silently they began to gather their belongings and harness the coons. With hearts pounding, they nudged Shawn, still half asleep, onto the sled. Now they could smell the Trogg's stench and hear the muffled whimpering of other Jumpers, captive in its pouch.

When Root peeked through the opening, the Trogg

came into view, thrashing wildly and yanking young birches from their roots, its tail sniffing. The noises scared Shawn, and he called out for Runnel. Shrieking, the Trogg spun around and raged toward their shelter. Root ripped open the hornets' nest and launched a colony of angry hornets out the opening. They swarmed into the face of the charging giant, stinging it again and again and again. The Trogg swatted the air, yowling in angry confusion.

Bursting out of their snowy shelter, Root steered the sled right between the Trogg's legs and sped down the slope. The hornets' fury couldn't last in the bitter cold. One by one, they fell out of the air and perished in the snow. The Trogg, its face swollen with red welts, charged after the sled. With pounding strides, the behemoth caught them from behind and yanked the sled into the air, tumbling Root and Runnel into the snow and dangling the helpless raccoons from their harness. The Trogg plucked Shawn out and prodded him with a scaly finger and sniffed him with its disgusting tail, mucus dripping from the nostril. The tiny human wailed.

Root and Runnel jumped onto the behemoth's hairy leg, but the Trogg shook them off like bugs. Desperate, Root sped up a birch tree to a branch eye level with the beast. The Trogg dangled Shawn over its mouth, ready to eat him in one gruesome bite, when Root drew a nugget of sparkling quartz from a pouch and showed it to the beast, then made the stone disappear. The Trogg hesitated, distracted by the Jumper's sleight of hand. Out of the corner of his eye, Root spotted a ten-pronged deer charging down through the woods behind the Trogg. Buying time, he revealed the quartz again, then made it vanish as the brave animal lowered his head and drove his antlers into the behemoth's leg. Howling in pain, the Trogg dropped the boy into the snow and lunged at the deer. The animal stamped backward, snorting, readying another charge, with Buck riding high on his neck. Buck drew the cattail plunger from its quiver and fired a torrent of cold water. The geyser struck the Trogg in the neck, momentarily stunning it.

While Buck sparred with the Trogg, Runnel and Root dug Shawn out of the snow and escaped on their sled toward a frozen lake at the bottom of the ravine. Once they were away, Buck began his retreat, but the vengeful Trogg sent him catapulting through the trees with a vicious swat of its tail. The deer bounded away as the screeching Trogg careened after the sled, ripping trees and bushes out of the ground as it went.

Root forced the coons onto the icy lake, where they slipped and slid, their paws barely catching hold. Knowing that Troggs couldn't swim, Runnel scattered a pouch of rock salt and sulfur dust off the back of the sled. As soon as the beast stepped onto the patch of softened ice, it crashed into the water. The Trogg bellowed in panic, flailing and kicking and furiously breaking ice all the way back to shore.

Grunting and heaving, it crawled onto the snow. Two Puddlejumpers wriggled out of its pouch, the bristles softened by water, and fled into the woods. The prehensile tail snatched the third Jumper just before he reached the trees.

On the other side of the lake, Root followed a deer trail up a steep gorge into the woods. When the sled reached the plateau, gathering clouds obscured the stars and snow began to fall. Root and Runnel could hear Buck's mournful cry in the distance. He was hurt, but they couldn't go back to help him.

In a hollow, two ridges away, Runnel stripped off Shawn's wet clothes, then bundled the shivering boy in the warm fleece. The storm showed no sign of letting up. Shawn drank the last of Pav's tea while Root fed the coons some honeycomb. Before departing, the Puddlejumpers brushed the snow to make it appear that no one had ever been there. They wondered what had happened to Cully and Chop. They hoped they could make it on their own.

Root and Runnel were farther from their den than they'd ever been, and the journey had barely begun.

Root and Runnel sledded through the night in a terrible blizzard. When the raccoons could no longer bear the weight of their prized load, Root was forced to abandon most of their supplies. Even with the Jumpers trudging alongside, the coons still struggled. They were beyond exhaustion.

On a treeless plain, icy and bare, the raccoons finally collapsed. Refusing to quit, Root and Runnel grabbed the coons by their halters and pulled with all their might. Step by step, they inched the sled through the drifting snow until the runners got caught in an icy trough. Root yanked on their harness and Runnel pushed from behind, but the valiant coons couldn't budge the sled.

Out of the dark, a rising stench and a coarse breathing gripped Root's spine. Runnel put her arms protectively around Shawn. They squinted into the raging snow and what they saw ended their last hope of escape. Four monstrous silhouettes, their tails arched overhead like scorpions ready to strike, emerged from the trees onto the frozen plain.

Suddenly a mechanical drone and an eerie light penetrated the storm. Root, Runnel, and the Troggs all turned to look into the glare of an enormous eighteen-wheeler as it blasted out of the darkness like a ghostly phantom, its air horn blaring. With snow flying off its locked wheels, the truck skidded along the icy surface until it stopped just inches from the sled.

The cab door, sporting the moniker *Bleacher Bum*, creaked open. A black man in his early fifties, wearing a Chicago Cubs baseball jacket and cap, descended from the cab. Joe Beason was a bear of a man with a day's worth of stubble on a round face. He waded through the snow to the front of his rig. When he crossed through the headlight beams, he thought maybe his mind was playing tricks. There in front of him were four raccoons harnessed to a small sled buried in a snowdrift in the middle of the Interstate. No matter how hard he tried to explain it to himself, it just didn't make any sense. And as much as he wanted to ignore the muffled cries coming from the bundle on the sled, he knew that he couldn't. He reached down and tentatively opened the wool covering. It was a boy—wide-eyed, trembling, and completely naked but for something draped around his neck that looked like a crystal in the shape of an acorn. "Hell's bells," he mumbled, crossing himself. "Now I've seen everything."

A shrill hoot pierced the night.

Beason felt the hair on his neck rise. He peered into the swirling snow, then shouted, "Hello? Anybody there?"

An unearthly bellow answered.

He buried his nose in his jacket sleeve. There was a stink he'd never smelled before and hoped he'd never smell again. Cussing under his breath, he opened his jackknife to cut the raccoons free from their harness, then hoisted the boy into the air. Shawn kicked and screamed with all his might.

"Settle down now, I got you," the trucker assured, tucking him inside his jacket. The raccoons crawled away as he hustled back to his rig. Whatever was out there, he had no intention of making its acquaintance.

Beason pinned the wild child on the seat beside him, revved the engine, and eased the truck into gear. The gargantuan tires crushed the sled as the eighteen-wheeler plowed onward down the Interstate.

The Troggs lurched onto the pavement, raging at the disappearing taillights. At the edge of the highway, beneath a road sign, NEXT EXIT, CIRCLE, Root and Runnel burrowed deep into the snow. They trembled in each other's arms, devastated.

The Puddlejumpers had lost their precious Rainmaker.

CHAPTER FOURTEEN

Trouble Behind, Trouble Ahead

FORGING THROUGH the blizzard, Joe Beason shifted his gaze from the road to the urchin beside him babbling some crazy gibberish he couldn't understand. Unnerved, he tugged his Cubs cap a little tighter and wondered what he'd gotten himself into. He picked up his radio mic to tell somebody, anybody, what had happened. All he got was static. Then he remembered. It was Christmas Eve and there wasn't another truck on the road.

"*Hooty-hoo!*" cried Shawn, lunging for the door, but Beason yanked him back by the foot and pasted him against the seat with his big hand. "You stay right where you are, mister," he warned. "I got enough problems without you taking a flyer."

His passenger's only response was to jabber indignantly. Still spooked, Beason furrowed his brow. "What language are you talkin', boy?" He lifted his cap to scratch his bald head as he pondered the hair bracelet on the boy's wrist. The kid smelled strange. It wasn't a bad smell, just different. It was as if somebody had bottled the great outdoors and sprayed it on him like cologne.

The storm showed no sign of letting up. Beason was tired and struggled to make sense of what was happening. He'd been driving for close to eighteen hours and was determined to reach Chicago for Christmas. He'd been invited to his sister's place for dinner, but, more than that, he had ideas about breakfast at the Kosmikon, a little diner on Martin Luther King Boulevard that he especially enjoyed. The pancakes and grits weren't on his new diet, but Shona, the pretty waitress who poured his coffee, always welcomed him with an especially warm smile. He wished he were looking at that smile right now, because that would mean all of this would be over.

Beason kept one hand on the wheel and the other on the crazy little kid, who was working himself into a full-blown tantrum. He reached across and buckled him into the seat belt. It was a loose fit, but it was better than nothing.

The cab interior was filled with Cubs memorabilia, including baseball cards pasted on the dashboard and ceiling. Joe Beason had named his truck Bleacher Bum because he was a dyed-in-the-wool Chicago Cubs fan. For him, there was nothing better than to see a game at Wrigley. If he was working, he loved listening to the game on the radio. But it was winter, he was a long way from Chicago, and the wild child was still bawling his eyes out.

As Beason downshifted on a tight curve, one of his baseball cards popped unglued from the ceiling and fluttered end over end to land smack-dab on the boy's lap. To Beason's great surprise, the kid went quiet for the first time. Being somewhat of a superstitious man, he took a long look at the familiar face on the card, then at the boy studying it in fascination.

"That's right—he's a man to live up to, and you can start right about now," declared Beason.

With one hand clutching the card and the other on the Crystal Acorn draped around his neck, Shawn blurted, "*Kadudee, matadie ra!*"

Joe Beason just shivered. "Listen up, Ernie Banks— you sit right smart in that seat and stop talkin' crazy. And don't be pointin' that rock at me neither."

It was still dark on a bitter cold Christmas morning, in lightly falling snow, as the eighteen-wheeler navigated past a silent Wrigley Field. Joe Beason thought about going to the authorities, but the more he thought about it, the less he liked the idea. *Who wants to spend Christmas explaining a*

story to the police they probably won't believe anyway? The best thing is to leave the boy with people who know what to do. Everybody will be better off in the long run. He turned his big semi onto a narrow street adorned with Christmas decorations.

The truck wheezed to a halt in front of an undecorated six-story tenement. The word ORPHANAGE was chiseled in concrete above the door. He knew the place because he'd spent the first seven years of his life there. Beason descended from the cab with the kid, finally asleep, swaddled in his Cubs jacket. He laid the bundle on the icy stoop, rang the bell, then hurried back to his truck.

Little Ernie would never know how he got there. No one would. Not even Mrs. Annie McGinty, the stern-faced matron of the Lakeside Home for Boys, who was up early that morning getting ready for Christmas. Mrs. McGinty was five feet tall, with thick arms and legs. Her red hair was coiffed with obsessive neatness and she always kept her nails well manicured. She had a ruddy complexion and her face turned bright red when she got mad, which was often. She was thirty-eight years old, but the worry lines etched around her eyes and her constant frown made her look much older.

Mrs. McGinty waddled down the hall and opened the

door just as the big semi disappeared in the swirling snow. She was surprised to find a bundled Cubs jacket on her stoop and even more surprised by what she found inside. In a tart Irish brogue, she muttered, "And on Christmas morn, what a shame. As if I didn't have enough trouble already."

The child was asleep and stark naked except for a strange necklace around his neck and a filthy hair bracelet on his wrist. He was clutching an Ernie Banks baseball card in one hand and a scribbled note in the other. The note read as follows:

> To Whom It May Concern, this is Mr. Ernie Banks.
> Please give this little Cub a good home.
> Yours truly,
> A concerned Bleacher Bum

Mrs. McGinty looked in both directions before fingering the ice-blue crystal hanging from the boy's neck on a dirty piece of twine. It was a perfect replica of an acorn and the most unusual piece of jewelry she'd ever seen. She held it to one eye and squinted through the glass like a greedy jeweler checking stolen goods. Her view of the naked child multiplied as the image fractured into a hundred Ernie Bankses. She leaned close to inspect his bracelet. "One thing's for sure—you won't be bringin' this disgusting thing into my house." She ripped it off his wrist and threw it in the gutter.

Unannounced, a stream of warm pee geysered up to squirt her in the face. McGinty recoiled in horror. Startled awake, Ernie Banks recoiled, too, and shouted something that sounded like "Hooty-hoooooo!"

From that moment on, Ernie and Mrs. McGinty began what would become a very difficult association.

Nine Years Later . . .

CHAPTER FIFTEEN

A Merry Little Christmas

BEFORE HER ALARM clock could ring, Mrs. Annie McGinty woke in her tidy room on the first floor of the Lakeside Home for Boys. With a stretch and a yawn, she got up and got started. She took off her flannel nightgown and put on her best outfit, a red business suit with white buttons and a bow on the side. Today was Christmas, the day she enjoyed more than any other, and this year she was ahead of schedule. The night before, the Salvation Army had delivered fifty wrapped presents and stowed them under the donated fir tree in the big front room on the second floor.

When Mrs. McGinty climbed to the second landing, she saw that the Christmas tree was lit, which she always unplugged just before going to bed. She also noticed that someone had pilfered Santa's cookies and drunk his milk. Not *someone*, she thought. It was Ernie Banks and none other. He craved milk like no other boy she'd ever met. "I swear that boy will be the death of me," she grunted, then squatted to pull the plug on the Christmas tree. Electricity was too expensive to waste, and Lakeside ran on a strict budget.

Mrs. McGinty glanced out the window. It was snowing and the city was already blanketed in white. She sighed, remembering it had been snowing like this the morning she'd found the boy abandoned on her doorstep. She silently cursed and wondered how her life might have been different if only she'd been able to find a home for Ernie Banks.

Mrs. McGinty climbed the back stairway to the third-floor kitchen, where she put a kettle on the stove. This was the one peaceful moment of her day. While she waited for the water to heat, her mind wandered back to the Lauers, the first family who took him home. Fred and Molly had been happily married for three years but unable to have children of their own. Beaming with pride, they left with Ernie walking hand in hand between them. Three weeks later, they returned with frayed nerves and sunken eyes, embarrassed to be returning him. But return him they did.

The problem, they said, was Ernie's bizarre behavior, which included his nonstop gibberish that no one could decipher. He also had a very unnerving tendency to hoot when least expected, and they practically jumped out of their shoes every time he did it. Even worse, he cried morning, noon, and night. He cried so much they couldn't get any sleep. But it was more than crying. Molly said it sounded like something not of this earth.

The Lakeside doctor examined him but couldn't find anything wrong, though he did remark on the strange spiral birthmark on the bottom of his foot.

As Mrs. McGinty sipped her morning coffee, she cringed at the memory of those early years. Ernie had refused to speak English and wouldn't eat anything that was packaged or canned. When she strapped him into his chair at mealtime, it was always a battle. He'd fling food in every direction, all the while protesting in high-volume mumbo-jumbo. To combat his ranting, she would turn her portable TV up loud and go about the daily chore of pulling bits and pieces of food out of her hair and scraping breakfast, lunch, and dinner off the wall, floor, and ceiling. Sometimes it got so bad that she just left him strapped in his chair and escaped to her room to eat by herself. Frankly, Ernie scared her.

Finding parents for a parentless boy was her favorite thing in the world, and she prided herself on putting together the right matches. She was good at it. In fact, the only time she'd failed in her long career was with Ernie, but she most certainly didn't think that was her fault. Either he misbehaved, or he frightened the other children, or he just didn't fit in. Never mind the reason, defeated parents always had a good excuse for returning him.

Mrs. McGinty rinsed her cup and saucer, then started up the back stairway, passing the fourth- and fifth-floor dormitories, where the younger boys resided. The boys twelve and older slept on the sixth floor and she woke them first. She huffed up to the final landing and opened the door to the dorm.

Mrs. McGinty stood in the threshold, taking in the stares of twenty-five boys all eagerly awaiting the Christmas festivities. Usually it was a chore to get them up and out, but today everybody was dressed and the beds were already made.

"Good morning, boys. Merry Christmas," she said.

"Good morning, Mrs. McGinty," the Lakesiders chorused in well-practiced unison. "Merry Christmas." These orphans knew that the best way to survive at Lakeside was to obey the rules and please Mrs. McGinty.

Her gaze zeroed in on Ernie, who was laughing with Nate LeCroix at the back of the room.

"Ernie Banks," she called. "Might you have any idea who ate the cookies and drank the milk we left by the tree?"

Ernie answered without blinking. "I wouldn't know, Mrs. McGinty. Probably Santa Claus."

The others snickered, but McGinty silenced them with an icy look. She knew that no other boy would ever turn him in. Ernie had been at Lakeside longer than anyone else and he'd earned a certain respect with his seniority. She'd also heard the whispers. Although Ernie was small for his age, he never gave up when he got in a fight. It wasn't a good idea to squeal on Ernie Banks.

"Oh, that's very funny, lad, very funny indeed," she said. "But in my book that's stealin', plain and simple. You'll be mopping the kitchen floor right after breakfast." A thin smile cracked her face, then she clapped her hands twice. "Line up, boys."

Everybody scrambled to form two lines facing the door. Mrs. McGinty waited until everything was absolutely quiet. Only when she was satisfied did she lead the boys out of the dorm and down the stairs.

The Lakeside orphans enjoyed a breakfast of pancakes and scrambled eggs in the cavernous third-floor dining room. There was even hot chocolate. Usually it was oatmeal or cold cereal and toast. But today was special.

Ernie and Nate sat next to each other, wolfing pancakes smothered in maple syrup. When Ernie's plate was clean, he reached into his pocket and pulled out a couple of chestnuts.

"My last two. I saved them for Christmas."

"From that tree on Fourth?"

Ernie nodded.

"I can't believe you still have chestnuts from September. What are you, a squirrel?"

"Maybe," he answered, grinning. "Want one?"

"No thanks. Why do you even like those things?"

He shrugged. "I just do."

Nate reached under his seat and gave Ernie a bag from Cleary's Sports Shop. "Merry Birthday," he said with a grin.

Although today was his thirteenth birthday, Ernie expected it to be lost in the Christmas festivities, as usual. McGinty had made Christmas his birthday because that was the day she'd found him.

Ernie opened the bag and pulled out a brand-new baseball cap. He held it in his hands as if it might break. He'd never gotten a gift from a friend before, and this was an authentic Chicago Cubs cap. He touched the red C on the front with his fingertips.

Nate smiled. "I would have bought you the whole uniform, but they didn't have your size. Try it on."

With a big grin, Ernie put on his new cap. The one thing he and Nate shared above all else was baseball. They both loved it, especially Ernie. Maybe it was because of his namesake, the legendary Hall of Famer Ernie Banks, or the fact that Wrigley Field was just down the street. Whatever it was, they both had it bad. The Cubs were Ernie's team and the Cardinals were Nate's, and they could talk baseball anytime, anyplace, anywhere.

From day one they'd spent hours and hours playing catch in the alley. Nate had been an all-star catcher on his Little League team in St. Louis. Ernie had always wanted to try out for Little League, but McGinty wouldn't allow it. Nate said it was a rotten deal because Ernie was the best pitcher he'd ever caught. He would get in his crouch, flash a sign, then Ernie would wind up on his imaginary mound and let fly. He had a decent curve, but nobody had a better fastball than Ernie. At least that was Nate's opinion. When they weren't calling balls and strikes, they were poring over Ernie's baseball card collection. He'd been collecting for almost five years, saving every penny, nickel, and dime from his meager Lakeside allowance and spending it on cards.

Ernie gave his friend a big bear hug.

"You're welcome." Nate laughed. "Now let me finish my eggs."

Suddenly Mrs. McGinty swooped behind them and delivered her famous "Irish Uppercut," which meant she took her hammy fist and pounded it on the top of each boy's head. They both winced, pretending it hurt more than it really did.

"You'd better stop your shenanigans," she scolded. She swiped the cap from Ernie's head and threw it in his lap. "No headwear at the breakfast table. Even you should know better than that."

"But . . ."

"Another word and you'll be cleanin' bathrooms all day," she warned.

As soon as she was gone, Nate scrunched up his face and did an uncanny impersonation. "You'll be cleanin' bathrooms all day . . . and using my fat head as a mop!"

That got Ernie laughing, and his laughing got Nate laughing. Tears rolled down their cheeks and their stomachs hurt from trying to hold back their laughter.

After Ernie finished mopping the kitchen, he sat next to Nate among a throng of boys in front of Lakeside's spindly Christmas tree. He adjusted his new cap as he waited expectantly to receive his present. One by one, they were called to the front, where Mrs. McGinty, wearing a Santa hat, doled out presents like a strict teacher giving out a set of bad report cards. Ernie reached into his pocket, pulled out a candy cane, and offered it to his friend.

"Where'd you get that?" asked Nate.

"Off the tree. I didn't think Santa would mind," he replied slyly. Before Nate could take it, Ernie passed one hand in front of the other and made it disappear.

"I can never figure how you do that," said Nate. "Okay, where is it?"

Ernie shrugged, then reached under Nate's armpit.

"What's it doing here?" he asked in mock surprise as he pulled out the candy cane.

"Ernie Banks," called McGinty.

He thought he was about to be reprimanded again, but instead it was his turn to receive a gift. He slipped the candy into Nate's pocket and hustled to the front.

"Thanks, Mrs. McGinty," Ernie said as she handed him his present. He tried to take it, but she wasn't letting go.

"Just be glad it's not a lump of coal," she said, then finally released her grip. "Merry Christmas."

Ernie ripped off the wrapping before he even sat down. It must have been a mistake or an amazing stroke of luck, because it was exactly what he wanted. *A Rocky Harmon wristwatch!* He was the star home run hitter of the Chicago Cubs. Ernie set the time by the clock on the wall. Rocky's arms twisted like a contortionist to point out the minutes and hours. Strapping it on his wrist, he decided it was the best gift he'd ever received, except for his portable radio from the year before, and of course his new Cubs cap.

When it came time for Nate's gift, Mrs. McGinty looked instead at Ernie and smiled a peculiar smile that he didn't understand. Not until she said, "Nate LeCroix won't be opening a Christmas present this year. Instead, he'll be getting a new family. Come on up, Nate, and join your parents."

Into the room stepped the Goodmans, a well-dressed,

middle-aged black couple Nate had met with several times. Nate shared a look with Ernie. Ernie knew his friend had liked them a lot, but they didn't say much about it because it was dangerous to hope for things when you were an orphan.

Nate walked shyly toward the Goodmans until they wrapped him in a warm embrace. Everyone applauded. Ernie sat frozen like a deer caught in headlights. He felt a hand on his shoulder. It was Kathryn Moss, the young social worker. She was pretty and funny and all the boys liked her, even Ernie, though he tried not to show it.

"You okay, Ernie?" she asked.

He swallowed the lump in his throat, then nodded. Kathryn didn't say anything more, but she sat beside him while Mrs. McGinty handed out the rest of the presents.

Up in the dorm, Ernie watched as Nate packed his belongings. They both knew they'd probably never see each other again. It was Ernie who broke the silence.

"Your new mom and dad look nice," he said.

"Yeah," answered Nate, without looking up.

Ernie wanted to do something for Nate, but he just wasn't sure what. Suddenly he reached under his bed and pulled out a shoebox that was hidden in the bedsprings. It contained his prized baseball card collection, with full teams and plenty of doubles for trading. He handed it to Nate. "This is for you."

Nate shook his head. "No way."

Ernie was adamant. "I want you to have them."

"Aw, Ernie, I can't. It's too much."

"No, man, they're yours now. You keep 'em."

"Are you sure?"

Ernie nodded. "I'm sure."

They tapped fists, then Ernie presented his thumb. With a grateful nod, Nate pressed his thumb tight against Ernie's, then they rotated a quarter turn. "Brothers," they whispered.

Mrs. McGinty bustled into the dorm, interrupting them. "Let's go, Nate, no time to socialize, the Goodmans are waiting."

"I have to go," said Nate.

"Yeah," answered Ernie, sadder than he'd ever felt before. He touched his heart, then reached out to touch Nate's. He wasn't sure why he did it, but the look in Nate's eyes told him it was okay. His friend balled his fist and tapped him back, then tucked the shoebox under his arm, picked up his suitcase, and started across the room.

Ernie called out, "Way to go, man. You made it."

Nate turned at the threshold and, with McGinty standing right beside him, said in his best brogue, "Ernie Banks, you'll be the death of me yet!" It sounded just like the old battle-ax.

Ernie couldn't help but laugh. McGinty cuffed Nate, then stormed over to whack him, too. "Now shut your trap," she hissed.

He watched as McGinty marched Nate down the corridor and out of his life. Alone now in the cavernous dorm, he stared out the window at the gray Chicago sky. A tear snuck down his cheek, but he angrily wiped it away.

The only thing he knew for sure was that he'd never let them see him cry.

CHAPTER SIXTEEN

Waterloo

A T THE BEGINNING of January, the Lakeside board of directors decided that every boy should know how to swim. Mrs. McGinty stationed herself by the door of the idling bus and checked off each boy's name as he got aboard. Ernie waited at the back of the line of nine- and ten-year-old boys. Lakesiders his age had been to the YMCA pool many times and were already able swimmers. But not Ernie. McGinty had always found a way to keep him from going. Now, because of the new policy, she was forced to include him.

Impatient, Ernie circled to the back of the bus, where he stomped on a row of ice puddles, which was one of his favorite things to do. Every puddle felt like an invitation, no matter the season, and he never passed one without romping through it.

"Ernie Banks!"

Looking up, he saw McGinty's disapproving glare, then jumped onto one last puddle, cracking the ice.

"You've got five seconds to get aboard this bus," she said. "Or face the consequences."

Once on the bus, McGinty made him sit next to her and lectured him the whole way across town about "responsibility" and "fulfilling his potential." He almost wished he'd stayed in the dorm.

After taking showers in their swimsuits, the boys pattered out to the pool for their first lesson. Ernie marveled at the water's dreamlike glimmer and the kinetic reflections that danced across the walls and ceiling. For as long as he could remember, he'd wanted to learn how to swim.

Mrs. McGinty perched atop a lifeguard tower like a bloated vulture surveying her prey. She'd rolled her nylon stockings to just under her fleshy knees, and her glasses dangled on a string across her bosom. From her lofty position she monitored the behavior of her boys shivering in a group huddle. That is, everyone except Ernie. He was on his hands and knees at the edge of the pool, stroking the shimmering water.

When their instructor arrived with an enthusiastic greeting, "Hey, tadpoles—ready to get wet?" the boys stood at attention, even Ernie. Mr. Franco Alvarez had been the freestyle champ in the city of Chicago when he was sixteen, but that was sixty years ago. Rail thin, with wrinkled skin and only a few wisps of white hair left on his bony head, Mr. Alvarez shuffled across the tile floor in a red-and-white-striped Speedo. His flip-flops made a sucking sound with each step. He blew the whistle dangling from his neck and announced, "First thing we're going to do is pick a swim buddy."

While the other boys grabbed a partner, Ernie drifted back to the edge of the pool. He had only one thing on his mind. The water. Unable to resist a second longer, he jumped into the pool, surprising everyone, even himself. He splashed about, flailing his arms and legs, then began to sink. Mrs. McGinty sprang to her feet. "Mr. Alvarez, do something!"

But Mr. Alvarez stood staring at Ernie as if he were walking on water instead of swallowing it.

"No Lakesider drowns on my watch," McGinty muttered. "Not even Ernie Banks." She pinched her nose and belly flopped into the pool, clothes and all. Blubbering to the surface, she gulped for air, then plunged back under.

But suddenly, to everyone's astonishment, Ernie began to wriggle across the bottom as if he'd lived in water all his life. By the time he reached the surface at the deep end, he was swimming with the grace of a porpoise, his face plastered with a giant grin. With the other boys cheering him on, he dove back under. From the bottom of the pool, he could see McGinty's blurry image paddling toward him. A thousand bubbles escaped her mouth as she screamed a garbled underwater rant. But the water felt so right, he decided to ignore her and swam several laps, sometimes underwater and sometimes on top.

When four YMCA staffers finally hauled him out of the pool, Ernie had an irrepressible grin because now he knew what it felt like to swim. It was the absolute best moment of his life.

McGinty greeted him with a stinging swat to his wet behind. "Ernie Banks, I'm gonna make you wish you never woke up this morning!"

When they got back to Lakeside, Mrs. McGinty kept her promise, and then some. For starters, she vowed he'd never see the pool again, not in this lifetime or the next, despite the fact that Mr. Alvarez said he was the best natural swimmer he'd ever seen. Then she made Ernie mop the entire basement, the damp, dirty underbelly of the old tenement, with the smallest sponge she could find. Finally she sat him in the corner of the dining room, facing the wall, while the other boys ate dinner, but McGinty still wasn't satisfied. After they washed their faces and brushed their teeth, the boys filed past Ernie standing outside the dorm in his underwear with a sign around his neck that read TROUBLE. It was long after lights-out before she let him go to bed.

After that night, something inside Ernie changed. He

just stopped caring. After losing his best and only friend, and knowing he'd never be allowed to swim again, he became more reckless than ever and challenged McGinty's authority at every opportunity. It became a battle of wills. Mrs. McGinty told anyone who would listen that Ernie Banks was well on his way to becoming a first-rate juvenile delinquent.

And she was probably right.

CHAPTER SEVENTEEN

The Unfriendly Confines

THE FINAL TROUBLE began on a summer afternoon perfect for baseball. It was the Monday of July 4th weekend and everybody from the sixth floor was going to Wrigley. Ernie had never actually been to a game, even though the field was just down the street. Mrs. McGinty knew how much he loved the Cubs, and when Lakesiders went on their annual trip to the park, she always found a reason why he should be left behind.

But that didn't stop him. He'd just sneak out onto the fire escape and climb the drainpipe to the roof, then jump to the adjacent building and sit with his legs dangling over the parapet while watching the game and listening on his portable radio. The play-by-play helped a lot, because he could see only a corner of the infield grass. The thing he wanted most in the world was to go to a game at Wrigley, but the roof was as close as he ever got. Until today.

On the previous Saturday, when the other boys went to the Y for their swimming lesson, he'd sprung open the corner fire hydrant, which had caused a minor flood in the street. The crime had put him in detention for seven days, and cleaning the kitchen floor that morning was his final task. He scrubbed and waxed the linoleum, buffing the floor until it shined like a pair of McGinty's patent leather shoes. He wasn't going to give her any reason to keep him from getting to the game. *Not today.*

He returned the mop to the supply closet, then bounded up the steps to the sixth floor. As soon as he entered the dorm, he saw five boys at an open window, waging a spitting contest to see who could hit a garbage can in the alley. A freckle-faced redhead invited him to join. "Ernie, you in?"

"Maybe later, " he said.

Everybody else was changing into their best T-shirts and jeans for the trip to Wrigley when a pigeon flew into the dorm. Panicked, the bird fluttered back and forth as the kids tried to catch it. Shouting, they threw their baseball gloves, hoping to knock it out of the air. One kid was even swinging his bat. When the terrified bird hit a closed window and fell to the ground, the boys swarmed.

"No!" Ernie shouted. "Leave it alone!"

Everybody froze. Ernie walked through the crowd and knelt beside the stunned bird. Cooing softly, as if he could speak its language, he gently picked up the pigeon. At first the bird pecked his hand, but calmed as Ernie stroked its chest and checked to make sure its wings weren't broken. The other kids watched dumbfounded as he stood up with the bird in his open palm, then walked across the room and slipped out the window onto the fire escape. The pigeon stretched its neck and chirped, as if thanking Ernie, then flapped its wings, taking off. He watched the pigeon catch a draft between the buildings and soar toward the roof. He wished he could fly away, too.

"Ernie Banks—get off that fire escape!"

As soon as he heard that voice, he knew he wasn't going to Wrigley.

This latest transgression put him on hands and knees scrubbing the toilets on the fifth floor. From the bathroom window, Ernie watched the Lakesiders merging with fans young and old, migrating toward the ballpark. In a way he couldn't explain, he felt more desperate than he'd ever felt before.

Tortured by the happy sounds of the crowd on their way to Wrigley, he noticed a *drip-drip-drip* coming from a nearby sink. He inspected the leaky faucet, but instead of trying to stop it, he stuffed paper towels into the drain and turned the water on full blast. He hustled from sink to sink, clogging each drain and cranking all the faucets. The basins filled with water, spilling onto the floor. Soon water was flowing into the hall and cascading down the stairway.

Mrs. McGinty was working in her first-floor office when a puddle swirled around her feet. Horrified, she followed the stream into the hall and looked up the stairs, where water poured from step to step in a series of waterfalls.

By the time the incensed McGinty hauled herself to the fifth floor, she found out-of-control boys splashing in ankle-deep water and a flooded corridor transformed into a water slide. With a running start, Ernie Banks slid head-first the length of the hall, a plume of water flaring behind. Unable to stop, he skidded between McGinty's legs, upending her. She tried to grab him, but he was already gone.

Ernie raced down the stairs, taking the steps two and three at a time. When he reached the third floor, he hopped onto the railing and deftly slid from landing to landing.

Four stories above, the soaked McGinty looked over the banister and spotted Ernie as he reached the first floor.

"Ernie Baaaaaaannks!" she screamed. "You stop right there!"

But he was out the front door and didn't hear her, though he wouldn't have stopped even if he had.

Ernie didn't stop running until he stood in the shadow of Wrigley Field. Still wet and out of breath, he watched enviously as fans entered the stadium. More than anything, he needed to get inside. He hovered near the turnstile, waiting for the moment to make a preemptive strike. When the ticket taker turned his head, he leapt the gate, then juked past the lunging security chief.

"Hey, you! Get back here!" the man shouted.

Ernie disappeared into a throng of fans, darting left then right. The barrel-chested chief grabbed his walkie-talkie from his holster. "Look alive, people, we got a jumper headin' straight up the concourse," he said with irritation in his voice. "Maybe eleven, twelve years old, a blue-and-white T-shirt with a Cubbies cap. Oh, and he's soaking wet."

Ernie was threading through the crowd when he noticed two security guards up ahead scanning the concourse. He checked over his shoulder and saw more security jogging toward him and closing fast. Putting on the brakes, he disappeared into the midst of a Boy Scout troop gathered around a concession stand. He slipped a scout cap from the pocket of an unsuspecting troop member, switched out his Cubs cap, then crouched down behind a pudgy scout who was licking an ice cream. After the guards hustled past, he returned the scout cap to its owner, then merged with other fans making their way to the field box level.

As Ernie walked out of the darkened tunnel into the

daylight, his jaw dropped and his heart skipped a beat. He gazed in awe at the field's diamond geometry, its rich velvety grass, and perfectly raked infield. Never had he seen grass so green or sky so blue. Like the pull of the ocean's tides by the moon, he was drawn down the aisle toward the field, where major leaguers stretched, played catch, and took batting practice. When he arrived at the rail just above the Cubs dugout, home run king Rocky Harmon emerged to swing a bat just in front of him. He stared for a minute, wondering if his voice had deserted him. Finally summoning his courage, he called, "Mr. Harmon? Can I have your autograph?"

The all-star first baseman was busy applying pine tar to the handle of his bat. "No kid's called me mister in a while. Got a pen? Paper?" asked Rocky.

Ernie shook his head.

"You got to be prepared, son," Rocky explained, then turned to a batboy. "Randy, you got a pen?"

The batboy tossed him a pen, then Rocky grabbed a ball from the ground. He turned to Ernie. "Okay, what's your name?"

"Ernie Banks."

Rocky gave him a look, suppressing a laugh. "You're kidding me."

Ernie shook his head and Rocky broke into a broad grin. "Yo, guys, catch this." Nearby players emerged from the dugout to gather around Rocky.

"Meet the man, Ernie Banks, Mr. Cub himself," he announced to his teammates. When the others saw the diminutive Caucasian kid bearing the name of their great Hall of Fame shortstop, they began to laugh.

"If he can hit like Ernie Banks, let's sign him," suggested one player.

"You got your spikes?" questioned another.

Rocky smiled. "Hey, Ernie, it's a beautiful day—what say we play two?"

Ernie wasn't sure what to make of their laughter, but the smile never left his face. Mesmerized, he couldn't believe that half a dozen major league ballplayers were actually paying attention to him. And because of that he didn't notice the security guards swarming down the aisle. His reverie was shattered when they clamped him in their grip from behind.

"Hey, people, not too rough. What's the problem?" asked Rocky.

The security chief arrived, angry and out of breath. "This kid's the problem. Jumped the gate without a ticket."

On the chief's command, the guards began to drag Ernie up the aisle, and none too gently. Fans near the dugout began to boo loudly.

"Hey, hold up!" shouted Rocky. Not willing to defy the great ballplayer, the guards waited. "Ernie Banks—keep your eye on the prize," he said, then tossed the autographed baseball to the youngster.

One of the guards tried to intercept it, but Ernie was quicker and he snagged the ball, to the crowd's delight. As security hauled Ernie up the aisle, the fans booed even louder. Before they disappeared into the tunnel, the entire stadium was thundering its disapproval. The Lakesiders in the right field bleachers swore it was Ernie, but their chaperones said that was impossible.

The beefy security guys lifted Ernie by his armpits and marched him along the concourse. When they reached the gate, the chief wrenched the autographed ball from his grip. "You're not taking this with you, that's for sure."

"I didn't want it anyways," Ernie blurted.

Outside the park, the goons manhandled him into the custody of two Chicago police officers. The cops tossed him up against their car and frisked him like he was Al Capone himself.

It wasn't the first time Ernie had been in the backseat of a police car. He didn't care about that, or even the McGinty punishment he knew was coming, but he did care about being thrown out of Wrigley on his very first visit. And that jerk had stolen his autographed baseball.

The police car made its way slowly against the flow of Cubs fans still arriving at Wrigley. Ernie stared out the window at a father and son walking side by side. The kid was about his age and wore an authentic Cubs baseball jersey with Rocky Harmon's number on the back. He said something to his dad, and whatever it was, it made them both laugh. Ernie wondered what it would be like to have a dad who appreciated the smart stuff you might say, or even the stupid stuff, or just anything at all.

The police car pulled to the curb in front of the Lakeside Home for Boys. The cops hustled him up the steps. To Ernie, they might as well have been walking him straight into the Cook County jail. He'd already been to the precinct station, where they got his fingerprints and took his picture. When they'd called Mrs. McGinty to come and get him, she'd refused.

The officer rang the bell and waited. Ernie could hear her heavy footsteps approaching the door. *This is going to be bad.* The door flew open and McGinty loomed on the threshold. The officer offered a crooked smile and handed her a clipboard. "Got a customer here for you, Mrs. McGinty."

"And a truer embarrassment you will not find," she seethed. She signed the paper that acknowledged his arrest. "Unfortunately, this little delinquent simply refuses to accept authority." She turned her attention to Ernie. "Next time I won't be signing anything, and they can take you straight to the Youth Authority," she threatened. "How'd you like that?"

Ernie stared right back.

She pinched his cheek and gave it a good shake. "And don't be giving me that look."

Shrugging her off, he slipped past her and down the hall. She shouted after him, "Ernie Banks, you wait in my office. In-my-office! Do you hear me?!"

He didn't answer. McGinty struggled to control her temper as she turned back to the officers. "Any property damage?"

In the dim corridor, Ernie paused beside her office. He looked inside. The room was intimidating and cold, just like McGinty. Ernie decided he couldn't bear to hear another lecture, especially after all he'd been through with the police.

He started quickly up the stairs, nearly colliding with Kathryn, the social worker. "Oops, Ernie, hi," she said, smiling. "They miss you at the pool. Mr. Alvarez asked about you today. He hopes they let you come back this winter."

Ernie was afraid if he opened his mouth he might start to cry.

"Hey, I thought you were going to the game. What's up? You okay?" she asked sympathetically. She reached out to put her hand on his shoulder, but he turned and fled up the stairs.

Ernie entered the fifth-floor dormitory on a mission. He knew his dorm would be locked, with everybody still at the game. The younger boys stopped what they were doing as he flung open a window and jumped out. They rushed over to get a look. The number one rule in the dorm was to never go out onto the fire escape, and now Ernie Banks was doing it twice on the same day.

He stepped off the metal grating. With his back pressed against the building, Ernie shuffled along the ledge, then shinnied up the drainpipe toward the roof. Halfway up, he stopped to acknowledge his fellow orphans by thrusting a defiant fist in the air. Twenty fists answered, along with shouts of encouragement.

Mrs. McGinty burst into the dorm. "Get away from those windows!" she screamed as she shoved away a clutch of boys and bellied up to the sill.

Ernie hoisted himself onto the roof. He could hear sounds from the elevated train and a roar from Wrigley Field, but McGinty's voice cut through it all.

"Ernie Baaaaanks!" she thundered.

Ernie looked down to see McGinty screaming through cupped hands. Every window was crowded with excited boys.

"If I have to call the fire department again, you'll be one sorry boy! Do you hear me?! Now get down from there!"

Ignoring her, Ernie sprinted across the roof to leap the chasm onto the adjacent building. He tumbled on the hard surface but jumped up running. He could barely hear McGinty's voice. "Ernie Banks! Don't make me come up there!"

Out of sight, he ran to his hideaway in the abandoned water tank. He pulled back the sheet metal, crawled inside, and found his portable radio. It was right where it was supposed to be, hidden inside an old milk carton.

Ernie crawled back out and sat on the parapet overlooking the street. Wrigley's infield grass was visible three blocks away. From his vantage point, the Tigers third baseman looked like an ant, but it was better than nothing. He turned on his radio. First static, then the announcer's voice squawked from the speaker, "Rocky Harmon calls for time as he digs in at the plate. Now he's ready."

"Get a hit, Rocky," Ernie whispered to himself.

The announcer rattled on. "The big left-hander looks in for the sign. Here's the windup, the pitch, and it's a weakly hit ground ball to the second baseman. He scoops it up and tosses to first. Another one-two-three inning for the Cubs. After seven innings in the not-so-friendly confines, it's Tigers three, Cubs nothing."

Ernie clicked off the radio with a weary sigh. He removed a loose brick from the facade, reached into his secret stash, and withdrew a single baseball card. He deftly snapped it faceup. It was the original Ernie Banks card, his most cherished possession—that and the Crystal Acorn he still wore around his neck. Those were the two things that proved he really did belong to somebody, somewhere.

A peal of thunder lifted his gaze to the sky. Huge black clouds were sweeping across the lake, accompanied by sheets of driving rain. It looked like the biggest storm he'd seen in a while. *This is going to be good.* He returned his Ernie Banks card to the stash and replaced the brick, then stuffed the radio under his shirt. At Wrigley, the ground crew was running onto the field with a big white tarp. It billowed up behind them like an ocean wave as they covered the infield. Ernie stood up on the ledge, preparing to meet the storm, and waited. Soon the rain pounded down, drenching him, while thunder and lightning cracked the sky with an awesome light. He felt like shouting, but didn't know what to say.

In the distance, he could hear the approaching sirens.

CHAPTER EIGHTEEN

Good-bye, Ernie Banks

FOR ONLY THE THIRD time ever, Mrs. McGinty demanded a meeting at the downtown corporate office of the Lakeside Home for Boys. Unfortunately, the first and second meeting had also been about Ernie Banks.

"I swear that boy will be the death of me! It took three firemen on a hook and ladder to get him off the roof. By God, I can't tolerate a boy who won't abide by the rules," Mrs. McGinty fumed.

Ernie sat wedged between his accuser and Kathryn Moss, the social worker, who was usually smiling, but not this morning. McGinty had been ranting for what seemed like forever and she wasn't losing any steam. On the other side of the desk was the person who would decide his fate, the Lakeside director, Antonio Vellani. A debonair sixty-year-old with a soft Italian accent, Mr. Vellani was a patient man with a natural sense of fairness, but the name Ernie Banks had come to his attention three too many times.

Vellani finally stopped McGinty's tirade with a raised hand. "All right, Annie, just a moment," he said, then turned calmly to Ernie. "Do you hear what Mrs. McGinty is saying?"

Ernie nodded.

Vellani tapped his pen on the desk. "And what do you think I should do?"

He thought about begging for one last chance, but figured it didn't matter anymore.

"If you won't talk, I can't help you," cautioned Vellani. "Do you realize what this could mean?"

Ernie felt like his chest was about to explode, but he just stared defiantly.

Vellani closed the Ernie Banks folder with a weary sigh. "Then you leave me no choice. I'm going to recommend you be placed under the supervision of the Illinois Youth Authority."

Ernie felt the floor go out from under him. He'd heard the stories from other kids about the Youth Authority. It was a prison for juvenile delinquents. Bad things happened there. *Real bad things.* He closed his eyes for a moment. *I might as well be dead.* He knew everyone was watching him, especially her, so when he opened his eyes, he looked straight at Mrs. McGinty and simply muttered, "Whatever."

"Okay, then. Wait outside," Vellani instructed.

Ernie shuffled out of the room. When the door closed, Mrs. McGinty nodded with satisfaction. "Thank you, Tony, thank you. And good riddance to him."

Vellani looked at his hands and sighed. "That's too bad. I can't help but feel like we've failed when a boy goes to the Y.A."

Kathryn sensed her opportunity. "Mr. Vellani, couldn't we try to place him in another foster home—just one last time?"

McGinty countered before Vellani could answer. "He's had more chances than most, and frankly, no family would even consider a boy his age, not with his record."

"Over the hill at thirteen?" asked Vellani, smiling ruefully.

"If we send that boy to the Y.A., he'll get crushed. He needs our help, not a prison," Kathryn pleaded.

"Maybe if you spent more time in the dormitory you'd be singing a different tune," snarled McGinty.

"Folks, folks, please," said Vellani, trying to keep the peace.

Kathryn suddenly had an idea. "What about the Summer Farm Program? Don't we still need to fill Doug McQuaid's spot?"

McGinty groaned. Every summer a few lucky orphans from Lakeside were chosen to spend some time on a working farm. The program had been running for several years and was a big success. Orphans from all over the state had benefited from the kindness of the Illinois farming community.

"You really think a few weeks in the country will make a difference?" asked Vellani.

"Honestly, I don't know. But it might give him something to feel good about, something to hope for," reasoned Kathryn.

Vellani turned to McGinty. "Annie, what about it?"

She was outraged. "Right now I could give you the names of fifty boys far more deserving than that hooligan."

"Maybe so, but I doubt you could name one who needs this chance more than Ernie Banks," appealed Kathryn.

Vellani sat back in his chair and weighed the decision.

The next day it was announced that Ernie Banks would spend three weeks in the country as a participant in the Summer Farm Program. When Mrs. McGinty gave the news to Ernie, she looked mad enough to spit. "Last Chance Texaco," she seethed. Ernie understood exactly what she meant. If he got in trouble at the farm, nothing and no one would be able to save him from the Illinois Youth Authority.

On the day of his departure, Mrs. McGinty was in a foul mood. She barely spoke to him except to complain about the way he'd made his bed, deride him for his messy hair, and issue extra morning chores.

After putting away the mop and bucket, he started upstairs to pack. As he passed McGinty's office, she stepped into the hall with a scowl. "Ernie Banks, you'll be wearing a coat and tie this morning."

Ernie nodded and slouched past her up the stairs. He could barely believe that he was really leaving and didn't want McGinty to see how excited he was. He was afraid she might still stop him from going.

With his Cubs cap pulled low over his eyes and dressed in a hand-me-down sports coat and mismatched tie, Ernie packed an extra pair of blue jeans, two T-shirts, underwear, socks, and his baseball glove into a battered suitcase plastered with Cubs emblems.

Feeling as if his feet weren't even touching the ground, Ernie said good-bye to a few kids, then lugged his suitcase down six flights of stairs and out the door. As he waited with Mrs. McGinty at the curb for a taxi, she made him open his suitcase and, just to spite him, confiscated his glove.

At the bus station, everything Ernie did annoyed her. She didn't like the way he scuffed his feet on the cement when he walked. She didn't like the way he slurped a drink from the water fountain. And she didn't like it that he was wearing "that ridiculous Cubs cap," which she made him fold and tuck into his back pocket. She was so agitated, she even smoked a cigarette, which came as a huge surprise to him. He wondered what other nasty things McGinty kept secret from the rest of the world.

When his bus was announced on the PA system, McGinty steered him by the collar through the crowded station, then shoved him up the steps of the waiting Greyhound. "If it was up to me, you'd be on a bus to the reformatory. But mark my words, if you come back from that farm with even one hair out of place, you're gone." Ernie only stared, which irritated her even more. She spat out her last words. "I'll be waiting for you, Ernie Banks. I'll be right here."

The bus door banged closed between them. Out of her reach, he snapped his Cubs cap back on his head, then marched up the aisle and settled into a seat. As the Greyhound revved its engine, Ernie looked out the window to see McGinty giving him the evil eye. As much as he hated to admit it, he felt a twinge of sadness in saying good-bye. The old witch was the only adult he'd ever really known, and suddenly he felt completely alone.

When the bus started out of the station, he waved at Mrs. McGinty's frowning face and, knowing it would make her mad, offered a colossal grin from ear to ear.

CHAPTER NINETEEN

Wrinkle in the Wheat

ERNIE FELT A SCARY enthusiasm as the skyscrapers became shorter and the gray pavement turned to green grass. He wasn't sure what it would be like where he was going, but he knew it couldn't be any worse than what he was leaving behind. He looked out the window at rolling hills and woods and wide fields planted with corn and wheat. After a while, the hypnotic passing of the checkerboard landscape and the rhythmic sound of the bus tires on the road lulled him to sleep.

"This is where you get off, son."

Ernie woke with a start. The bearded face of the driver was staring down at him. Disoriented, he grabbed his suitcase from the adjacent seat and shuffled down the aisle. The few remaining passengers craned their necks when he tripped on his untied shoelace and tumbled down the steps, landing facefirst in the dust of the Illinois countryside.

"You all right there, pardner?" the driver asked.

Ignoring the question, Ernie jumped to his feet and brushed off the dust.

"Okay, then—happy trails," said the driver as he closed the door and noisily shifted into gear.

Ernie watched the bus motor away. He was standing in front of a dilapidated grocery store named The Trading Post. The plate glass was cracked and someone had nailed a sheet of plywood across the entrance with the words OUT OF BUSINESS scrawled across it in red paint.

Ernie sat on a weathered bench beneath a rusted sign that read BUS STOP. All around him, fields of withered wheat baked in the hot sun. He hadn't known what to expect, but it certainly wasn't this. Even a city boy could see that something was wrong. Everything was brown and dusty. The trees looked haunted. It felt like it hadn't rained forever.

Suddenly thirsty, Ernie swallowed and loosened his tie. A quarter mile down the old state highway, two church steeples rose above a small town. He could just make out a couple of signs, THE TURKEY ROOST and THE WILLOW LOUNGE, but it didn't look like there were any customers. He perked up when a car started in his direction, but then it turned and disappeared from view. Across the street and a few hundred feet in the opposite direction was a gas station, but it, too, was closed. Beyond that, there was nothing but parched fields.

Ernie remembered Mrs. McGinty telling him that some guy would be waiting for him at the other end, but he hadn't been paying much attention. Now he wondered if she'd made a mistake, or maybe this was her plan to get rid of him for good. Not sure what to do and roasting in the hot sun, he crossed the street and walked toward the shade of the abandoned gas station.

A big green dinosaur peered down from the dented sign. The gas pumps had white circular lamps on top with the same green dinosaur and the word SINCLAIR in red lettering, but the handles and hoses were missing.

Ernie looked back toward the town to see if anyone was coming. No one was. That's when he noticed the sign, WELCOME TO CIRCLE. It was about sixty feet away, just like the distance from the mound to home plate in the big leagues. He scooped up some stones from the side of the road, snugged his Cubs cap low on his head, scratched a line in the dirt, and zeroed in on the sign. He cleared his throat, then, imitating a play-by-play announcer, broadcast in a loud voice, "It's unbelievable, folks. The ninth inning, two outs, and Ernie Banks is on the mound for the Cubs, facing the most dangerous hitter in the game, the King of Swat, Babe Ruth." He spit into his palm, then rubbed the stone. "Here's the windup, and the pitch . . ."

Ernie fired the stone, pegging the sign with a metallic clang. "Steee-rike, on the outside corner! The Babe took a mighty swing and connected with a big chunk of nothing." He took another stone out of his pocket and jiggled it in the palm of his hand behind his back. He squinted at the road sign. "Banks, wasting no time, looks in for the sign."

Suddenly laughter interrupted his game. Embarrassed, Ernie watched a kid on a black-and-white pinto pony canter from the field onto the highway, between his pitching mound and the sign. When Ernie heard her say, "Whoa, Sassy," he realized the intruder was a girl.

Joey Woodruff was wearing a faded T-shirt boasting the slogan ROOSTERS DON'T CROW FOR NOTHIN'! and an International Harvester cap pulled tight over short brown hair. He thought she was somewhere around his age, with lots of freckles on her nose and a fierce look in her light brown eyes. He wondered how long she'd been spying on him.

Determined to maintain his pride, Ernie decided to ignore her. He stared in at his target, now mostly obscured by the pony and its rider, then went into his windup. He fired a stone that whizzed past the girl's nose and pinged the sign loudly. "Steee-rike two!"

Joey lowered the brim of her cap. She stared first at the sign, then at Ernie. "That's public property, you know."

Ernie pretended she wasn't even there. In fact, to show how little he cared about her presence, he even exaggerated his radio broadcast. "Wrigley Field is going absolutely gaga, Cubs fans. One more out and we've got the Series. The whole season rides on this pitch. Banks looks in for the sign."

"I wouldn't do that if I was you," warned Joey.

"Here's the windup, the pitch . . ."

He reared back and fired his best fastball. It flew straight as an arrow, beaming for the sign, until Joey unexpectedly doffed her cap, caught the stone in its crown, then flung it deep into the adjacent field.

"That ball is outta here!" she cried.

Ernie stared dumbfounded as Joey trotted her pony up alongside him. She leaned down to read the name tag on his suitcase.

"You Ernie Banks?" she asked.

Exasperated, Ernie grabbed his suitcase and started for the Sinclair station. Joey watched coolly from her mount. "You always wear a tie when you travel?"

Ernie pressed on until the sound of beating hooves made him glance over his shoulder. He tumbled out of the way as Sassy galloped past.

"Are you crazy?" he yelled angrily.

Joey reined Sassy about and reared her up like a trick pony in the center ring of the circus. Ernie rolled in the dirt to avoid her clopping hooves. Joey expertly rode Sassy into position, leaned out of the saddle, and swooped up Ernie's suitcase before trotting into the wheat.

Ernie couldn't believe the audacity of this girl. "Hey, that suitcase is private property!" was all he could think to say.

"Can it, Mr. Cub. You're not in Chicago anymore."

"Wait a second! I'm supposed to get a ride from back there."

"This is your ride," she said flatly.

Ernie watched, baffled, as Joey tied his suitcase to her saddle while trotting away down a narrow tractor lane sandwiched between two fields of dying wheat. He looked back at the bus stop. Beyond it, the town still looked empty. With no other recourse, he reluctantly followed, trudging a safe distance behind his new adversary.

"So how come they're dumping you on us?" asked Joey without looking back.

He didn't answer.

"I guess they got to dump you orphan kids somewheres," she explained. "Last year we had a real runt. Lasted three days. Year before that was even worse. I told Russ to quit this 'be nice to orphans' thing but he says we got to share the good Lord's earth with rejects, I mean people like you less fortunate than ourselves."

"Just keep it up," warned Ernie.

"Keep it up what?" mocked Joey.

"Just get me there," he snapped.

Joey wheeled Sassy around, reining her wide flanks into Ernie, and stared down fiercely. "Look, orphan—me and Russ got to harvest the wheat, least what's left of it, and we got no time for the likes of you. I'm sayin' it right now— you get in our way or even look at me or Russ sideways, I'll bust you raw!"

She untied his suitcase and dropped it to the ground, spilling his clothes in the dirt. Ernie stared in disbelief as she turned Sassy and started back down the lane. "And another thing, orphan . . ."

Her warning was interrupted when a dirt clod splattered against the back of her head. "Oww!" she screamed, then jumped from her pony and charged Ernie, tackling him. They grappled in the dirt like two snarling dogs determined to prove who was stronger. Only the sound of screeching brakes prevented them both from losing some fur.

The frozen combatants stared into the vintage grillwork of a black Cadillac scowling at them like an iron beast. They scrambled out of the way on hands and knees, Ernie to one side of the lane and Joey the other. The Cadillac accelerated, crushing Ernie's suitcase. He watched openmouthed as it sped away in a cloud of dust. Joey swung up into her saddle. "Come on, I'm supposed to bring you back!" she yelled. "Get on!"

Ernie spit dirt from his mouth with a defiant look. "That's your problem, Rooster. Not mine."

She reined Sassy sideways, prancing. "Listen up, Ernie Banks—there's a war on out here and Russ' life could be at stake!"

"What are you talkin' about?" he demanded.

"Get on or get lost!" she said, then offered her hand.

The only thing he knew was that he didn't want to be left alone in this used-up and good-for-nothing boondocks. Swallowing his pride, he grabbed hold of Joey's hand and pulled himself awkwardly onto Sassy's rump.

"Next time, you're on your own. Git up!" she shouted, and Sassy galloped off. Not wanting to hang on to a girl, Ernie gripped the saddle with both hands in a desperate bid not to fall.

CHAPTER TWENTY

Grand Theft

SASSY GALLOPED down a sloped field of pitiful, dried-out wheat. As they came in sight of the farmhouse, Joey insisted they dismount and steal through what had once been a flower garden but was now nothing more than clumps of hard dirt. Motioning Ernie to keep quiet, she led Sassy past a grave marker under a stooped willow. Carved into the wood was the name PITCH and the inscription BEST DOG IN THE WORLD. Joey touched the marker before crossing past a silo to the back of a big barn. She sidled along the old wooden structure to peek around the corner. Wondering what all the fuss was about, Ernie spied past her shoulder. Two overgrown twenty-year-olds, with no necks and brutish faces, lumbered from the backseat of the black Cadillac, one the hulking shadow of the other.

"Those two ugly ones are the Holsapple twins, Angus and Axel," Joey whispered. "They don't say squat to me and I'm not even sure they can talk. I'd feel bad for their mom, but she's already dead."

When Angus cleared his throat, Axel spit, but Ernie couldn't tell them apart. Another man, sinewy, with a face like a ferret—sinister eyes, bad teeth, and a jagged scar on one cheek—slunk from the driver's seat.

"That guy is Dicky Cobb, the foreman," she pointed out. "I been chased by him plenty." She lowered her voice and spelled "C-R-A-Z-Y." Ernie started to ask a question, but she shushed him with an expression that made it clear she was the only one allowed to talk.

Dicky Cobb opened the passenger door and out stepped an aged man in a dark suit with unruly white hair, a gnarled face, and a bent posture supported by an ebony cane.

"The old crooked man is Harvey Holsapple. Got the biggest oil operation in all of Illinois."

Sassy whinnied, which caused Joey to duck for cover and bump into Ernie. "Watch it," she hissed. "Pay attention!"

He gave her a disgusted look as she eased back around the corner. They watched undercover as old Holsapple hobbled to a modest one-story farmhouse, its red paint peeling, and rapped on the door of the screened porch with his cane.

"Dude's got no heart, either," whispered Joey. "He ever catches you alone, you're dead."

A man emerged from underneath an old combine parked in the shade of the barn. "What can I do for you gentlemen?" he asked in a friendly voice.

The Holsapple clan turned in surprise.

The man approached, wiping his hands on a rag. Though walking with a slight limp, he reminded Ernie of Rocky Harmon. He wasn't as big, but he carried himself with the same easy confidence. Instead of a bat, he had a large wrench in his hand. Ernie thought it would make a good weapon, if needed, but the composed expression on the man's face said that he wasn't looking for a fight.

"Who's that?" asked Ernie.

Joey shot him her most disdainful look. "Dumb Cub, that's the guy who's supposed to act like your dad for three weeks. That's Russ Frazier." She scanned the yard surmising the situation before slapping Sassy's reins into his hand. "Make sure nobody sneaks up from behind," she ordered.

"Where you going?" Ernie asked.

"I said, watch my back!"

Ernie watched her scuttle along the rear of the barn and disappear around the corner. Sassy nudged him with her nose and snorted. "Shhhhh," he hushed, more than a little unnerved by this big animal. "Good horse," he whispered, then cautiously patted her nose.

Reaching the side of the house, Joey scaled a rickety trellis like a lizard climbing a rock face. After clambering to the crest of the steep roof, she looked back to the barn, where Ernie watched from his concealed position. She gave him the high sign, but he chose to ignore it.

Like three hungry vultures, Angus, Axel, and Dicky Cobb surrounded Russ as Harvey Holsapple used his cane to scratch $275,000 in the dirt. "It's a good price, Russ, considering the way things are," said Holsapple.

"Well, my answer's still the same, Harvey—my farm is not for sale."

Shaking his head in disbelief, Holsapple slashed the 7 with his cane, changing the offer to 285.

"Sorry, Harvey, but thanks for the offer," Russ said firmly.

"What's the matter, scared to make some real bucks for once in your life?" spat Holsapple.

The old man was starting to get his dander up, but Russ refused to be baited. "This might sound corny to you oil fellas, but I just don't get up in the morning thinkin' about dollar bills, never have and never will."

Ernie, still holding Sassy's reins, watched Joey pad across the crusty shingles. He wished he were up there, too.

"What are you going to do when your wheat dries up and the bank forecloses on your farm?" challenged Holsapple.

Russ smiled. "Faith, Harvey, you got to have faith in Mother Nature. Rain'll come."

"Oh I see . . . faith," mocked Holsapple as he scanned

the cloudless sky. "Like tonight the sky's going to open up and rain down Noah's flood?"

Dicky Cobb and the twins guffawed at Harvey's joke.

"Stupid farmer," said Cobb with a voice that sounded like his throat was full of gravel. "You people are a dying breed."

Russ kept his smile, but Holsapple gave Cobb a harsh look. "Take no offense, Russ. Sometimes my foreman wants to talk when he should be listening."

On the rooftop, Joey's sneaker caught on a broken shingle that tipped her off balance. Flapping her arms, she barely righted herself. With a deep breath, she continued along the roof, hugging it a little closer than before.

Russ extended his hand in a neighborly gesture and shook hands all around. "Now, if you folks don't mind, I've got a guest comin' today and there's some work I need to get done."

Joey crabbed along the eave in time to see Holsapple take Russ' arm and walk him toward the porch below her.

"Come to your senses, man. The only harvest you're going to get this year is a hundred bushels of dirt."

Joey leaned out a tad too far and lost her grip. She slid off the roof in a flurry of arms and legs, landing on Holsapple, collapsing him in the dirt. Dicky Cobb jerked her up in a crushing headlock. Joey thrashed about like a wounded tiger. "You chicken-belly corncob!"

"Get your hands off her!" shouted Russ as he rushed in to break Cobb's stranglehold. From behind, Angus knocked Russ to the ground with a hard punch to the head, then Axel delivered a kick to his ribs, knocking the wind out of him.

"Russ!" screamed Joey as she kicked Cobb's shin with all her might and scratched his cheek. Howling in pain, he was about to backhand her a good one when a car engine suddenly fired to life. Everybody froze, then watched dumbfounded as the driverless black Cadillac began to motor past the barn and down a tractor lane, all by itself.

"Get my Cadillac!" screeched Holsapple.

Dicky Cobb threw Joey to the ground and bolted after the car, followed by the hulking twins.

Joey crawled over to Russ, who was still gasping for breath. She buried her face in his chest and hugged him close. The dark shadow of Harvey Holsapple loomed over them, blocking out the sun. He raised his hand and she cringed, but he only brushed the dirt from his shoulder. "I'm sorry, Russ," he said. "I always hate to see violence. You think about my offer." Then he turned and hobbled off after the others.

Scrunched low in the Cadillac, Ernie steered with one hand while jamming a rock against the accelerator pedal. He knew this wasn't his fight, but he couldn't just watch those thugs beat up on that poor farmer. If there was one thing he couldn't stand, apart from Mrs. McGinty, it was a bully.

As the Caddy motored along the tractor lane, he

opened the door and watched the ground rush past. Steeling himself, he jumped from the car and tumbled across the hard-packed dirt. Scraped and covered in dust, he belly-crawled to a concealed position in the wheat as Cobb and the twins ran past in pursuit of the car. Smiling with satisfaction, he watched until they disappeared over a knoll. Suddenly a gnarled hand jerked him to his feet and he found himself staring into the flushed face of Harvey Holsapple.

"What do you think you're doing?!" snarled Holsapple.

Ernie recoiled from the old man's grip, but Holsapple twisted even tighter. He smacked the boy's back with his cane, hard, as he spit out each word, "That"—WHACK!—"Caddy"—WHACK!—"cost"—WHACK!—"sixty"—WHACK!—"five"—WHACK!—"thousand"—WHACK!—"dollars!" He throttled Ernie by the tie, yanking him nose to nose. "What's your name?!"

Ernie was gasping for breath, surprised by the old man's strength. "Stop . . . can't . . . breathe," he choked.

Holsapple started to throttle him again, but froze when the Crystal Acorn, dangling on a shoestring around Ernie's neck, popped out from under the boy's shirt. Catching the sun at just the right angle, the ice-blue crystal refracted a sharp light directly into the old man's eyes, blinding him enough so that Ernie was able to break free. He swiped the ebony cane and hurled it into the wheat. Holsapple charged, but Ernie scrambled back just beyond the reach of the old man.

"What is that?" demanded Holsapple.

Ernie whipped the Crystal Acorn off his neck and stuffed it into the pocket of his jeans.

"I'm talking to you, boy," he threatened.

Ernie glared defiantly. "My name is Ernie Banks."

Calming himself as quickly as he'd flared, Holsapple cackled good-naturedly. "All right, Ernie Banks. Now let's have a look at that thing." Wheezing, he hobbled forward, but Ernie retreated, step for step.

"You owe me for one suitcase and all my clothes," said Ernie.

"You think so, huh?" said Holsapple gruffly. Belying his age, he raged toward the boy like an angry tornado. Ernie stumbled backward through the wheat, only to run smack into Russ Frazier, who protectively put his arm around him. Ernie wasn't used to being touched by a stranger, or anyone, for that matter, but at this moment he was pretty glad for the help. Joey ran up to slip beneath Russ' other arm.

"That little thief hijacked my Cadillac!" ranted Harvey. Holsapple was scary when he got angry, but Russ held his ground.

"I think that's about enough for today, Harvey. If you've got damages on your car, send me the bill."

"Oh, you're going to get more than my bill, sir!"

Ignoring the old man's threat, Russ steered the shaken Ernie and Joey back toward the house.

"Mark my words," Holsapple shouted. "That boy got there is bound for trouble!"

CHAPTER TWENTY-ONE

The Mystery

I T FELT STRANGE to be with someone he didn't know, but Ernie thought the house seemed friendly and so did Russ. He followed him into the kitchen, where Russ poured tall glasses of cold milk from the fridge.

"You sure I can't make you something to eat?" asked Russ. "A sandwich, maybe?"

"No thanks, I'm not really hungry. Milk's good."

Russ drained his glass, then, with a wink, smacked his lips and made an exaggerated *ahhh* of satisfaction. Ernie smiled. It was just the two of them. Joey had volunteered to retrieve his suitcase from the outskirts of town.

"C'mon, Ernie, let's check the damage," said Russ, motioning him toward the bathroom.

Russ glanced at Ernie's scraped chin before opening the medicine cabinet and removing several bottles. He began to line up medicine by the sink. Ernie sat on the edge of the old claw-foot tub, feigning disinterest but studying Russ' every move.

"So how's life treating you back in Chicago?" Russ asked while mixing his concoction in a small basin.

"It pretty much sucks."

Russ nodded sympathetically. "I can imagine." He added a few drops of iodine to his potion. "Sorry I wasn't able to pick you up today."

"Doesn't matter."

He glanced at the boy in the medicine cabinet mirror. "I'm having some trouble with my combine and we're getting pretty close to harvest. At least I hope to have a harvest."

Ernie shrugged. He didn't know what to say and wondered why Russ was trying to explain everything. He wasn't used to it.

"Okay, Dr. Frazier's anti-Holsapple pain reducer and fungus fighter is ready. Guaranteed satisfaction or your money back," said Russ as he turned from the sink with his basin of red brew.

Ernie stared apprehensively at the blood-colored concoction.

"C'mon, it won't hurt but a minute," assured Russ. To prove his point, he lifted his own shirt and dabbed the abrasions where he'd been kicked.

Ernie winced. "Those jerks were pretty big."

Russ chuckled. "Yeah, well, like my dad used to say, 'The bigger they are, the harder they fall.'"

Ernie laughed. The man had to be kidding. Russ had gotten the worst of it, by far.

"Okay, Mr. Banks, your turn."

Ernie self-consciously removed his shirt. When Russ got a look at the welts on the boy's back, his face flushed with anger but his voice remained calm.

"Brace yourself—here comes Mr. Smarts," he gently warned as he dabbed the concoction on the boy's back. Ernie sucked in his breath and gritted his teeth.

"You got some first-class welts here," said Russ.

"I've had worse."

"This stuff is supposed to burn some, you know."

Ernie just tucked his chin a little tighter.

"So what's your prediction on the Cubs this year?" asked Russ.

"They still need a left-hander in the pen, and one more big bat," he answered, trying to ignore the pain.

Their conversation was interrupted when a crushed suitcase banged onto the windowsill. Joey popped into view with a grin. "Suitcase is shot but the clothes got a good press," she reported.

Ernie found his pulverized Rocky Harmon wristwatch buried in the dusty clothes. "That old geezer busted my watch, too," he said angrily.

"I'd like to kill those Holsapples!" chimed Joey.

"Whoa, now I don't want to hear that kind of talk, and I don't want you getting into it with the Holsapples," said Russ.

"But if they're beatin' up on you, Russ, I'm gonna tussle," she protested.

"You just go tussle with a telephone and call the sheriff. We stay clear from those people. They go their way and we go ours. Is that understood?"

She nodded regretfully.

"Ernie, that goes for you, too," he added.

Ernie shrugged. Russ clapped a hand on his shoulder. "All right then, let's get you settled."

Russ led Ernie and Joey into the old nursery. Ernie could see right away that some effort had been made to prepare for his arrival. Against the wall, just inside the door, was a wood-frame bed. Next to it was a small bedside table with a reading lamp and a vase of wildflowers with a few wheat stalks mixed in. There was also a ceramic pitcher shaped like a goose and a drinking glass. But what captured Ernie's attention was an old crib in the corner. Above the crib he noticed a faded photograph of a younger Russ with a baby in a back-harness holding a rattle.

"Joey and I spiffed it up best we could, but feel free to fix it so you're comfortable. Make yourself at home, that's the main thing," said Russ.

Nodding, Ernie wandered over to the crib. It was empty, except for a folded red quilt. His gaze lifted to an elfin mobile attached to the rail. He fingered the empty woolen harness at its center. He was wondering what used to be in it when Joey broke the spell. "It ain't much, but it's all you paid for."

"This your crib?" he asked her.

Behind Russ, Joey frantically waved her arms and shook her head, mouthing "No!" But it was too late. Russ answered, "The crib belonged to my son."

"Oh. Where is he?" asked Ernie.

Joey shot him a punishing look.

Russ responded softly, "I lost him, Ernie, a long time ago. Maybe we'll talk about it some other time, okay?"

Ernie nodded.

"Well, I'll let you get settled. Just give a shout if you need anything. I won't be far," said Russ. On his way out, he gave Joey's shoulder a squeeze.

She smiled weakly. As soon as he was gone she charged at Ernie. "Don't you got any idea what you're not supposed to talk about?!" she said in a disgusted whisper.

"How was I supposed to know?"

"I was giving you signals! Don't you pay attention?!"

Turning away, Ernie casually snapped a finger against each of the mobile's wooden elves. "How'd your dad ever lose your brother?" he asked.

"First off, Shawn wasn't my brother, and second, Russ isn't my dad."

"Who is?"

"None of your beeswax."

Ernie continued to snap each elf into orbit, as if that were far more interesting than the present conversation.

"You live here?" he asked.

"I live with my mom next farm over."

"So what did happen to Russ' kid?"

"I told you we don't talk about it."

Ernie stepped back to admire his work. Now all the elves were dancing by their threads.

"Who's stopping us?"

Joey shook her head in exasperation. "He got stole, all right?"

"Stole? Who stole him?"

She looked at him with disdain. "I'm not telling no rookie."

Ernie raised his empty palms to Joey, snapped his fingers twice, waved his hands in front of her face, then reached behind her head to produce a set of keys. She stared in disbelief. The keys dangled from a black leather case embossed with gold double Hs.

"Harvey Holsapple's keys!" she exclaimed. "How'd you ever get 'em?"

Ernie stuffed the keys into his pocket. "Not telling no rook. Now why don't you just run along—I got stuff to do," he said nonchalantly. He sauntered across the room and flopped onto the bed, only to wince in pain. He'd forgotten about those welts.

"You crazy Cubber—when Harvey finds out you pulled a fast one . . ."

"Hey, Rooster—stop crowin' about something you know nothing about."

"I swear, you're the know-nothin'," said Joey.

"If you don't know what happened to Russ' kid, just admit it," goaded Ernie. There was a long stare-down. Ernie thought she looked ready to burst.

"All right, already," she finally said. "I'll tell it, but only this one time, and don't ever tell Russ I told you. Got it?"

Ernie wasn't ready to agree to anything. But he did want to hear the story, so he just nodded. It must have satisfied her, because she closed the door, then marched to the window and gazed outside.

"Okay then. There was a big storm that night, rained like nobody around here had ever seen before or since. The sheriff found a trail comin' down through the field. He said it was a bloodthirsty gang of four, maybe five, broke right through this very window." She abruptly threw open the window, as if to relive the awful crime. Intrigued, Ernie watched as she tiptoed to the crib, her voice dropping low. "They crept over to this crib and just . . ."

"Where was Russ?" interrupted Ernie.

"I dunno, somewheres else, outside maybe, and don't butt in," she said impatiently.

"What about his mom?" persisted Ernie.

"Dead," said Joey gravely.

"How?"

"You want to hear this story or not?"

He tried not to answer, but the look on his face gave him away.

"I thought so," she said smugly. "So this gang just lifted baby Shawn Frazier right up." She cradled the red quilt in her arms as she acted out the scene. "Took the whole shebang—his bottle, clothes, and all the toys laying around and the entire time this kid never made a peep, almost like he enjoyed getting stole." She reached the window and pointed toward the fields. "Then they beat out into the wheat, and not even the sheriff's hounds could track 'em."

Ernie joined her at the window to gaze out toward the great beyond, his imagination working overtime.

In a spellbound voice, Joey whispered, "Only one thing ever got found." She thrust the quilt into his face and he flinched, despite himself. "This old quilt, up on the plateau."

"Did they fingerprint it?" asked Ernie as he ran his hand across the soft red fabric.

"Did it all, everything, but all they got were raccoon prints."

"And nothing else was ever found?"

"Nothin'. End of story. Around here we got to calling it 'the Mystery of the Quilt Baby.'"

Ernie frowned. "A baby doesn't just disappear."

"Quilt Baby did," retorted Joey.

Ernie pondered the mystery. There was something about her story that didn't add up. "Did the sheriff find the quilt?"

"Pitch found it. She was Russ' dog."

"Do you know where, I mean, where exactly?"

"'Course, but that's Holsapple property now."

Ernie looked her in the eye, challenging her with an impish grin. Joey caught his drift and began to shake her head. "That is trouble, Mr. Cub. Big-time trouble."

But the grin had crept onto her face, too.

CHAPTER TWENTY-TWO

Voyagers

ERNIE TRAILED JOEY across the yard to the corral. He felt like he'd escaped from jail, even if it was only for three weeks. Knowing he'd be back at Lakeside soon enough, he decided to put Chicago out of his mind and make the most of his time on the farm.

He wasn't sure what to make of Joey. She wasn't like anyone he'd ever met before. For one thing, she was a girl, and there weren't any of those at Lakeside. But she was a good fighter and didn't mind getting dirty, plus he liked the way she stood up to Dicky Cobb and the Holsapples. Most important, he was pretty sure Mrs. McGinty would have hated her, which definitely counted for a lot.

At the corral, Joey ordered Ernie to hold Sassy's reins

while she cinched the saddle. He reluctantly did as he was told and reminded himself that she was also bossy. He looked over at the barn, where Russ was working on the combine.

"Keep your fingers crossed," Russ called. "Here goes nothin'." He cranked the starter. The engine sputtered, then died. "God-zilla," he cussed. "Hey, Ernie, you know how to fix an engine?"

Ernie didn't know what to say, so he looked to Joey.

"Dumb Cub—he's kidding," she muttered.

"What are you guys up to?" asked Russ.

Joey whispered out of the side of her mouth, "I'll do the talking," then called to Russ, "Ernie wants to get a look at the spread."

"Great. Give me fifteen minutes and I'll take you guys around on the tractor."

"But he wants to ride Sassy, Russ. We won't be long."

Russ laughed. "All right, glad to see you two are coming around."

Joey slipped her foot into the stirrup and swung into the saddle. "Yeah, I got him straightened out pretty quick."

"Ernie, how about you and me take that tractor ride tomorrow, that is, if you can fit me into your schedule," Russ joked.

"I don't know, Russ—he's pretty busy," she answered, then whispered to Ernie, "C'mon, let's go!"

Ernie scaled the fence, then swung his leg over the

pony's flank to sit behind Joey. She nudged the horse with her heels and Sassy broke into a fast trot along the drive. Ernie bounced up and down against Sassy's rump, his teeth clicking like a windup toy.

"Supper's in an hour," called Russ. "I'm making my famous beef stew."

"Don't forget the oregano," reminded Joey. She started to gallop up the tractor lane.

"Stay away from Holsapple's now, you hear me?" shouted Russ.

"Act like you didn't hear him," instructed Joey, but Ernie glanced behind anyway. He thought the man looked awfully lonely all by himself in the yard of his dried-up farm. When Russ waved, Ernie waved back. He could hear the distant sound of the combine engine sputter and die just before Sassy crested the ridge, galloping into the upper field.

When the pinto pony reached a split-rail boundary fence, she began to whinny and prance nervously. Joey nodded gravely at the wasteland on the other side of the fence. The entire surface had been strip-mined for coal, and now the scorched land seemed to suffer from a mortal thirst. Scattered across the vast expanse were tall derricks and noisy pumps that looked like prehistoric birds pecking crude oil from the earth. In the distance, a four-story stone farm-house, with gabled windows, spires, and turrets, stood in the shadow of a sheer black cliff.

"Holsapple's," said Joey.

Ernie just stared. He could hardly believe his eyes. Both the land and the mansion had a haunted look.

"It used to be a big old church, before Holsapple got his hands on it."

"I never saw anything so creepy in my whole life," he whispered.

"I know," she agreed. "All this land used to be a big for-est with a stream running right through it."

"What happened?"

"What do you think happened?" she said sharply. "Holsapple cut down the trees and sucked it all dry, and I got that right from Russ."

Ernie shook his head. "Did Holsapple live up here when the Quilt Baby got kidnapped?"

"I don't know, I guess," she said, then pointed to a dis-tant spot. "They put up a derrick right where Russ found the quilt." She dismounted and tied Sassy to the fence. "It's way out there. If we get caught, it's certain torture and pos-sible death."

"Are you always this dramatic?" scoffed Ernie as he hopped from the saddle onto the top rail of the fence. He walked along the narrow beam with the assurance of a tomcat.

"I know what I know," she asserted.

"Ever been caught before?" he asked.

"No way, but I heard you been caught plenty."

"Says who?"

"Says your paperwork, and I didn't get caught doin' that, neither," boasted Joey as she grabbed the knapsack and coil of rope from her saddle.

"What's all that for?"

"Just in case. Two years ago a kid from school fell in some old mine shaft out here," she explained. "Broke both legs. You sure you want to do this?"

Without a word, Ernie jumped down on the Holsapple side of the fence. Joey patted Sassy's flank. "Don't worry, girl—we'll be right back."

She jumped the fence to join him on enemy terrain, but Ernie had already started across the field. She ran as fast as she could and finally caught up with him crouching beside a derrick.

"Which one?" he asked.

"Follow me," she said, and took the lead.

They threaded through the maze of derricks and pumping wells like commandos advancing through a mine-field. Joey suddenly dove for cover behind a bulldozer. When Ernie landed beside her, she pointed to a cloud of dust moving across the field. A pickup truck was coming toward them, fast. Alarmed, they hid behind the dozer blade as the vehicle wheeled to a stop next to the derrick in front of them. The driver, a man with coarse skin, spiky hair, and yellow-stained teeth, spit a stream of tobacco juice out the window. Ernie was afraid the man had spied them and was shooting them a sinister wink, until he realized that the guy's left eye was completely seared shut.

"One Eye," Joey whispered.

In the back of the pickup were a dozen laborers, all smoking and spitting and grousing. Their faces were sunburned and smeared with oil. They looked just as ready to fight each other as work on the rigs.

"Holsapple's thugs," Joey whispered. "My mom says they all belong in cages."

One Eye jumped out of the truck, a ring of iron keys jangling from his belt. He unlocked a steel-mesh cage housing an oil gauge, then tweaked the pressure valve. Satisfied, he got back behind the wheel and fishtailed away. The workers in back cursed his neck-snapping acceleration. Joey and Ernie coughed and covered their eyes from the swirling dust.

"That was too close," exhaled Joey. "If we were smart, we'd turn around right now."

"Forget it, they're long gone."

"So you say," she doubted, but started counting the derricks anyway. "That one," she said, then dashed back into the open with Ernie right behind.

They skidded to a stop beside the tall derrick. A crudely painted sign identified it as DERRICK 19. Next to it was a rusted oil pump enclosed in a chain-link fence with barbed wire along the top. Joey pointed to the soil just beyond the machine's iron arm that ratcheted noisily up and down, pumping crude oil from deep underneath.

"There. It was right there," she shouted. "That's where they found the quilt."

Ernie knew getting to the spot was going to be dangerous. The only break in the fence was at the ratchet arm. He started toward it, but Joey grabbed him by the shirt. "You want your head chopped off?"

"Try not to worry so much," he said cockily, but he wasn't feeling so brave. Setting his jaw, he dove headfirst past the ratcheting arm and rolled to a dusty stop.

"You look like a pig in a slop trough," Joey yelled over the noise.

"Least I'm not a chicken, Rooster," he yelled back, brushing himself off. He fished Holsapple's keys out of his pocket and used them to dig around in the dirt.

"What are you doin'?!" she shouted.

"What do you think I'm doing, I'm looking for clues."

"Well, hurry up. Holsapple can smell trouble on his property like no other person alive!"

Ernie struck something hard a few inches beneath the soil. He looked past the ratcheting arm to Joey. "I hit something. C'mon, help me."

"Forget it," she replied. "It's probably just a rock."

"I'm telling you, I found something—don't be such a wuss!"

Joey glared at him. He glared back, which really made her mad. Gritting her teeth, she swayed back and forth to match the timing of the iron pendulum, then jumped. The huge arm caught her heel on its back swing, tumbling her into the dirt at Ernie's side.

"You okay?"

"'Course," she said as she rubbed her throbbing ankle.

Pulling a jackknife from her pocket, she helped dig until they uncovered a three-by-three-foot sheet of plywood. They shoved it aside to reveal a narrow shaft descending into the darkness. Ernie cupped his hands around his mouth and called, "Quilt Babyyyyy . . ."

Joey laughed nervously. "Right, like anybody's down there."

Ignoring her, Ernie dropped a stone. It hit the ground with a thump. He turned to Joey. "Well, what are we waiting for?"

She took a flashlight out of her backpack and shined it downward. The hole was twenty feet deep.

"For nothin'. It's some old mine shaft," she said.

"Maybe not," countered Ernie.

"Maybe what, then?"

"Maybe something."

"Maybe some people think they're smarter than Russ, the sheriff, and all the detectives," she suggested sarcastically.

Ernie smiled. "Maybe I am." He tied the rope to the

base of the pump, then tossed the free end down the shaft. She shook her head. "Maybe you're crazy."

He started down the rope. "Maybe you don't care what happened to Russ' kid."

Joey watched as he descended the rope hand over hand. "Maybe you wanna get us trapped down there so Holsy can eat us for supper, piece by piece," she yelled as he disappeared into the black.

Ernie touched down at the bottom of the pit. When he looked up, he could see Joey's silhouette at the top of the shaft. "Maybe you should throw down the flashlight," he shouted.

"Maybe you should . . . aww, forget it," she muttered, then began to shinny down the rope. Halfway down, she lost her grip and fell in a heap at Ernie's feet.

"You okay?"

"'Course I am," she said with a wince.

Joey flicked on her flashlight and panned the beam across the rugged surface of a subterranean cavern. A passageway receded into the darkness.

"Jeez Louise, a tunnel," she sputtered.

Ernie pointed to the left. "Shine the light over there."

Joey illuminated a thin wooden pole that ran horizontally along one wall before disappearing into the earth. They shuffled over to examine it. Joey trained the flashlight along its surface. The wood was a whitish color with peeling bark.

"It's just an old piece of birch," she said.

"But what's it doing down here?" He tapped it with his knuckles. "It's hollow."

"So?"

"Gimme the light," he said as he swiped the flashlight from her hand. He shined it deeper into the tunnel. The light glistened off a puddle in a rock basin about twenty yards away. "What's that?"

"Water! It must be some underground spring!" blurted Joey excitedly. "C'mon."

They eagerly approached it. Joey knelt beside the puddle and swirled the water with her fingers, then tasted it. "It's fresh, all right," she confirmed. Kicking off her shoes and socks, she waded into the puddle. The water rose above her ankles. "Come on in, the water's great," encouraged Joey as she reached down to splash some of the cool spring water on her face. "If Russ and Gramps could get hold of this water, they could beat the drought! God-zilla, wait'll they hear about this!"

Not listening, Ernie stared trancelike at the puddle. Cupping his hands around his mouth, he called out, "*Hoo . . . hoo.*"

"What's that for?" asked Joey, spooked.

"I don't know."

Then he did it again, his voice echoing eerily in the dark tunnel. "*Hooty-hoo, hooty-hoooooooooo.*"

"Hey, don't get weird on me. Not down here."

He crouched by the puddle, lost in thought.

"Hey, Cubber, wake up and stick with the program, okay?"

He met her worried gaze. "This is not a mine shaft," he declared.

"Okay, it's a tunnel with a spring in it."

"Don't you understand?" he asked incredulously.

"Understand what?" she answered, equally exasperated.

"You said the Quilt Baby just disappeared, right?"

She nodded.

"No clues, nothin', not even the dogs could track it, right?"

She nodded again, not yet sure what he was trying to say.

"Well, he did just disappear . . . right into this kidnappers' hideaway."

Joey frowned.

"That hollow piece of birch could've been their air shaft," Ernie continued, "and they got their water from this spring. Air and water, that's all they needed. That gang could've been down here days, maybe weeks."

"Okay, so what if the gang did keep him here for a day, a week, a year, which I doubt and double doubt," said Joey, standing ankle-deep in the puddle. "So what? That was twelve years ago and you ain't got a clue where they took him next."

Ernie spotted another piece of birch, this one running vertically up the wall of the cave. He tried to budge it, but it was anchored in the dirt.

Joey splashed him playfully. "Get in here, Cub. The bottom is like this really soft sand—you can dig your toes in it and everything."

Handing her the flashlight, Ernie kicked off his sneakers and socks and stepped into the puddle. The moment his foot touched the surface, they rocketed through the water, landing in a heap ten feet below, wet and gasping for breath. Ernie had never felt anything like it before. It was weird, like exploding through a black ring of wetness that soaked him from bottom to top.

In the darkness, it was Joey who spoke first. "Ernie Banks, you okay?"

"Yeah, I think so," he answered. There was a tremor in both their voices.

Joey picked up the flashlight and shined it on her knee. It was bleeding. She aimed the light overhead. The puddle hovered in the ceiling, defying gravity.

"What is that?" she whispered.

Ernie stared at the water suspended in the ceiling hole.

"I don't know," he muttered.

Joey put the light on his face. His chin was cut. "How are we going to get out of here?" she whimpered. "We're done for."

"Be quiet and shine the light."

She panned it across some sort of chamber. As

the light moved, they saw a fallen ceiling beam atop a splintered table, then chairs, pottery shards, a stone sink with a birch-pipe faucet, and finally a row of walnut cabinets, each one bearing an oak tree insignia carved into its face. As impossible as it seemed, someone had once lived here, but even more impossible was the fact that everything was in miniature, so small that they towered over their discovery.

"What is this place?" gasped Joey in awe.

Ernie dropped to his knees in front of the cabinets. He ran his hand across the carvings, then turned the faucet on the tiny sink. A hairy spider emerged and he toppled backward, landing on his backside.

"I hate spiders," declared Joey.

Ignoring her, Ernie tried to open one of the cabinets, but it was stuck. He dislodged a piece of timber from the ceiling. Dirt sprinkled on them from above and Joey covered her head. "Oh my God—we're going to get buried alive!"

"Shhh!" he insisted as he rammed the face of the cabinet with the timber, collapsing it inward.

"You're the one making the racket!"

He managed to get one hand inside and began to feel around.

"I've got something," he said, wide-eyed.

"What is it?" she whispered.

"Something," he grunted.

Whatever he had a hold of, it didn't want to come out. He twisted his arm and positioned his body at a different angle and finally extracted a cedar chest, no bigger than a bread box.

"Holy smoky!" exclaimed Joey. There were cherrywood handles on each side and sturdy oak hinges at the back. But what they saw next changed everything. There was a baby's face hand-carved on the vaulted lid. In amazement they whispered, "Quilt Baby."

Suddenly a digging sound grabbed their attention. Joey panned the light to the opposite corner, where a dirt wall was beginning to crumble, as if something were trying to tunnel in from the other side. She froze, and the flashlight dropped from her hand. It rolled into a crevice just out of reach, its beam of light now projecting dimly against the far wall.

His heart racing, Ernie looked for a way out. The dark puddle was ten feet above, but there was a birch pipe running parallel to the ceiling beneath the water. He gave the chest to Joey.

"We'll never get out, we're going to die here," she croaked.

With surging adrenaline, Ernie took a running jump and scratched and clawed and kicked up the wall until he could catch hold of the pipe. Dangling, he rocked back and forth like a gymnast, gathering enough momentum to swing his feet up through the puddle and hook his calves on the floor of the tunnel above. Hanging upside down, he could feel the water seeping into his jeans.

"You made it!" cried Joey.

"Give me the chest!" he ordered, stretching down as far as he could.

Joey stood on tiptoes, holding the chest high, and Ernie was able to grab it. He curled at the waist and heaved the chest through the puddle into the tunnel. He again unfurled his body until he was looking at an upside-down Joey. "Okay, use me like a ladder, c'mon!"

She jumped up and grabbed his arms, but lost her grip and fell back into the chamber. It was then that Ernie glimpsed a shadow crossing in front of the beam from the abandoned flashlight. "Joey, quick, behind you!"

Screaming, she scrabbled full throttle up his arms and chest, frantically grabbing his shirt, ripping the collar and popping buttons, then clawed up his legs and disappeared through the puddle. When her hands came back through the water, he grabbed them and held on tight as she pulled him up into the tunnel, where they collapsed on top of each other. With hearts pounding, they grabbed the chest and their sneakers and scrambled toward the shaft of light. They tied the chest to the end of their dangling rope, then Joey, followed by Ernie, shinnied back to the surface.

On top, the noisy clatter from the pump was a welcome relief. In the fading twilight, they leaned over the hole and hoisted the rope until Ernie could untie the chest and shove it past the ratcheting arm. Timing their jumps, they dove past the iron tusk to the other side of the fenced enclosure. Without a word, they each grabbed a chest handle and raced across the scorched landscape toward the sanctuary of Frazier land.

At the open shaft, a tiny Puddlejumper clambered to the surface, followed by another holding a boy's dirty sock in his hand. Runnel and Root looked weary and tattered and parched. They'd been in search of water and were near the abandoned outpost at Red Moss Point when they'd heard the unexpected "Hooty-hoo." Sniffing the air beneath the noisy pump, they watched, mystified, as the intruders fled across the field.

CHAPTER TWENTY-THREE

Rattled

I T WAS DARK when Joey and Ernie emerged from the wheat field to find a sheriff's sedan, three pickups, two cars, and a Jeep parked in the Frazier yard. They dismounted and put Sassy in the corral. Crouching low, they snuck between the vehicles, carrying their chest of unknown treasure. From inside the house, they could hear the sounds of heated adult voices.

"What's going on? Who are all these people?" asked Ernie.

"Neighbors," answered Joey. "Probably more trouble with the Holsapples."

"What kind of trouble?"

"He's buyin' up all the land for his oil operation," she explained.

Joey led past the porch to a storm-cellar door that angled almost flat against the ground on the side of the house. She flipped the latch and pulled back the door. They hurried down the cement stairs, silently closing the door behind them.

Joey flicked on a switch that provided a dim light from an overhead fixture. Against one wall was a workbench with a set of wrenches, assorted screwdrivers, and woodworking tools hanging on a Peg-Board. Glass jars containing screws and nails of various sizes were attached to the ceiling. There were shelves of canned pickles, beets, peaches, and plums in mason jars. Stored along the adjacent wall were a cake mixer, a high chair, a baby stroller, and cardboard boxes with the name *Dolores* written on the outside. There was even an old baseball glove, a bat, and an open box of dusty trophies in the corner. Ernie thought it smelled a little like the basement at Lakeside, only sweeter, more like old wood and fallen leaves.

They hurried to the workbench, where Joey tugged on a string to light a bare bulb dangling over the work area. Ernie placed their treasure on the coarse tabletop. Like two expert archaeologists, they studied their discovery with intense concentration. Though they could hear the rumble of adult voices overhead, they were too involved with the chest to care. The baby's face was carved in intricate detail, and under the light his mischievous expression came alive. Ernie tried to open the lid, but it was locked. He ran his fingers over the curves of the baby's face, searching for a hidden lock. He peered into its mouth.

"Wax," he said at last.

"What?" whispered Joey.

Ernie opened the bench drawer and rummaged around until he found a pack of matches. He ripped out a match and lit it. Joey helped him tilt the chest upside down while he held the flame to the baby's lips. Wax dribbled down its chin.

"Quilt Baby's lips were sealed," he whispered, then blew out the match. He wriggled a small screwdriver inside the baby's mouth until he heard a clicking sound. When he opened the lid, a few dandelion puffs floated into the air. Euphoric, they carefully examined the items inside the immaculate interior: a rattle, a baby bottle, an acorn cap, a mobile of hand-carved farm animals, a small belt made from bark with tiny pouches, a braid of wheat looped like a lasso, and a Snow White lamp.

Joey rattled around in the drawer for batteries. She popped two double AAs into the back of the lamp and the bulb lit beneath her skirt. "Good as new," Joey whispered excitedly. She picked up the mobile and spun it while Ernie emptied the belt's pouches. There was nothing but dust inside. He pondered the rattle, even shaking it a couple of times. Suddenly he turned to Joey. "The picture!"

"What picture?"

Sticking the rattle in his pocket, he hustled toward the cellar stairs that led up into the house.

"Wait up!" said Joey in a hushed voice. She stuffed Snow White and all the baby things back into the chest, hid it beneath some burlap sacks, then hurried to catch up.

At the top of the stairs, Ernie cracked open the door and spied through a narrow slit. He had a clear view into the living room, where the sheriff, a pudgeball of a man with small eyes behind thick glasses and thinning hair on a round head, was doing his best to placate an agitated group of neighbors. A vivacious woman with long, brown hair and fiery brown eyes, in faded jeans and a red tank top, was laying into him with both barrels.

"That's bunk, Tom—this whole town is elbow deep in Harvey Holsapple's pocket, and you know it. Everyone in this room tonight has made complaints to you about any number of problems, but you haven't done squat about it."

Joey gave Ernie a jab in the ribs and proudly mouthed the words "That's my mom."

Sheriff Dashin was just as emphatic. "That isn't true, Betty, and unless you got hard evidence, you can't go around accusing that family of foul play."

Betty's reply was sharp and quick. "Oh, yes I can, and it won't be the last time, either!"

At the cellar door, Ernie made his move. Joey grabbed his shirttail. "Wait!" she whispered, but he pulled out of her grip and slipped into the kitchen. Frustrated, she followed. They tiptoed down the hall until they had to stop at the entry to the living room. It was a large opening, and if they continued, the adults would see them. Ernie peeked into the room, waiting for an opportunity to cross and get to the crib room.

"What about Russ' combine, Tom?" blurted Emil Goetz. He was on the sofa next to his wife, Elsie, and their strapping son, Neal.

Joey whispered in Ernie's ear, "Before the drought, the Goetzes had the prettiest farm on the whole plateau—apple orchards in back, a string of cherry trees . . ."

"Shhh!" Ernie ordered.

The pudgy sheriff seemed to have an answer for everything. "A blown engine ain't no crime in itself and you know it."

"Like hell it's not," fired Betty. The room erupted with angry accusations.

Tugging Ernie's shirt, Joey urged, "Now's our chance, let's go!" She shoved him forward, but just at that moment Russ spoke and the room fell silent. Retreating abruptly, Ernie bumped into Joey. Wincing, she rubbed her forehead as they crouched in their hiding spot.

"Listen, folks," said Russ. "We've had rough years before and always found a way to make it. Let's just stick together. We've done it before and we'll do it again."

"Fine and dandy," said Emil gloomily. "But who's gonna fill my wells? Who's gonna make it rain? Russ Frazier?"

"C'mon, Emil—you're not going to sell the land your

folks worked and their folks before that, are you?"

"With this drought, I'll be lucky to get ten percent of what I planted." Emil tried to say it matter-of-factly, but his voice cracked.

Elsie took her husband's hand. "It's not just the drought, Russ. We're sick of the strong-arming and the threats."

Flushed with anger, old Doc Thorpe set down his coffee. "Jack Voisine's not here tonight, but just last week I treated him for two cracked ribs and a broken thumb. He was afraid to file a complaint, but I'm not."

In the hall, Joey pressed against Ernie, whispering, "That was Dicky Cobb and the twins, no doubt about it— the sheriff acts like a big shot, but he never does diddly."

"Sorry, Doc, but Jack Voisine will have to speak for himself," said the sheriff. "I'm open for business at eight sharp. If he wants to file charges, he knows where to find me."

"No, Tom," he said. "I suspect where he'd find you is up at that monstrosity they call a house, drinking Harvey's coffee. Isn't that where you start your day?"

The sheriff laughed, though his face reddened with embarrassment. "That's a good one, Doc. Monstrosity— I'm gonna write that down."

"Here's the thing," said Gramp Atwater. "Those dollars Holsapple's offering are nothing to sneeze at." He was on the love seat next to Eleanor, his wife of forty-five years.

"Oh, Dad, please," pleaded Betty. "Not you, too."

Joey was back in Ernie's ear. "Those are my grandparents. They're really old."

Ernie shushed her again, keeping his attention on the room.

"What you don't know, Betty," Gramp continued, "is they were out to our place this morning."

"Ours, too," added Neal Goetz.

Ernie was running out of patience. Motioning for Joey to get low, he crawled past the opening. She followed, scurrying across the floor. When they got to the other side, Ernie spied back around the corner. Russ was staring straight at him and he looked none too pleased. Ernie expected he'd be cleaning the bathroom and maybe the kitchen, too. He thought Russ was about to come over, but Joey's grandfather started talking, and Russ stayed put.

"We just can't keep up anymore," Gramp said sadly. "Gram and me are thinking, what with the debt growing every year and now this drought . . . it might be time to get out of farming altogether."

"There's a way out of this, John, and we're going to find it," assured Russ. "We can't let ourselves be intimidated by the likes of the Holsapples. We're not quitters."

Ernie figured there was no time to waste. He hustled to the door at the end of the hall, with Joey on his heels.

In the living room, Russ tried to make eye contact with Gramp Atwater, but the old man refused to meet his gaze. He turned to Betty. "We'll fight back, we'll help each other."

She nodded her agreement, but the others just stared at the floor.

The crib room was dark. Joey wanted to turn on the overhead light, but Ernie insisted on using the matches so they wouldn't attract attention. They went directly to the old photograph hanging on the wall. Ernie struck a match, then compared the rattle from the cedar chest to the one baby Shawn held in the picture. The decorative pattern was identical—farm animals in alternating colors of pink and blue. Ernie gave the rattle a shake as if to punctuate their discovery.

"One and the same," he whispered as the match burned out.

They hadn't noticed that the voices in the living room had shifted to the kitchen. A sudden knock and the overhead light came on. They spun around to face Russ standing just inside the room.

"What's going on in here?" he asked. Ernie's shirt was ripped and missing most of its buttons. He was wearing only one sock, and there was dried blood on his chin. Joey's knees were scraped and the smell of sulfur from a burned match was in the air. "Are you guys okay?"

Joey couldn't contain her excitement. "Oh, Russ, you won't believe what we found . . ."

". . . yeah, some bear tracks," interrupted Ernie. "Up in that field across the ridge." He nervously fingered the rattle concealed behind his back.

Catching on, Joey stammered, "Oh, oh yeah, up there behind Emil's bee keep. Can you believe it, Russ—bears, right here in Illinois."

Russ raised an eyebrow but went along good-naturedly with a look to Ernie. "And I'm guessing you got to wrestling with that same bear and looks like you got the worst of it."

Ernie was starting to regret the bear story when Betty entered looking stressed. The sight of her daughter standing next to a wild-looking boy in a dusty Cubs cap and ripped shirt didn't brighten her outlook. "I hope you have a good reason for getting back after dark, Jo Virginia—I'm already on the boiling point, and when my spout blows, I'm not going to be whistlin'," she warned.

Joey improvised, "Well, Mom, you see, we were playin' a big old game of hide-and-seek and Ernie was having some trouble finding me, and it got late, but I didn't want to leave him, seeing as he's new around here, so I finally just came in."

Betty laughed. "I'm sure you don't expect me to believe that."

"It's all true, mostly, hey, Mom—meet the Cubber, just in from Chicago."

Betty extended her hand while keeping a skeptical eye on her daughter. "Hi, Cubber. I'm Betty Woodruff."

Ernie slipped the rattle into his back pocket before shaking Betty's hand. "Ernie Banks," he said.

"It must be nice for you to get away—from the city, I mean."

Ernie shrugged.

"We sure hope you enjoy your stay," she said with a smile.

"He can do magic, Mom," proclaimed Joey, then tugged Ernie's arm. "Make something disappear."

Ernie looked pained under the glare of the adult spotlight. Betty squeezed her daughter in a hug and kissed her forehead. "Think you could make this one disappear?" she asked playfully.

"Mom!" complained Joey.

Betty frowned. "How on earth did your clothes get wet?"

"It's called water, Mom. You know, like what comes out of the hose."

Betty shook her head. "And you shouldn't be wasting it."

"No baths tonight," joked Russ as he herded everyone out of the room. "C'mon, I want Ernie to meet everybody, and we better get you guys some supper before it's all gone. Oh, one more thing—I'll take those matches now."

Ernie sheepishly handed them over. As they walked toward the kitchen, he gave Joey a look, warning her to keep silent.

CHAPTER TWENTY-FOUR

The Secret

AFTER SUPPER, Ernie and Joey wandered out to the corral and sat on the top rail of the fence. Beneath a moon that hung so low in the sky Ernie felt he could touch it, they discussed their discovery. *Why was everything so tiny in the kidnapper's hideout? What made that puddle float in the air? Where was Shawn Frazier now?*

They fell silent when Russ and Betty came outside to bid the neighbors good night. Joey and Ernie listened to the friendly exchanges as everyone got into their cars and pickups, then watched the parade of vehicles motor up the dusty drive. Russ and Betty lingered by the porch, looking at the stars. Her Jeep was the only vehicle left in the yard.

After a few moments, Ernie turned to Joey. "I like your mom."

"Yeah. So does Russ. He says she's the only mom in the whole county who can fix her Jeep and paint a picture and do it on the same day. She paints barns, mostly. Not real barns, just pictures of barns and some other stuff, too. Russ says they belong in a gallery somewhere, but most of them end up in people's houses. Oh, and our mailbox, too. It looks just like that," she said, pointing to the stars.

Ernie nodded as he considered his next question. "So what happened to your real dad?"

She answered matter-of-factly. "My daddy got run over by his tractor on a mud slide up along East Creek when I was a little kid."

"Oh." Ernie wondered if a father dying was worse than never having one at all. "You think your mom and Russ'll ever get married?"

She shrugged. "She sure talks about him enough."

Ernie tried to stop himself from asking the next question, but it just spilled out. "Would you like it if you got a new dad?"

"Yeah," answered Joey.

"You'll probably get the crib room," he speculated.

"I doubt it. My mom says if it don't rain soon, Russ is gonna lose this farm."

"He can't lose his own farm," protested Ernie.

"Shows you know nothin' about economics—the

bank can take it when he don't make a cent on one acre out of twenty-five."

Ernie wasn't exactly sure what she was talking about, but he gave her the benefit of the doubt, considering she was a farmer and all. He decided to change the subject. "How long has Russ been bringing orphan kids out here?"

"Ever since I can remember. My mom says it makes him feel like he's doing something for little Shawnie."

"What's that bat and glove doing in the basement?"

"It's Russ'," she replied. "He used to play ball with the Tigers."

Ernie's jaw dropped. "No way! The Detroit Tigers?"

"Yup," she said casually. "Didn't you see all those trophies? Russ didn't get 'em riding the pine—he was a star, until he blew out his knee sliding into home plate."

"Wow," he said, shaking his head in awe. "Is that why he limps?"

"Obviously."

Their conversation was interrupted when Betty called from the porch, "Joey, time to be getting home."

"Don't worry, Mom, I'll have Sassy fed and watered before you get there."

"Don't give her too many oats—that pony's wild enough already."

"I know, just one can," she answered, then turned to Ernie with a shy expression. "Now it's time for their big smooch." They watched as Russ and Betty disappeared arm in arm into the kitchen. Joey whistled for Sassy. Her pony trotted over and nuzzled against her.

"You afraid of blood?" asked Ernie.

"Not hardly," she responded.

"Good," Ernie said as he pilfered a sliver from the fence. He didn't like the sight of blood any more than the next person, but this was something that had to be done. He pricked his thumb and blood oozed from the wound.

"You crazy?" she blurted. "What'd you do that for?"

Ernie looked Joey in the eye. "You and me know something nobody else knows in the whole world, and now we got to trust each other, like family."

"Oh, jeez—why's everything got to be such a big secret with you?"

"'Cause grown-ups mess things up and that's no maybe—it's a fact," he asserted.

"But it's Russ' kid we're talkin' about here, not some stranger," she reminded.

"We'll tell him when the time is right and not before."

Joey gave him a long look. "So what you're asking is for me to be your blood brother?"

"Yeah, basically, for the sake of Shawn Frazier."

She sighed deeply, then held out her thumb. He pricked it with the sharp sliver.

"Ouch!" she cried.

All business, Ernie took her thumb and pressed it

against his, then looked her in the eyes with a solemn gravity. "You promise to never abandon a brother in time of trouble or war?"

"Yes."

"To never tell what can't be told?"

"I guess," mumbled Joey.

"Yes or no," snapped Ernie.

"Yup."

"You promise all the way to Kingdom Come and back?"

"Where's that?"

"Just promise!"

"Yes!"

Ernie pressed his thumb tight against hers and rotated a quarter turn. "We're brothers now."

"Brother and sister, but don't get soppy," she said as she put a foot in the stirrup and swung up into the saddle. Sassy snorted and pranced impatiently, ready to go home. "What about tomorrow?" she asked.

Ernie dangled Holsapple's keys.

Joey's eyes grew wide. "No way, nohow, never."

Ernie smoothly palmed the keys, banged his fists together, then magically made them disappear.

"Yes," he insisted. "The kidnappers' hideout was up on Holsapple property, and it's up to us to find out if there's any connection. The answer could be somewhere inside that house."

Joey considered his logic with a wry smile. "You're dangerous, Cub. You could really get a girl in trouble." She reined Sassy to the side and gave her a quick kick with her heels. "Giddy-up!"

Ernie watched the pony and rider depart in a cloud of dust, then wandered back across the yard, mulling all the questions surging through his mind. He padded across the porch to peer through the screen door. Inside, Russ and Betty were doing the dishes, but he could tell it was more than that. They were laughing and whispering. Embarrassed, he slipped inside and, averting his eyes, walked through the kitchen. Betty looked up, suds on her cheek, and smiled. "Hey, Ernie."

He stopped just inside the hall, caught.

"Anything special you'd like to do while you're here?" she asked.

He pondered the question. "Well, I really like to swim. Is there a pool anywhere?"

Russ smiled. "Sorry, no pools." He shared a wistful look with Betty. "I used to have a beautiful water hole, even had an old tire swing."

"Geronimo," recalled Betty.

"That's what Joey called it," said Russ. "Unfortunately, that hole dried up with the drought. Even the river's nearly gone."

Ernie seemed disappointed.

"Tell you what," said Betty. "How about later in the

week you and Russ come over and we'll go horseback riding."

"Okay," he said flatly.

"Or we could do something else," she offered.

"Well, it's just my butt's pretty sore already, from Sassy."

She laughed. "Well, then—I guess we'll give you a few days to recover."

"Okay, g'night," he muttered as he hurried down the hall.

"Good night," she said.

"I'll be down in just a minute, Ernie," called Russ.

When Betty heard the crib room door close, her expression turned serious. "So what do you make of him?"

"What do you mean?"

"He's kind of odd. All he did tonight was stare. Never spoke a word to anyone," she pointed out.

"He's just taking it all in, everything's new," explained Russ as he dried a dish and placed it in the cupboard. "I was the same way at his age."

Poised outside the crib room at the end of the hall, Ernie reversed direction and tiptoed back toward the kitchen. He'd closed the door to make them think he'd gone inside. It was an old Lakeside trick he used when he needed to get information from Mrs. McGinty. He peeked into the kitchen, where Russ and Betty were at the sink with their backs to him. When Russ turned to wipe the counter, Ernie jerked his head back and pressed up against the wall, listening.

"But there's just something, I don't know, just a little off-kilter about him," said Betty softly, her hands working in the sudsy water. "And that report you got from Lakeside, quite a laundry list to compile in just thirteen years. I wonder if he's going to be more difficult than some of the other boys you've brought out here."

"Well, Joey seems to like him—that's a first."

"I guess, but he's pretty rough around the edges. I just hope he won't be a bad influence."

"They'll be fine," assured Russ as he splattered some suds on her nose. "She's plenty tough herself. Just like her mother."

Betty laughed and kissed Russ quickly on the lips. Russ looked in her eyes, then kissed her back.

Entranced, Ernie watched for as long as he dared before creeping back down the hall to the crib room.

Dressed in his underwear, T-shirt, socks, and Cubs cap, Ernie stood at the window watching Betty's Jeep depart up the driveway. There was a knock on the door.

"Ernie?"

"Yeah?"

"Can I come in?"

"Yeah," answered Ernie as he hustled to get under the covers.

Russ poked his head into the room. "Anybody thirsty?" He came over to the bed and handed Ernie a tall glass of milk.

"Thanks," said Ernie, then downed it in one breath.

Russ chuckled. "I guess that answers that. Need anything else before you turn in?"

"Nope."

"How's your backside doing?"

"Better."

"It'll take a while." Russ took the empty glass. "Is it true?" he asked. "Can you really do magic?"

"A few things."

"Love to see a trick sometime."

Ernie considered the proposition. "I could show you one now."

"Great," said Russ as he sat on the edge of the bed. "Need an assistant?"

Ernie shook his head, then reached under his pillow and pulled out his Ernie Banks baseball card. He showed it to Russ.

"Hmm, Ernie Banks—any relation to somebody I know?"

Ernie smiled and shook his head, then passed one hand in front of the other and the card disappeared.

"Wow," said Russ, impressed.

Ernie reached behind Russ' ear and produced the

card. Russ slapped his thigh and laughed appreciatively.

"Man-o-man, how in the world did you ever do that?"

Ernie smiled crookedly. "Trade secret."

He propped the card against the lamp on the adjacent nightstand. Russ took note of the watch next to it. Rocky Harmon's face was disfigured, his arms broken. "Well, you're really good at it."

Ernie sat up a little straighter. "Listen, Mr. Frazier, about what happened today, you know, the Cadillac and all . . . I was hoping maybe you wouldn't have to tell anybody, you know, in Chicago."

"What happened this morning I guess we'd all just as soon forget. As far as I'm concerned, you and I are working on a clean slate. Fair enough?"

Ernie nodded, relieved.

"Good. Tomorrow I want you to meet some friends of mine from the barn. They know a little magic, too," said Russ.

"Okay. There's one other thing I was wondering about."

"What's that?"

"Joey told me you played baseball for the Tigers. Is that true?"

Russ shook his head with a smile. "She's exaggerating, but I did play for the Toledo Mud Hens, their triple-A team."

"What position?"

"I was a pitcher."

"So am I."

"No kidding? How's your curveball?"

"Not so great. The fastball is my best pitch."

"Well, if you'd like, I'll show you a few of my trade secrets. You bring your glove?"

Ernie shook his head.

"No worries," said Russ. "I know just where to get one for you."

Ernie nodded. He could hardly believe his luck. *A pitcher!*

"All right then, good night, Ernie. Pleasant dreams." Russ turned out the bedside lamp and started to leave.

"Mr. Frazier?" Ernie sat up in bed. He wanted to talk about the abandoned hideout and the mysterious puddle and the cedar chest and Snow White and . . . but at the last second he blurted, "You think it's ever gonna rain?"

"I'm praying for it just about every second of the day," said Russ, silhouetted by the light from the hall. "Think you can do some talkin' with the Man upstairs?"

"I don't think He listens," answered Ernie.

"I know, sometimes it feels that way, but that doesn't mean we don't keep trying."

Ernie nodded.

"See you sunrise. I got a rooster tends to crow on the early side," warned Russ, then closed the door behind him.

Ernie settled back to his pillow, but he wasn't sleepy. He was more awake than he'd been in a very long time.

CHAPTER TWENTY-FIVE

Kingdom Come

DEEP IN A FIELD of stunted wheat, a puddle glistened in the moonlight. The water rippled just before Root and Runnel vaulted feetfirst out of the puddle, landing like a secret between the furrows. Instead of shaking themselves dry, they rubbed the excess water into their chapped skin, cherishing the moisture. In these days of drought, there wasn't another surface puddle within a hundred miles, and it had taken all their resources to make this one. The anxious Puddlejumpers knew it was dangerous to venture into the Up Above, but they felt it was a necessary risk. They sniffed cautiously in all directions before setting out.

The soft amber light from their lantern lit the way down through the wheat. In the distance, there were rumblings of thunder and flashes of heat lightning. The Jumpers emerged at the farmyard and went straight to the back of the house, where they scampered up a drainpipe onto the window ledge. Root and Runnel stared wide-eyed through the glass. Inside, the old crib room was dark.

The little ones squeezed past the screen, then, using all their strength, pried open the window and slipped into the room. They scooted up the leg of the bed onto the mattress, then tiptoed to the edge of the pillow, where they could study the boy's face by lantern light. His eyelids were flickering and his breathing was steady. On his head was a blue cap with a red C stitched on the front.

Through the years Runnel had wondered what Wawaywo would look like when he grew up, and now she thought she knew. Root wasn't convinced. He jumped to the nightstand and inspected a card propped against the lamp. It was a picture of a dark-skinned human wearing the same cap as the boy. On the bed, Runnel warbled excitedly, her hand on the Acorn bulging beneath his T-shirt.

Suddenly Ernie turned in his sleep, pinning her with his arm. Root leapt back and tried to free her, but the arm was too heavy. Flipping on his back, he pushed it with his legs until Runnel could wriggle free. Ernie stirred again and they slid down the bedpost to the floor. Just above, his foot was jutting off the mattress. Standing on tiptoe, they gripped his sock and coaxed it off. There, wound into the ball of his foot, was the Spiral Tattoo, the very one Runnel had stitched so many years before. Enraptured, they traced the spiral with their fingers.

"Wawaywo," they whispered. Their Rainmaker had returned.

But there was a very big problem. The boy was six times their size and wouldn't remember anything about them or his life in the Kingdom. *How could he?*

In the next instant, Ernie sat up in bed and scratched his foot. The window he'd closed to silence the constant chirping of the crickets was now open, and the curtains billowed with a gust of wind. Feeling like someone was in the room, he flicked on the lamp, then cautiously got out of bed to shut the window. A lightning flash illuminated something on the glass. Perplexed, he inspected more closely. *Tiny handprints!* He looked down to discover a dusty trail of miniature footprints leading back to his bed, where he found his sock on the rug. He listened, waiting for the intruder to make the next move.

Something rustled under the bed.

Holding his breath, he peered underneath. Just then the door squeaked open, which in the dead quiet sounded like a scream. He nearly jumped out of his other sock.

Ernie peered down the hall. It was empty. The only sounds were the ticking grandfather clock and Russ' snores. With his heart pounding like a jackhammer, he padded down the hall into the living room. Another door squeaked open. He hurried through the dark into the kitchen, where he found the cellar door ajar. A light went on downstairs.

Grabbing a broom for protection, Ernie slowly descended the cellar stairs. The lit bulb was swinging on its cord over the workbench, casting macabre shadows back and forth. Snow White and all the baby paraphernalia lay scattered on the workbench. Suddenly the storm door banged closed, sending his heart to his throat. He scrambled across the cellar and up the steps to peek out the storm door. Thunder rumbled across the plateau and a flash of heat lightning provided a glimpse of something small scurrying into the field.

Determined to see whatever it was, Ernie gave chase. He raced up through the wheat, pursuing shadows he could no longer see. When he finally reached the split-rail boundary fence, the moon was hidden behind the clouds. In the pitch-black night, he could hear the derricks pumping in the Holsapple wasteland. He pinched his nose. There was a terrible odor like nothing he'd ever smelled before. Suddenly something huge erupted from the dark with an unearthly howl. He raised his broom in defense, but before he could swing, the behemoth batted it away and clawed his chest, knocking him to the ground, hard. Feeling like his chest was on fire, he crabbed across the furrows, retreating in panic. He heard something small skitter through the wheat, but didn't see Root and Runnel grab his broom on either end and trip the beast just before it could pounce. When the giant landed, the ground shook with a violent thud.

Ernie wasn't sure what had just happened, but he didn't wait to find out. He scrambled to his feet and sprinted back down the slope. A wicked howl knifed along the plateau, followed by a strange and mournful hooting.

It haunted him all the way back to the farm.

CHAPTER TWENTY-SIX

Bigfoot

IN HIS JUMBLED DREAM, a strange sound was coming out of Mrs. McGinty's mouth as she angrily screamed in his face. She was ten feet tall and had claws and grungy red hair covering her body. When he woke, he realized the strange sound was a rooster crowing in the yard. Somebody was holding a cup of hot chocolate and shaking his shoulder. "Morning, Ernie—time to make this day sing."

Gaping wide-eyed, Ernie sat up in the big easy chair next to Russ' bed. He looked around the unfamiliar room. He was still dressed, but one foot was bare and a dirty sock dangled from the other.

"Was there a problem with your bed?" asked Russ, puzzled as to why the boy had come into his room during the night.

Ernie realized where he was, and felt ashamed that he'd been too afraid to sleep by himself. "Morning," he mumbled, then jumped out of the chair, sprinted down the hall, and shut himself in the bathroom. There was a knock on the door. "Ernie, you all right?"

"Yeah," he answered, then lifted his shirt and stared at the bloody claw marks scarring his chest. He wasn't all right. Not by a long shot. Shuddering, he clutched his Crystal Acorn, still on the shoelace around his neck. He looked at his face in the mirror and saw pure terror looking back.

It wasn't a dream after all.

Ernie stayed close to Russ as they entered the gloomy barn. The only light came from sunlight streaming through cracks in the wall. It was like a spooky cavern with too many dark places. Something was crawling through the hay, and he heard a fluttering in the rafters. He jumped when Russ stopped him from nearly walking into a huge spiderweb.

"Careful," said Russ. "Charlotte's been there a long time."

The boy stared at the hairy black spider vibrating just in front of his face.

"Isn't she beautiful?"

"Yeah," agreed Ernie, knowing that Mrs. McGinty would have killed it immediately and flushed it down the toilet. Russ grabbed a stool and pail from wall pegs, then sat beside the cow and took hold of the udder. "Mornin', Beulah." He winked at Ernie. "This is Ernie Banks—you two are going to be working together."

Ernie patted the cow's flank. "Hey, Beulah."

"You want to be firm, but gentle at the same time," Russ instructed, drawing several streams of milk into the pail. "Your turn, don't be shy."

Smiling sheepishly, Ernie sat on the stool and reached under to grab the udder, but he was having a difficult time focusing on the cow. The night's events kept turning in his mind. There had to be some explanation. He'd read about a giant creature called Bigfoot and thought it was just a big hoax. Now he was having second thoughts. Remembering whatever that thing was that attacked him at the fence sent a prickle of fear up the back of his neck.

Russ' voice pulled him back to the barn. "Some days it's almost like somebody milked her before I got here— who can figure it? Maybe we'll have better luck tomorrow." He picked up the pail with its meager contents. "Come on, Ernie Banks. I'm putting you in charge of our feathered friends."

Russ plodded out of the barn in his galoshes, but Ernie remained behind, his attention riveted on an old bear trap nailed to the wall. Reaching up, he gingerly touched its rusted teeth.

"Ernie?" Russ called.

Flinching, Ernie backed away from the trap, then hurried outside. He found Russ waiting for him inside the chicken coop, a small enclosure stuffed with tiers of nesting chickens that clucked and cooed. His nose twitched from the smell.

Russ chuckled. "You'll get used to it." He scooped a coffee can into the feed bin and showed it to Ernie. "About this much, and don't forget to give 'em fresh water. Spigot's just outside. Make sure you shut it off tight—water's a precious commodity around here." He looked at his distracted helper with amusement. "Ernie?"

"Yeah?"

"I'll need you to get the eggs once a day," instructed Russ as he gently lifted the breast of a sitting hen and deftly reached underneath to pull out an egg. "Just reach under and pick 'em clean." The hen obliged with a contented clucking. "Okay, give it a go."

Ernie stared, lost in his own thoughts.

"Hey, partner, you haven't heard a word I've said. What's on your mind?"

There was a lot on his mind. *A whole lot.* Nothing seemed normal here, and now he was trying to decide if what happened last night was somehow connected to the Quilt Baby. He took a deep breath. "Has anybody around here ever seen Bigfoot? You know, that big old hairy Neanderthal people talk about?" Ernie was proud of himself for knowing the word *Neanderthal.* He'd sometimes used it at Lakeside when he needed just the right insult.

Russ laughed. "Bigfoot? Well, not lately, but I have seen a few big barn rats. Don't worry, I know it's a little adjustment out here after living in the big city. Give it a few days, you'll get used to it."

Ernie nodded. There was something else he wanted to ask and he figured now was as good a time as any. "Well, I hope you don't get mad at me for asking, but . . . did the kidnappers ever send a ransom note for the Quilt Baby, I mean, for Shawn?"

Russ collected himself before responding. "No, Ernie, they never did. I guess whoever took . . . the Quilt Baby . . . didn't do it for money."

"So you figure the kidnappers took him far away? Or maybe they hid him somewhere close?"

"Well, Ernie, that's something I really don't like to think about anymore," he said. "I guess I just pray that he's okay."

"It's not right what happened," said Ernie. "I mean, getting stolen like he did and never knowing his mom and dad."

Russ struggled with his emotions.

"I'm gonna help you, I really am," Ernie declared. "I'm going to find out what happened to Shawn, I promise."

Though taken aback by Ernie's pledge, Russ couldn't help but smile. "You think you got time enough for that in three weeks?" he asked.

"I hope so."

"All right, Sherlock, glad you're on the case," Russ said, squeezing Ernie's shoulder. "Now let's get back to feathers—reach under and get those eggs."

Ernie reached for the next hen, but she squawked a warning.

"Just a little spooked because she doesn't know you yet. Go again," encouraged Russ.

When Ernie slipped his hand beneath the hen, she flapped into the air, inciting the entire coop. They both ducked for cover as hens squawked every which way in a whirl of chaotic feathers. Huddled together beneath the cramped nesting racks, Russ and Ernie shared a chuckle, then Russ laughed, which made Ernie laugh, which made Russ laugh all the harder.

After chores, Russ retrieved two gloves and a baseball from the cellar. They played catch in the shade of the weeping willow. Every ball Russ threw went hard to Ernie's chest. The man really knew how to pitch. Russ worked with Ernie on his mechanics, just like a big leaguer. He added a high leg kick to Ernie's delivery, then showed him how to push hard off his back leg. Soon Ernie's pitches zipped into Russ' glove with a loud, leather-cracking pop.

Russ finally called it quits, grinning as he took off the

glove. "That's about all my poor hand can take—you're really throwing some heat. Let's get some lunch."

As they walked back to the house, Russ looked down at Ernie and smiled. Ernie suddenly realized that he'd talked more with Russ, while playing catch, than with any other adult in his entire life.

CHAPTER TWENTY-SEVEN

Jaws of Death

ERNIE CAREFULLY camouflaged the bear trap near the wheat trampled during the previous night's attack. He'd taken it from the barn when Russ went into town to pick up a few things. Sassy grazed on some stubborn crabgrass while Joey, wearing her favorite rooster T-shirt, sat atop the split-rail fence.

"That's disgusting," she muttered, pointing at a patch of black slime just inside the Holsapple property.

Ernie joined her at the fence to see what she was talking about. "What is that?"

"I don't know, but it stinks. I think it spills off stupid Holsapple's oil trucks."

"Doesn't look like oil to me, Rooster." He swung under the fence to get a closer look.

"Don't touch it!" she warned. "It burns, and it's hard to get off. One time my mom had to throw away my jeans when I fell into some. And they were brand new, too."

Ernie leaned close to sniff the black slime, but quickly recoiled, pinching his nose against the fetid smell. "It stinks worse than rotten potatoes," he said as he swung back under the fence.

"Told you." She hopped down and picked up a broken wheat stalk. Holding it like a fork, she pretended to eat, chewing and swallowing loudly. "Mmmm, this sure tastes good!" He thought she said it just like somebody in a TV commercial. "Oh yes, thank you, Gram, I'll have another piece of that homemade apple pie. What about you, Cubber? Yeah, dish it out!"

Ernie laughed. She reminded him of his friend Nate doing one of his impersonations.

"Well, that's where we'd be if we had any brains. You just better hope my mom doesn't call my gram."

"You said she doesn't check up on you," reminded Ernie as he placed two sticks to mark the trap's center.

"Sometimes she's unpredictable."

"We'll just have to take our chances."

As far as Russ and Betty knew, they were scheduled to spend the night with Gram and Gramp Atwater. As far as Joey's grandparents knew, they were spending the night at Russ'.

"I just don't think this is such a smart idea," cautioned

Joey. "Number one, Russ told me never to touch that trap, and number two, you better hope he doesn't notice it missing from the barn. You absolutely positive we need it, Cubber?"

"Did you forget this little detail?" He pulled up his T-shirt to reveal the red claw marks on his chest.

She gulped, sobered, but caught a glimpse of something else as he pulled down his shirt. "Hey, what was that?"

"What?"

"That diamond thingy around your neck."

"Nothin'."

"Come on, let me see."

"Maybe sometime," said Ernie as he retrieved the splintered broom from the trampled wheat. He shuttled backward to the fence, erasing his footprints.

"Some blood brother you are."

"I said sometime, okay?"

She burned a gaze into the back of his head while he used her jackknife to carve a big X into the fence post, marking the spot. "It's personal," he said at last.

"What's that supposed to mean?"

Ignoring her, he fastened a string that ran from the trap to a cowbell dangling from the lower rail of the fence.

"Okay, fine," said Joey with disgust as she mounted Sassy. "You can go on up to Holsapple's by yourself. Why should I risk my life if you're not even gonna be straight with me?" She untied their gear from the saddle and dropped it into the dirt.

"All right, already," he muttered, then pulled out his Crystal Acorn and held it up for her to see. She stared openmouthed at the one-of-a-kind ice-blue crystal.

"Jeez, Cubber," she marveled. "Where'd you get that?"

"When I was a little kid, I got left at a boys' home in Chicago, and it was the only thing I had on me. Now it's the only thing I've got to prove I belong to somebody somewhere, okay?"

She offered a sympathetic nod.

"And I think that thing last night was trying to steal it."

"Why?"

"I don't know, but Harvey Holsapple wanted it, too, and I'm gonna find out why." They glanced toward the distant Holsapple manse with a shared look of apprehension.

"He probably thinks it's worth a lot of money," suggested Joey.

"Maybe." He put his crystal back under his shirt, then picked up the broom handle. "Watch this." He approached the marked piece of ground and nosed the broom toward the trap. "Beware, Bigfoot, here comes . . ."

The broom triggered a spring mechanism and the bear trap hammered shut, snapping the handle like a toothpick. The cowbell clanged until Ernie smothered it.

"The jaws of death!"

CHAPTER TWENTY-EIGHT

The Blood Trail

THEY TOOK THE roundabout way to the east end of the plateau. Joey claimed they'd be less likely to get spotted if they crossed into Holsapple property through the old bee keep on Emil Goetz's land. As they made their way across the hard-packed dirt, she told Ernie that the keep used to be her favorite place to spend a summer day, with the bees purring in the clover and the sweet smell of honey in the air. A few times Emil had even let her lift the lid on some of the wooden boxes that housed the honeycombs so she could get a look inside. Thousands of bees busily crawled in and out of the comb, making sweet Warbling River honey. Now the clover was dried up like everything else, and the bees had all gone away.

They led Sassy up a slope of oak and pine to the

summit of a craggy bluff known as Black Rock. They dropped onto their stomachs and crawled to the edge of the sheer-faced cliff. Only thirty yards away was the four-story manse of gables, turrets, and spires. A gargoyle water-spout glowered from each corner of the steep roof. The black Cadillac was parked in the courtyard.

Joey gave Ernie a hard look. He knew she was hoping he'd call it off, but that wasn't going to happen. They hunkered down and watched and waited. But they didn't have to wait long.

The back door banged open and Harvey Holsapple and the twins lumbered across the barren ground behind the manse. They stopped beside an iron wheel attached to a pipe six feet in diameter that ran from the adjacent oil field directly under the house.

"Open it up, boys," ordered Holsapple. "She wants all we can give her."

The twins gripped the rusted wheel and cranked it, hard. A rush of oil flowed down the pipe.

"Let's hope that'll satisfy her," Holsapple said.

At the top of the cliff, Ernie and Joey watched, perplexed, as the men returned inside.

"Her? Who are they talking about?" he asked.

"And why are they pumping oil into the ground instead of taking it out?"

"And why right under their house?"

Without answers, they looked back to the manse.

It was late afternoon and all was quiet. Chewing a wheat stem, Joey kept watch with binoculars while Ernie practiced sleight of hand with a pack of matches.

"Russ must like you some if he told you all that," she mused.

"Can you believe it? No ransom!" he recalled.

"'Course not."

"Just shows you've got no clue when it comes to economics, Rooster—a baby's worth plenty," cited Ernie.

"Oh, please! Babies suck up greenbacks faster than Uncle Sam can print 'em," she declared knowingly, then put down the binoculars. "I'm starving."

Joey retreated to the copse of tall pines where Sassy was tied. She got a box of crackers and a jar of peanut butter out of the saddlebag. Sitting cross-legged on the ground, she spooned the gooey spread onto some crackers, then let Sassy lick the spoon. She called softly, "Mr. Cub, you hungry?"

When he didn't answer, she started to repeat the question, but he twisted around and gestured for her to zip her mouth. She hustled back, dropping on her stomach to crawl the last few yards to the precipice. He was looking through the binoculars, but she could see it plainly with her own two eyes. "It's the Corn-Cobb," she whispered.

They watched as Dicky Cobb removed what looked

like a blanketed cage from the trunk of the Cadillac. A muffled cry sounded from inside the cage as he carried it across the courtyard.

"Good night and sleep tight!" blurted Joey.

He quickly covered her mouth, but she kept right on talking, her voice muted. "What is that?"

"Probably another baby," whispered Ernie.

She pushed his hand away. Her eyes were bigger than Sassy's as she murmured, "Kidnappers in our own backyard!"

"Professionals."

As Cobb entered the manse with his victim, Ernie and Joey felt a sinking feeling in the pit of their stomachs.

As twilight fell, the cicadas screamed in the dry pine needles and some crows cawed from the trees. Keeping their vigil, Ernie and Joey avoided each other's gaze. Both were frightened by the coming darkness, but determined not to show it.

"Holsapple!" he whispered.

Below them, Holsapple, Cobb, and the twins walked across the courtyard and got into the Cadillac. Ernie and Joey watched it motor down the long drive and turn onto the highway. When it was out of sight, they probed each other's eyes for a glint of fear.

"We might get in, but I'm not so sure we're going to get out," she warned.

"Keep your eyes out for any kind of clues or evidence," he instructed.

"I'm keeping my eyes out for Holsapple," she muttered, gathering her backpack.

"If by some miracle we find Shawn, he's probably brainwashed, so be prepared to take him by force."

Joey swallowed. "If we don't get decapitated first."

Looking her dead in the eye, Ernie presented his thumb. "Brothers."

"Sister," she countered with a nervous laugh as they cranked their thumbs a quarter turn.

Ernie grabbed the rope, tied one end around a pine, then tossed the coil over the edge. He descended hand-over-hand down the cliff. Joey followed. Touching down, they bounded across the courtyard to the manse portico, where they slowed to a stiff walk. The gloomy walkway was covered in thorny vines and lined with pillars and statues like something from ancient Rome.

Up ahead, two stone Chimeras guarded the steps leading to the front door. The sentries had enormous wings on lion bodies, with dragon tails, vulture claws for feet, and reptilian heads, whose granite faces seemed to leer at them as they passed.

At the massive door, Ernie drew Holsapple's keys from his pocket. He studied each key before inserting one into the lock. "Get Shawnie's rattle out of the pack."

"What for?" whispered Joey.

"For luck."

"Won't make no difference."

"Go on, shake it," he insisted.

She reluctantly retrieved the rattle from her pack and gave it a shake. Satisfied, he tried the key. The door clicked open. Suddenly a car started up the driveway, its headlights washing over them. They collapsed in a heap and belly-crawled across the threshold into the manse. Ernie eased the door closed as Joey peeked out a window.

"It's the sheriff!" she exclaimed.

"What's he doing here?!"

In the courtyard, Sheriff Dashin got out of his cruiser and trained a spotlight on the front door. Joey ducked down to avoid its harsh beam. "We are so dead," she moaned.

Dashin cautiously approached the door. He shined his flashlight through the window and peered inside. The intruders pressed against the wall as his flashlight beam washed just over their heads. The light illumined an enor-mous oil painting of Harvey and his twins on the wall fac-ing them. Too scared to even breathe, Ernie and Joey looked at each other as if they'd just entered their worst nightmare. They didn't blink until the sheriff's flashlight went out. They didn't budge until they heard his car motoring away.

"I knew this was a bad idea," she muttered.

"C'mon," he said, then started off. Joey wanted to go home in the worst way, but it was too late to back out now. So she did the only thing a blood brother could do—she followed.

A chill swept over them as they crossed through the vestibule. The air felt dank and cold. Rugged stone walls were framed by long black drapes and adorned with iron sconces holding thick candles. Two lifelike mannequins, dressed like Samurai warriors, threatened with upraised swords. Joey put a finger to her throat and drew it slowly from ear to ear.

Doing his best to ignore her, Ernie noticed something on the stone floor. He knelt down to touch a tiny red spot, then held his finger up to Joey's flashlight.

"Blood!" gasped Joey. "If it's a baby, Holsy killed it, or worse."

"Shhhh," hushed Ernie, trying to stay calm, "or we'll be next. Keep your eyes peeled—there might be more."

He grabbed her flashlight and proceeded past a grand staircase that led upward into the dark. It was Joey who saw the second spot of blood. He found the third. They tracked the trail down a corridor into a large room with a vaulted ceiling made of rough-hewn timber. Ernie scanned the walls with the beam of light. It was as if they'd entered the stronghold of Genghis Khan. A collection of Mongol and Chinese swords covered one wall. Around the room were sculpted busts of fierce warriors, golden figurines, and jeweled icons from the Far East.

"These people are even weirder than I thought," whispered Joey.

"Look, more blood."

They followed the trail into the next room, which was ornate and lavish. The antique French furniture was upholstered in red and purple velvet. Huge paintings of gory battles adorned the walls.

"Where'd these creeps get all this stuff?" wondered Ernie.

"Stole it, probably."

They crept into another room. This one looked like the Old West, with cowboy and Indian paraphernalia and a stuffed buffalo whose glass eyes were frozen in a dead stare.

The blood trail led to the dining room, its walls lined with hunters' trophies—heads of lions, tigers, bears, and a black panther. They gagged at the sight of flies buzzing around a half-eaten hog's carcass splattered across a long wooden table.

"This is too sick," shuddered Ernie, backing away.

"Watch out! Stop!"

He shot her an exasperated look. "What?"

"Look what you almost stepped in," she said, pointing at a pool of black slime.

He crouched down to examine it, recoiling from the smell. "This is the same gunk we saw up by the fence. What's it doing here?"

"Maybe Holsy drinks it with his dinner, how should I know? C'mon, let's keep moving—maybe we can save that baby."

They pressed on into the next room, which turned out to be the kitchen. Everything was oversized. There were four ten-foot doors and cupboards that stretched from floor to ceiling. But what riveted their attention was the blue flame surging on the stove and the sound of something bubbling inside a big iron pot. They stood on tiptoes to peer inside.

"What is that?" asked Ernie.

"I can't tell. It looks like something with a bone."

"It smells awful," he said, on the verge of throwing up.

"All I know is my mom never leaves the house with something on the stove. I don't like this, Cubber, let's go, let's get out of here."

"Wait."

Ernie traced the drops of blood across the polished floor. His light froze on the blanketed cage Dicky Cobb had carried in from the Caddy. It was set on a butcher's block below a rack of medieval knives. A bloodstained cleaver lay beside it. Horrified by the prospect of what they might see, Joey took a step backward and covered her mouth in case she needed to scream. Ernie slowly pulled off the blanket. It was a birdcage. And it was empty.

"Poor little thing," said Joey softly. "That's probably him in the big pot, half eaten."

"Never had a chance," added Ernie.

"Cannibals, right here in Circle, Illinois," she said, repulsed.

"Yeah. It's probably what happened to Shawn Frazier."

From another room, an antique clock struck the time. Its gong echoed eerily throughout the manse. Nine strikes. Once the final gong rang out, Joey was adamant. "All right, that's it, I'm leaving!" she declared, grabbing the flashlight.

Ernie didn't need any convincing. He draped the blanket back over the cage so no one would know they'd been there, but, just as they turned to go, two black wolfhounds bounded through a dog door into the kitchen. Scrambling, Ernie and Joey escaped into separate rooms, slamming the doors behind them. The wolfhounds barked viciously.

"Ernie?" she called.

He answered in a loud whisper, "Joey!"

"Where are you?"

Ernie was in complete darkness. Her voice sounded far away. "I don't know, you've got the flashlight."

Joey'd forgotten it was in her hand. She panned the light across the windowless room. The shelves were stocked with foodstuffs she'd never seen before, with strange labels in unreadable languages. There were animal parts floating in murky glass jars along with pickled snakes, centipedes, and worms. Something smelled rancid and she tried not to breathe. "This place really stinks!" she called.

Ernie heard but didn't answer. He dug the pack of matches from his pocket and struck a match. His pupils dilated with the sudden flare. He could see that he was on the landing of a steep cellar stairway. A collection of bizarre

African and Asian masks lined the walls. When the flame singed his fingers, he was again in darkness. He cracked the door to peek into the kitchen. A wolfhound lunged with bared teeth and he slammed the door on its nose. The dog howled angrily.

"You okay?" shouted Joey.

From below, Ernie could hear a faint whimpering. "There's a baby crying in the cellar. I'm going down."

"Ernie, no, don't do it!"

Ignoring her warning, he descended the stairs, striking a new match each time one went out. From up above, he could still hear Joey calling his name. When he reached the cellar, he tracked the whimpering to a large storage bin set in the floor. The lid was secured by a padlock in the shape of a skull. He tried to force open the lock. The whimpering got louder. He fumbled in his pocket for Holsapple's keys. Choosing the skeleton key, he inserted it into the skull's eye socket. Its jaws popped open. He removed the lock and opened the bin. An iron ladder disappeared into the darkness. It wasn't a storage bin, but he wasn't exactly sure what it was. He clenched his jaw and listened. The whimpering had stopped.

In the pantry, Joey was frantic. "Ernie!" she shouted again. The only reply was a low growl from the other side of the door. She swept her flashlight in every direction to find another way out. Nothing. She felt like the walls were closing in around her. She leaned her forehead against a shelf, closed her eyes, and tried to calm herself. *What was I thinking, breaking into Harvey Holsapple's? Stupid!* When she opened her eyes, she realized she was staring into a jar filled with eyeballs. Recoiling, she bumped against a hidden switch, which triggered a secret panel. It creaked open to reveal a dark passageway. She listened. Everything was quiet. Desperate to find a way out, she hurried into the passage, turning left then right then left again, until it dead-ended at a brick wall. She tried to retrace her steps, but soon realized she was lost in a labyrinth of passageways. Like a rat trapped in a maze, she kept moving, but her light was growing dimmer and dimmer. When her flashlight finally died, she couldn't stifle the sobs escaping her throat. She was in a darkness so black, she didn't know if her eyes were open or closed.

Ernie felt his way down the ladder, one step after another. It delivered him to the steel floor of an oval chamber with walls of rusted iron fastened by thick rivets. There was some kind of instrument panel in the center, and round windows, like portholes, around the perimeter. Ernie stood on tiptoe to look outside one of the portholes. All he could see was a vast blackness and, far below, an eerie, reddish glow.

An anguished whimper spun him around. Straining to see in the dark, he could barely make out a crumpled shape beside a mesh of hydraulic gears. When the shape moved, he struck his last match. In the flickering light, he saw a tiny, badly beaten creature struggling for breath. He gasped aloud, amazed. He'd never seen anything like it in his whole life, and yet something about the creature felt familiar. *How could that be?* She was no bigger than a ruler and wore colorful clothes that looked like they were made from plants. *She? Yes!* It was a girl.

The spell was broken by noises from above. Ernie instinctively scooped up the injured creature and clambered up the ladder into the cellar. When the kitchen door opened above, he dove beneath the staircase. A pair of heavy boots clopped down. His blood pounding in his ears, Ernie watched Axel Holsapple track suspiciously to the open bin.

The moment the twin disappeared down the ladder, Ernie shot up the cellar stairs, cracked the door, and squinted into the harsh glare of the brightly lit kitchen. "Joey . . . Joey!" he whispered. A door slammed somewhere in the manse. When he heard Axel's angry curse from below, he dashed across the kitchen and slipped out a corner door.

Ernie found himself in a dark garage. He nestled the tiny creature inside his jacket. She was barely conscious. He crept along the wall, his heart almost beating out of his chest. Shouts of alarm and barking sounded from inside the house, and he hoped Joey had gotten away. He heard the whir of a motor. The garage door began to rise. He took cover behind a pile of raccoon and beaver pelts as the Cadillac pulled inside. When the door started back down, he scuttled along the floor and tumbled outside just before it closed.

With two lives in the balance, Ernie sprinted across the courtyard, then tore out across the barren oil fields. The moon was struggling to break through thick clouds, which meant he couldn't see much, but it also meant no one could see him. The wolfhounds' howl faded behind as he raced past the shadowy derricks that stood like angry iron sentinels. Finally he slowed down, for the sake of the creature.

When Ernie looked back, he thought he saw the silhouette of something humongous loping across the field toward him. He started to run. When he looked again, the monstrous shape was only two derricks behind. Cupping his hand against his jacket to protect the creature, he ran as fast as he'd ever run.

He raced along the Frazier boundary fence, looking frantically for the post marked with the carved X. In the dark, he couldn't tell one post from another, and he could hear a horrid growl gaining against his every stride. Just when he was sure he wouldn't make it, there it was. He hurdled the fence as the beast crashed through the rails right behind. He felt its rancid breath on his neck just before the bear trap slammed shut with a vicious *thwack!*

Losing his cap, Ernie tumbled head over heels through the dirt but bounced to his feet and never lost stride, running to the accompaniment of a jangling cowbell and a bitter howl.

CHAPTER TWENTY-NINE

A Familiar Stranger

ERNIE RIPPED DOWN the slope through the dark, never once looking back until he reached the Frazier porch. Struggling for breath, he hovered by the screen door. He could see inside, where Russ was surrounded by bills at the kitchen table. He heard him sigh. Ernie checked inside his jacket. The wounded creature was barely breathing. He needed to do something right away. He repositioned her, then slipped inside.

Russ looked up in surprise when Ernie entered with a studied nonchalance. "Well, Mr. Banks, this is a surprise. What are you doing home?"

"Hey, Russ," said Ernie casually.

"I thought you two were staying at Gram and Gramp's tonight."

"Well . . . uh," he sputtered, forgetting momentarily where he was supposed to be. "We were, but then Joey had something to do, so we left."

"Don't be too disappointed. I've learned over the years that girls can be somewhat unpredictable. How'd you get home?"

"Ran, I mean, walked." Not wanting to answer more questions, he continued into the hall.

"Ernie?"

"Yeah?"

"Come here a sec."

Folding his arms to cover the bulge in his jacket, Ernie stepped back into the kitchen. His face was flushed, and his tousled hair visible for the first time without his customary Cubs cab.

"You and Joey getting along?"

Ernie shifted uneasily as the creature stirred inside his jacket. "Good enough."

"She's not giving you a hard time, is she?"

"Nothin' I can't handle."

"Well, that's good. What you got in your jacket?"

"Um, just a big old toad."

Russ smiled. "How 'bout a look-see?"

"Could we do it later? He's, uh, sleeping right now."

"Come here, Ernie."

Fearing the worst, Ernie walked slowly across the room, but Russ only emptied a shoebox of its receipts and offered it to him. "Just don't let it loose in the house," he cautioned.

Ernie took the box and escaped down the hall. He rushed into the bathroom and locked the door. He spread a bath towel in the tub, then gently laid the injured creature on top of it. Runnel's once-robust brown skin was pale and sickly, her hair tangled and matted, and her eyes sealed shut. Awed, Ernie knelt over her and whispered, "Can you hear me?"

She didn't move, didn't make a sound. He gently laid a finger in the palm of her tiny hand. "If you can hear me, just squeeze my finger."

Her eyes fluttered open. They were bright turquoise, but glassy and unfocused.

"Oh, man!" His whole body shook with excitement. Bursting into action, he ran hot water and scoured the medicine cabinet with the hope of re-creating Russ' concoction. "Just hold on. You're safe now—I'm going to help you," he promised. As he mixed the dark red brew, thoughts of his blood brother tightened his stomach into a knot. *Did she find a way out? Or did the Holsapples catch her?*

Ernie turned to the creature with his medicine. "Brace yourself," he warned. "Here comes Mr. Smarts." He gripped her delicate foot and began to dab a nasty wound in the webbing between her toes. "This stuff is supposed to burn some, you . . ."

His mouth dropped open and he nearly fell into the tub.

Tattooed into the ball of her foot was a spiral, a marking identical to his. It shook him to the core. *What could this little creature have to do with me?*

Reeling with the mystery, Ernie finished his doctoring, then prepped the shoebox with a soft hand towel and placed the creature inside. He found an eyedropper in the cabinet, wedged the box under his arm, and peeked out the door. Russ had gone into his bedroom and turned on the radio. It sounded like some kind of weather channel. They were saying it was the tenth straight year of decreasing rain. Ernie hurried to his room, closing the door behind.

He deliberated on a hiding place before putting the shoebox in the crib beneath the red quilt. "Don't worry, I'll be right back," he reassured, tucking a T-shirt around her. When he looked up, the seven carved figures dangling from the mobile were staring him in the face. One of them looked like the creature in the shoebox. He took another look. *Exactly like her!* Even the clothes were the same. His head spinning, he closed the lid and hurried from the room.

Ernie tiptoed to the kitchen and scanned a list of telephone numbers posted next to the wall phone. Her number was the first one on the list. He dialed, then, with the phone cradled at his ear, got a glass and poured himself some milk. When Betty answered, Ernie took care to disguise his voice. He wished he had Nate's talent for impersonation.

"Hello, is Joey there?" he asked hoarsely.

"Who's calling?"

"Ah, it's . . ." he stumbled, surprised by the question. Finally he said, "It's Shawn."

"Shawn?" she asked suspiciously. "Shawn who?"

Ernie didn't answer. Approaching footsteps forced him to hang up. Trying to look busy, he gulped some milk.

"Did Gramp Atwater show you his old tractors?" asked Russ as he went to the sink to pour himself a glass of water.

"Nope."

"Well, that's a first," he said. "So what did you guys do?"

Ernie shrugged. "Just looked around." He desperately needed to change the subject. "Hey, Russ—you know what time it is?

"Right behind you." Russ chuckled.

Ernie turned to see a large wall clock. It read 10:05. He turned back to Russ and smiled sheepishly. "Oh yeah, I forgot about that. Is it okay if I get something to eat?"

" 'Course it is. You want me to whip something up? I make a mean grilled cheese."

"No, thanks."

"Okay, get a plate then, help yourself."

For once, Ernie did as he was told. Rummaging through the fridge, he wondered what his little creature would like to eat. Russ watched, amused, as Ernie grabbed an armful of disparate items: bologna, celery, crackers, sugar cubes, olives, peanut butter, pickles, and cheese.

"Didn't Gram feed you two?"

"Not really," said Ernie as he grabbed his glass of milk off the counter.

"That's funny, she usually puts out a spread and a half."

Ernie changed the subject. "Hey, Russ—where'd you get that mobile? The one on the crib."

"It was a gift."

"From who?"

"Well, to be honest, I never found out. It's a mystery. Why do you ask?"

"Oh, just wondering." Ernie shut the fridge with his foot, then slipped into the hall. "Well, good night," he called over his shoulder.

"Good night," called Russ as he watched him shuffle down the hall burdened with his late-night feast. He picked a cookie jar off a high shelf. Inside was a felt pouch containing an antique gold pocket watch on a brass chain. Russ clicked the crown to open the lid. He gave the watch a quick wind, and was glad to see that it still worked.

Ernie closed the crib room door with his foot and dumped the food items on the rug. He retrieved the shoebox, then sat cross-legged on the floor next to his bed and took off the lid. The creature was covered with a mishmash of bandages, and Ernie felt a surge of pride over his first-aid work. He tried to feed her a cracker, but she barely looked at it. He tried cheese and peanut butter, bologna and pickles, even the sugar cubes, all to no avail. Finally he filled the eyedropper with milk from his glass and squirted a couple drops into her mouth. She drank it gratefully.

"Oh yes, oh boy, you like it! Yes!"

"*Ko, baa,*" she murmured.

Thrilled, he jumped up and flopped back on the bed. The posts gave way and the bed crashed to the floor, nearly crushing the shoebox. Footsteps, a preemptive knock, and Russ was in the room.

"You okay?" he asked with concern.

"I think so," said Ernie, sitting up. Out of the corner of his eye he could see the creature peeking out of the shoe-box, just inches from Russ' work boot.

"What in the world happened here?"

"I had the toad over on the windowsill," said Ernie quickly as he eased himself to the edge of the collapsed bed. Waving the eyedropper, he deftly directed Russ' attention to his hand while using a foot to slide the box under the nightstand. "That was after I fed him, of course," said Ernie in his most innocent voice. "And I was on the bed, showing him how to hop, 'cause he was kind of injured and all, and then the bed just caved in on me, and he hopped away gone and here I am. Sorry about that."

"Well, don't worry about it. That old frame was bound

to go someday," said Russ, while putting a steadying hand on his shoulder. "Ernie—you sure everything's okay?"

"Oh yeah, and don't worry about that toad. He jumped right out the window. He's probably halfway home by now."

Russ laughed. "Well, okay, we'll fix the bed up tomorrow. Tonight you get to camp out on the floor. Good night."

"Night," said Ernie.

Russ paused on the threshold. He took the gold watch from the pocket of his flannel shirt. "I was thinking . . . this might help you get to supper on time." He handed him the watch. Ernie could hardly believe it. Apart from his Cubs cap, it was the first gift he'd ever gotten from somebody he actually knew. At Lakeside, gifts came from people you didn't know, like the Salvation Army. Genuinely touched, he turned the watch over in his hand, unsure what to say.

"It looks really old."

Russ laughed. "Take good care of it. My dad gave it to me."

"I will. Thanks, Russ."

"Sure enough. I hope you put it to good use."

For a moment, they just looked at each other.

Finally Russ said, "Okay then, get some sleep," and started out of the room. "I'll be waking you early. I know you can't wait to meet up with those chickens."

When the door closed, Ernie made a beeline for the

shoebox. The creature opened her eyes and smiled weakly. He smiled back, then fed her a few more squirts of milk. Each drop seemed to give her more strength.

When she finally closed her eyes, Ernie covered her with the T-shirt and whispered, "Sleep tight, pleasant dreams." He set the lid askew for air, then put the box in the top drawer of the bureau. He checked the time on his new watch and breathed on its face and polished it on his shirt. He admired it one last time before closing the lid. He attached the brass chain to a belt loop on his jeans and tucked the watch in his pocket.

Then he turned out the light and slipped out the window into the night.

CHAPTER THIRTY

Midnight Run

IT WAS ALMOST midnight when Ernie found the mailbox painted like a starry night. *Just like Joey said.* He ran up the dirt driveway past a corral and a Jeep parked in front of the modest ranch house. Keeping low to the ground, he crept along the face of the house and peered in a front window. Betty was sitting in front of an easel, painting a picture of a barn.

He skulked along the side of the house to a corner room. Gripping the ledge, he pulled himself even with the open window. The interior was dark, but he thought he could see posters of horses on the wall. *This must be the room.*

"Joey," he whispered. "You there? Joey!"

A light came on in the hall and the bedroom door opened. He noticed that Joey's bed was still made before he dropped to the ground and pressed against the house, out of sight. Just above him, Betty looked outside before shutting the window and locking it. The room went dark again.

Ernie swallowed hard. If Joey wasn't home that meant she was still at the Holsapples. *What would they do if they caught her? Torture? Or even worse.* His mind fixated on the blood trail, the bloody cleaver, and the bubbling pot on the stove. He felt like his chest was caught in an invisible vise that kept squeezing him tighter and tighter.

The stars glittered above like ethereal jewels as Ernie hustled up the backside of Black Rock. Sassy was still tied to the pine. He nuzzled the pony's nose and fed her some sugar cubes from his pocket, then crawled to the edge of the cliff.

There were lights on downstairs, and he thought he saw Holsapple draw the curtains in an upstairs room. He'd wait until everyone was asleep, then sneak back into the manse and rescue Joey. He checked his new watch. It was a quarter after one. His eyelids were heavy and he was glad to be able to rest, even for a few minutes.

In the eerie light just before dawn, Ernie woke cold and shivering and mad at himself for falling asleep. Knowing he couldn't break into the house in broad daylight, he backed away from the cliff. He clambered onto Sassy and retreated back down Black Rock, overwhelmed with a feeling that something bad had happened. He whispered encouragement to Sassy, thankful that she knew the way and could negotiate the precarious trail.

CHAPTER THIRTY-ONE

Who's Who

IN THE CHICKEN COOP, a hen stared hypnotized at the pocket watch oscillating on its chain. Ernie gently snatched beneath her fanny, then added the egg to his basket, then dangled the timepiece before the next hen. Collecting eggs was much easier with his new watch. In fact, it would've been fun if it weren't for Joey. *What am I going to do?* If he told Russ, he was sure to get blamed for breaking into the Holsapples' and they'd ship him back to Chicago, probably before lunch. But the longer he waited, the worse it might get for her. Whatever it was, he had to do something, and soon.

He entered the barn in a rush, set the basket of eggs in the hay, then grabbed a milking stool and bucket off wall pegs. He was anxious about finishing his chores so he could get back to his room and feed his little creature. He squatted on the stool beneath the big black-and-white cow and tried to remember Russ' instructions. As hard as he worked, he couldn't coax even a squirt of milk from the cow's udder.

"Look, Beulah," he said. "This isn't just for me, you know."

The cow turned her head and looked at Ernie.

"It's for this little person," he said while holding his hand eleven inches off the ground. "About so big, and milk is the only thing she wants in the whole world."

Beulah mooed and Ernie milked several squirts into his pail. He rubbed the cow's flank. "That a way, girlie," he said gratefully.

Ernie was hustling across the yard with milk and eggs when Russ, standing over a hole near the side of the house, waved him over. "Want to see what I'm doing?"

Ernie reluctantly joined him and looked down a narrow shaft.

"This is how we measure the water in a well." He hoisted a line of insulated wire hand over hand until a depth gauge came to the surface. He looked at the dripping meter. Ernie could see the worry on his face, but Russ' voice remained cheerful. "Know any rain dances?"

"Not really."

"Me neither, but I'm ready to learn. I'd try just about anything to get us some rain."

"You know, Russ, I should probably put this stuff in the fridge."

"Sure, you go ahead."

Forcing a smile, Ernie hurried into the house. He put away the milk and eggs, then picked up the kitchen phone and dialed Joey's number while prepping a breakfast tray. *Please be home, please.* When Betty answered, he hung up. His stomach churned as he grabbed the tray and hurried down the hall.

He closed the crib room door with his foot, then set the tray on the bureau and opened the top drawer. His creature stirred awake in the shoebox. They shared a smile. Ernie gave her a shot glass brimming with frothy milk. She drank it. Smiling proudly, he gave her a strawberry. "They're pretty sweet. I had some on my cereal."

While she munched the berry, Ernie ripped off his sneaker and sock, then balanced on one foot so that he could show his spiral birthmark. "It's like yours," he said.

She nodded knowingly as Ernie hopped about on one foot. "Why? What is it?" he asked.

She spoke in a language Ernie couldn't understand, except he did hear the word *root* two times. "Oh, oh, I get it," he said excitedly. He unhooked the mobile from the crib and pointed to the carving that looked like her. "This is you. Is your name Root?"

She shook her head, then pointed to herself. "Runnel," she said in a voice that sounded almost musical, then pointed to a different carving. "Root."

"Oh, okay—that's Root. And you're Runnel?"

She nodded.

"Great! I mean, it's fantastic!" gushed Ernie. *There's more of them.* He returned the mobile to the crib, then twirled it so the figures spun in a circle like a carnival ride. He pointed to himself. "My name is Ernie Banks. Er-nie Banks."

Runnel shook her head. In the kitchen, the telephone rang.

Ernie laughed. "Yes! Er-nie Banks!" He picked his Ernie Banks card off the nightstand and pointed to the boldfaced print. "See? Er . . . nie . . . Banks."

Runnel jabbered insistently. This time he heard the name *Shawn* several times.

"No, that's him," Ernie explained, pointing to the wall photo above the crib. "That's Shawn. I'm Ernie."

Adamantly shaking her head, Runnel pointed to the photo and then to Ernie and said "Shawn" both times.

"Me? No, you don't understand. Shawn used to live here. I'm just visiting."

Runnel reached out and touched the Acorn hidden beneath his shirt. "Shawn Frazier."

"Shawn Frazier?" muttered Ernie in astonishment.

There was a quick knock at the door. Ernie slid the drawer closed a second before Russ entered the room.

"Ernie?"

"Yeah?"

Russ stood on the threshold, visibly upset. Ernie stared as if seeing him for the first time, wondering if this man could possibly, by some miracle, be his father.

"Betty's on the phone. She says Sassy came in by herself this morning. She called her folks and Gram said you two weren't over there at all yesterday. Just what is going on? Where's Joey?"

CHAPTER THIRTY-TWO

A Reckoning

THE SHERIFF'S CRUISER led the Frazier pickup down Highway 99 at a fast clip. In the cab, Ernie rode wedged between a grim-faced Russ and a distraught Betty Woodruff. She was so mad she wouldn't even look at him. Before leaving the house, Ernie had tried to explain what happened. He told Russ how he and Joey went into the Holsapples' looking for clues about Shawn Frazier, and how they got separated, and why he thought the Holsapples were up to no good, and why he was sure Joey was still somewhere inside that creepy house. He left out the part about the little creature he'd rescued and what she'd told him.

As the cars turned up the Holsapple driveway, Ernie

could feel Russ' eyes on him, but he stared straight ahead. In the courtyard, they parked beside the sheriff's cruiser. Ernie stepped tentatively from the pickup. Holsapple's oil riggers were loitering by the garage, staring with crossed arms and mean faces.

"Morning, boys," greeted the sheriff. "You all workin' hard or hardly workin'?"

Nobody answered. One Eye, jangling the ring of keys on his belt, spit a big wad of tobacco. Ernie, feeling like the whole gang was staring at him, stood rooted to the ground. Russ took his arm and nudged him along.

The adults escorted Ernie under the thorny vines of the walkway's canopy, then between the winged Chimeras at the end of the portico. Sheriff Dashin rapped the front door's iron knocker. They waited in silence for what seemed like forever. Russ squeezed his shoulder. "It's all right, Ernie. Just tell the truth."

Finally the door opened and Dicky Cobb greeted them with a phony smile. "Good morning, sheriff, Russ, Betty."

"And a good morning to you, Dicky," answered the sheriff cheerfully. "Lordy, what happened to that leg?"

Ernie's gaze fixed on the foreman's right leg encased in a plaster cast.

"Got her jammed out in the rigs," Cobb said with a smile. "Ain't hardly scratched."

"Not to worry, time is the healer, yes, sir," said the sheriff.

"Come on in," he said. "Mr. Holsapple will be right down."

The visitors shuffled inside the vestibule. Ernie was the only one to see Cobb's welcoming smile change to a threatening leer. The foreman ushered them into the main hallway, where a swooping staircase led to the second floor. Harvey Holsapple was coming down the stairs with an obedient black wolfhound on either side. "Good morning, all," he said with a good-natured smile.

"Morning, Harv," said Dashin as he proudly presented Holsapple's keys in their gold-embossed leather case. "Got the keys. Kid stole 'em out of your glove box the other day."

The old man accepted the keys and slipped them into his pocket. "What a shame we should have to meet under such difficult circumstances. Can I get anyone anything?"

"No, thanks," said the sheriff. "We don't want to take up too much of your time."

"Angus just put on a fresh pot," offered Harvey.

"Appreciate it, cream and sugar then. I like it sweet."

"Anyone else?"

Russ and Betty muttered "No, thanks" as the group moved down the hall. Ernie noted the rooms still looked strange, though they weren't nearly as scary in the light of day. There was no sign of the hog carcass or the black slime, and the blood trail had been washed away.

In the kitchen, all eyes were on Ernie as he studied four closed doors. He recognized the one to the cellar and the one to the garage. Of the two remaining, he wasn't positive but he had a feeling it was the door on the right. He remembered the sound of Joey's voice as they were calling back and forth. Harvey Holsapple waited impassively, the wolfhounds well behaved at his heel. Dicky Cobb and the twins hovered like flies on a wall. Finally Ernie pointed. "That one."

"You sure? You sure Joey went through that door right there?" asked the skeptical sheriff.

Ernie nodded.

When Holsapple grunted, Cobb limped over to open the door. Dashin waddled behind to scan the well-ordered pantry. The jars of snakes, centipedes, and eyeballs had been taken away. Even the smell had been scrubbed clean.

Dashin smirked. "And exactly where were you at this point?"

Ernie pointed to the other side of the kitchen. "Behind that door."

"I thought you said you could see her. If you're behind that door, you must have X-ray vision."

Ernie smoldered. He knew it didn't look good and the sheriff was making it worse.

"I know where she was, I heard her."

"Oh really," said Dashin, rolling his eyes. "Okay, then what?"

"I went down to the cellar," Ernie said, then with a look to Holsapple, "all the way down."

The sheriff smugly crossed his arms. "Then in fact, she could have departed the house at that time and left you to your own devices, isn't that possible?"

Ernie stared unblinking. "No."

"So you say," Dashin chided. "Mr. Holsapple—you got time to finish the nickel tour?"

Holsapple chuckled. "Sorry, Tom, the cellar's going to cost you a quarter."

The sheriff clapped a hand on Ernie's shoulder. "All right, kid, lead the way."

Holsapple opened the cellar door and allowed everyone to pass—everyone except Angus and Axel. He whispered something and they hurried away.

The search party descended the well-lit stairway. The tribal masks were still on the walls but, like the rest of the house, didn't seem half as scary as the night before.

In the cellar, all eyes were again on Ernie. Crouching by the storage bin, he noticed that the skull lock had been replaced with a simple latch. He glanced at Holsapple as if the old crooked man might stop him, almost wishing he would.

"Well, what is it, boy?" demanded the sheriff. "What happened then?"

"I opened this," Ernie said, then opened the lid. He couldn't believe it. The iron ladder down to the oval chamber was gone. It was just a bin full of potatoes. He looked up at the adults pressing around him. They'd tricked him. He could see it in Holsapple's mocking eyes and Dicky Cobb's crooked smile.

Desperate, Ernie burrowed into the bin, tossing potatoes every which way, digging to uncover the ladder. Russ hauled him to his feet, restraining him.

"Oh my God," moaned Betty, overwhelmed.

"No," cried Ernie. "It's underneath! They hid it! It was like a spaceship or something. It's down there. It was . . ."

"That's enough, Ernie," cautioned Russ.

"But, Russ . . ."

"We'll talk about it later," he said, and he meant it.

Ernie glared at Holsapple. "If you hurt her, I swear I'll . . ."

Dicky Cobb stepped forward to grab him, but Russ stepped between them, standing nose to nose with the foreman. "We're sorry, Harvey," said Russ. "We won't be taking any more of your time."

"You got that right," sneered Cobb.

Holsapple stooped down to latch the bin closed. "Tall fences do good neighbors make."

"How true, how true," chimed the sheriff.

To Ernie, it seemed like the stone Chimeras were sneering at him as the adults conferred by the massive front door.

"I'm sure these folks appreciate you not pressing charges," said Sheriff Dashin. "Breaking and entering is a very serious crime."

Holsapple shrugged graciously. "I'll have my boys check out the fields. It's possible she got into one of the old mine shafts."

"Real good, and I'll keep you posted on any developments on our side," said the sheriff.

"Please do. We'll all sleep a little better when Joey's back home," reassured Holsapple.

Putting an arm around Betty, Russ ushered Ernie along the portico. The sheriff caught up with them by the pickup. "This kid really owes Mr. Holsapple an apology. And no offense, Russ, if he was mine, I'd have tanned his rear good, two or three times by now."

"Well, he's not yours," snapped Russ.

Betty, her temper flaring, added sharply, "And my little girl is still missing, so why don't you just do your job for once in your life."

"Slow down, Betty, just slow down," said the sheriff. "We'll find Joey. I got no doubt."

"No you won't!" fired Ernie.

The sheriff grabbed the boy's arm. "I swear, if you don't shut your mouth pronto, I'm going to do it for you."

"I don't think so, Tom," warned Russ.

Ernie yanked his arm away and looked the sheriff in the eye. "Those people are lying—Joey's a prisoner somewhere inside that house!"

"Ernie Banks!"

Everyone turned to see Holsapple standing in the portico waving the Cubs cap. "You forgot your cap!"

Unnerved, Ernie looked to Russ.

"Go ahead, get it."

As Ernie reluctantly retraced his steps, Sheriff Dashin settled his wide girth behind the wheel of his cruiser. "Listen, folks—if you ever get the truth out of that kid, you know where to find me."

A somber Russ and Betty watched him motor down the driveway.

Harvey Holsapple waited between the granite Chimeras as Ernie slowly approached along the portico. He stopped just short of the old crooked man. He was out of Russ' sight and didn't want to get any closer. Dicky Cobb leered from the threshold.

"Come here, son," Holsapple said, motioning with his hand. "You don't need to be afraid. I got your cap right here."

Ernie inched forward. In a flash, Holsapple hooked him by the neck with his cane, yanked him close, and snapped the cap home, forcing it snug on Ernie's head. "We know who you are," he hissed.

Coming to life, the stone Chimeras snorted and flapped their wings, blasting air that would have knocked him down but for Holsapple's iron grip. The old man blew his terrible breath on Ernie's face and snarled, "Welcome home . . . Shawn Frazier."

Ernie trembled as Holsapple unbuttoned his shirt, only to find scabbed claw marks on a bare chest. The Crystal Acorn was missing. When the old man saw that he was no longer wearing the Acorn, he smacked Ernie's chest and snarled angrily as thorns sprouted from his tongue, warts bubbled on his forehead, and his eyes boiled. But only for an instant. The gnarled old man spun him on his heels and whispered into his ear, "Joey tasted good."

The Chimeras snapped their dragon tails against his back, knocking him off his feet. He sprawled in the gravel, scraping his hands. His back throbbed, and the skin on one leg felt hot. He looked down and saw a patch of black slime on his jeans. Trying to ignore the burn, he jumped up and sprinted under the portico to the courtyard. *Where did that come from? Holsapple?*

Russ was waiting with an open door, but Ernie hopped instead into the bed of the pickup.

"Come on, Ernie. Sit with us," offered Russ.

Afraid his voice would break if he tried to speak, Ernie waved off the invitation.

"Let him be," snapped Betty.

Ernie wanted to tell Russ that Holsapple was some kind of terrible monster, but he knew he wouldn't believe him. Nobody would. If he tried to tell what happened, they'd think he was crazy. *Poor Joey.* He'd doubted everything she'd said about the Holsapples, but it turned out she was right. *Dead right.*

The pickup departed down the Holsapple driveway. Ernie stood on the flatbed, gripping the cab roof. He wiped away tears that leaked from the corners of his eyes, then reached into his sock and pulled out the Crystal Acorn. At least he'd managed to hide it and keep it out of Holsapple's hands. *But why does that wicked old man, or whatever he is, want it?*

Ernie could feel the manse watching him from behind as he slipped the Acorn back around his neck and stuffed it under his shirt. He refused to turn around. He didn't want to see that evil house ever again.

At the bottom of the driveway, Holsapple's riggers were digging a trench in the field. As the pickup turned onto the highway, One Eye raised his shovel in the air and slowly swung it back and forth, as if he were waving good-bye. The trench looked just like a grave and, this time, Ernie couldn't turn away.

CHAPTER THIRTY-THREE

The Puzzle

IT WAS A LONG, windy ride down Highway 99. Crouching in the bed of the pickup, Ernie secretly cracked open the cab's panel window so he could hear what Russ and Betty were saying. Out of the corner of his eye, he saw Russ reach for her hand. "I know it's a wild story, but what if he's telling the truth?"

Betty pulled her hand away. "What are you talking about? Now you think there's a spaceship in Harvey's basement?"

Russ clenched his jaw but didn't reply.

"Joey would never go inside that house on her own," Betty declared stormily. "Look at his background—a dozen foster homes, no respect for authority, constantly in trouble. We don't know what that kid's capable of doing. What if he hurt her?"

When Russ' gaze shifted from the road to the rearview mirror, Ernie averted his eyes. He was surprised that Russ would still stand up for him after everything that had happened. "I just don't think so," he heard Russ say. "I don't think he'd do that."

"Well, maybe it's time you think again."

Ernie's attention shifted from the distraught couple to the black Cadillac approaching fast from the opposite direction. He stood up as the Caddy zoomed past with the twins in the front seat. He watched even after the car disappeared around the curve. His back ached and his leg still burned from the black slime on his jeans.

The pickup was coming to a stop when Ernie hopped out and ran for the house.

"You stick close," called Russ. "I want you right by my side, you understand? Ernie!"

Ernie bolted through the kitchen and down the hall. He banged open the door to the crib room and stopped in his tracks—everything was tossed and thrown and ripped and ruined, the bureau overturned and the crib destroyed. He searched madly through the wreckage until he found the shoebox torn in half, the eyedropper shattered. He pictured what must have happened and felt sick to his stomach. *The twins.*

Ernie searched desperately, hoping against hope to find Runnel somewhere in the room. As he came along the wall, he saw a fragment from his baseball card sitting on the windowsill. He picked it up and realized he was looking into the eyes of Ernie Banks. Perplexed, he scanned the ground outside the window. There was another card scrap lying in the dirt. He hurried to the door and checked down the hall. He could hear Betty crying in the kitchen.

"We'll find her, I promise," comforted Russ. "Let's check with your mom again, then start calling the neighbors."

Ernie shut the door, then slipped out the window and collected the fragment. Scouring the ground like a bloodhound, he recovered a third card scrap near the corral. He matched it with his other pieces to form the face of Ernie Banks. He found another fragment by the wheat and flattened stalks that indicated a tiny trail. Mesmerized, he followed it.

Standing on the kitchen threshold, Russ stared at Ernie's closed bedroom door while Betty talked on the phone. "I don't know, Joey said she wanted to show that boy Dad's old tractors." She paced back and forth the length of the phone cord. "No, Mom. He came back by himself last night. Russ just figured she was home with me." She watched Russ stride down the hall. "That's right. The Goetzes are organizing a search party. Everybody's meeting here at noon."

Russ rapped on the crib room door. "Ernie?" Not waiting for a reply, he opened the door into the ransacked room. "What in God's name?" At his feet was the photograph of him and baby Shawn, now shredded. It felt like a punch in the stomach. Through the window he could see Ernie racing up the field.

Russ climbed out the window and ran across the yard, shouting, "Ernie, get back here! Ernie!" The boy was already disappearing over the first knoll. Furious, Russ turned back to the house as Betty hurried from the porch. "What happened?" she asked.

"He's gone. We'd better call the sheriff."

With his gaze fixed on the ground, Ernie hustled through the field, claiming card scraps. At the boundary fence he found an arrow-shaped fragment pointing toward the scorched Holsapple wasteland. He set it in his palm with the other pieces. The Ernie Banks puzzle was almost complete. With a defiant look to the distant manse, he jumped the split rail and hustled across the blistered earth like a hawk searching for its prey. Up ahead, something glinting in the sun caught his eye. He sprinted past derricks and ratcheting oil pumps, not slowing until he realized what it was.

There, waiting patiently at the heart of the wasteland, was a puddle. As he got closer, he could see a tiny Cubs insignia floating in the water. He picked up the soggy emblem and added it to his puzzle, now a fully restored Ernie Banks card. He gazed at his reflection in the mirrored surface, swirling the water with his fingertips, then looked back at Ernie Banks in his palm. It seemed to be the end of the trail. *But why here? Why a puddle? And how can a puddle even be in this dried-out place?*

The sound of a car engine broke the spell. He spun around to see the black Cadillac zooming along the boundary fence. Fighting the urge to flee, he kept his focus on the puddle. *The puddle.* There was something about the puddle that he had to understand. The Caddy veered onto the field in a cloud of dust. It was coming fast and bearing straight for him. His mind raced back to the underground spring beneath Derrick 19. It was like a secret door that opened into the hideaway. *But how?* He probed the shallow water with his hands, unsure what he was looking for.

The Cadillac charged like a raging bull eager for the kill. Ernie jumped up and down in the puddle, but nothing changed. Then he remembered the one thing he shared with Runnel. He ripped off his sneaker and sock and planted his foot with the spiral birthmark squarely in the puddle. The earth instantly opened, plunging him downward just before the Cadillac shot past at seventy miles an hour.

As the puddle hatchway closed behind him, all that remained were the fragments of the Ernie Banks card floating in the water.

CHAPTER THIRTY-FOUR

Underneath

ERNIE LAY SPRAWLED in the dirt of a decrepit tunnel. It smelled dusty and stale like an abandoned house. Groaning, he rolled onto his back and stared up at the puddle through which he'd just fallen. It was like a window floating in the air. He squinted into the sunlight filtering through the water, still mystified that it didn't spill down.

Suddenly two ugly faces appeared in the puddle, Angus and Axel. Ernie sprang to his feet, but when the twins didn't react, he realized they couldn't see him. The puddle was like a one-way mirror—you could only see through it from underneath. The frustrated twins kicked and stomped in the water. They looked like a heat mirage shimmering in the desert.

Ernie sensed something moving in the dark just beyond the shaft of sunlight. A tiny figure emerged from the shadow. Runnel limped into the light, gripped Ernie's jeans, and rested her bandaged forehead against his knee.

"Shawn . . . Fra . . . zier," she whispered.

"Runnel," he whispered back.

Ernie wasn't sure what to do, so he just touched the top of her head and grinned. When dirt from the tunnel ceiling sifted onto their heads, they looked up to see Angus and Axel digging at the edges of the puddle. As they slung the dirt faster and faster, they began to transmogrify into something hideous. Black slime oozed from their pores and claws grew from their hands and feet. Their heads bulged to three times their original size and their noses became grotesque snouts. Coarse hair sprouted over their entire bodies and their leathery tails pounded the earth.

Ernie gaped in fear as the monsters clawed down so fast that heaps of dirt nearly buried Runnel. A thick tail smashed into the Underneath and knocked him off his feet. His head struck the ground hard. Runnel cried, "*Mata-ki, mata-ki, lo!*" as the tail raked across the dirt. She tugged his arm, but Ernie was woozy and couldn't move, like in a nightmare when something's chasing you but you can't run. She jumped on his chest, slapped his face, and squealed, "*Lolo, lolo!*" He struggled to his knees just as the monster jammed its head into the tunnel and screeched, its hideous breath fouling the air. A raspy tongue shot out like a giant lizard's, but Runnel and Ernie scrambled just beyond its reach. They escaped into the dark tunnel, where the beast was too big to follow.

With a terrible snarl, Axel yanked his head out of the ground. The twin Troggs, standing in two fresh pools of black slime, yawped angrily as they shrank back to human form. They'd almost captured the boy who had come to destroy them.

Ernie ran hunched over so he wouldn't scrape his head on the tunnel ceiling. Riding on his shoulder, Runnel released fireflies from a pouch on her belt to light the way in the pitch black. They swarmed ahead with their lantern torsos flashing in a changing constellation. She chirped, "*Akadie-lo! Akadie-ru! Kaday, kaday!*" while pointing left, right, and straight, guiding him ever downward. Ernie lost his sense of direction, and even for Runnel it was difficult. The Holsapples had ravaged much of the Underneath with their blasting and mining and drilling.

As they wound deeper and deeper into the earth, Ernie felt fear in the pit of his stomach. *Where is she taking me?* He couldn't help but wonder if he'd ever breathe fresh air again. Just when he didn't think he could run much farther, Runnel pointed to a faint glow up ahead where the tunnel seemed to end. They passed through a snarl of dead vines to emerge on a ledge overlooking a vast cavern. Ernie had the strangest feeling he'd been here before, at least in his dreams, but it was different now.

Like the world above, everything was parched and dry. A giant oak tree stood with exposed roots in the middle of a fissured lake bed. It looked like it was about to fall over. The tree was glimmering with a feeble blue light that seemed to haunt the deserted cavern.

As they descended the dusty slope, Ernie was careful not to fall into any of the numerous holes dotting the hillside. Looking down, he could see that they were homes where little creatures like Runnel must have lived. It reminded him of the secret hideaway he and Joey had found. Like that one, these dens were dark and abandoned. It was clear that something terrible had happened.

Ernie stepped over a thin stream threading across the lake bed. He glanced at Runnel riding on his shoulder. Her expression was pained. He didn't know if she was still suffering from the wounds inflicted by the Holsapple monsters, or if it was from the sadness of returning to this ruined place. She pointed to a stone hut at the top of a knoll.

As they approached, Runnel climbed down his body. Ernie watched her limp to the hut and disappear inside. He hurried to a window chiseled out of the stone and sprawled on his stomach. Through the opening, he saw Runnel reuniting with four other tiny creatures. One spun her in a circle while the others jabbered excitedly. Runnel finally quieted them. "Wawaywo," she said, then pointed to the window. They turned and looked at Ernie as if he were a ghost. No one said a word.

Ernie rose to his knees as the little ones came outside. They approached with timid smiles. Runnel introduced each one by name. Ernie's mind flooded with long-forgotten memories. *So that's Root.* He thought he remembered jumping through a puddle with him. And he'd gone down a big waterfall with the littlest one. He remembered laughing in a thunderstorm with the one she called Cully. And Buck, the one with the scar on his cheek . . . *had they slept with bears?* Though initially hesitant, they soon surrounded him, their kindly eyes brimming with joy, touching him as if to make sure he was real.

When Cully beckoned him into the hut, Ernie squeezed through the front door on his belly. Above him, a mobile dangled from the ceiling, vibrant carvings of hundreds of creatures that covered the room like a canopy. He couldn't help but wonder what had become of all the others. Sitting in a circle, they shared a meager meal of ground wheat paste. Ernie thought it tasted like cardboard but ate it anyway.

As impossible as it seemed, Ernie sensed that he belonged with these little creatures. They felt familiar, like members of a long-lost family.

CHAPTER THIRTY-FIVE

The Choice

THE LAST OF THE Puddlejumpers hurried across the dry lake bed, chattering nonstop. Ernie couldn't understand what they were saying, but there seemed to be some disagreement, and he was sure it had something to do with him. As they passed beneath the giant oak's drooping branches, Ernie reached up to touch one of the last crystal acorns clinging to a branch. It was identical to the Acorn he was wearing around his neck, except this one flickered with a pale light. He'd always wondered where his Acorn came from, but he could never have imagined anything like this.

When Runnel pointed toward a hollow at the base of the tree, he entered the dark interior. His first step launched him headlong down a water-polished groove. He slid down and down the oak's intertwining roots until he tumbled into a bed of soft sand. The others tumbled right behind. This place, too, was bone dry and eerily quiet. A gray crust coated the walls, muting veins of gemstones and silver.

They trudged across the sand, then passed through a threshold in the rock. Buck and Cully's lanterns lit the way down a winding stairway. To keep his balance, Ernie kept one hand on the outer wall, its surface polished smooth. He stopped to peer over the side, but the others nudged him on, as if they were late for a very important rendezvous.

They reached an oak platform suspended on ropes of hemp over a gorge that led even deeper into the earth. A torch embedded in the wall provided a shadowy light. When Ernie crossed onto the platform, it swung precariously under his weight, and, for a moment, he was afraid the ropes might snap and they would tumble into the blackness, never to return.

At the edge of the swaying platform, a lone Puddlejumper was moistening the rock wall with a sponge affixed to a birch pole. She was taller than the others and had long white hair. Runnel called out her name. When Pav turned and saw Ernie, her eyes filled with tears. Ernie watched as she put down her pole and came toward him. Gazing into his face with piercing green eyes, she touched her heart, then stood on tiptoe to touch his. It was the same way he'd said good-bye to Nate, and now he understood why.

As Ernie's eyes adjusted to the light, he began to see the most astonishing creature in the texture of the rock. It was a face two stories high. A woman's face, the same one from his dreams. Her emerald eyes twinkled for an instant, and Ernie gasped in wonder, disbelieving he could be under the scrutiny of such an awesome creature. She seemed to be in pain, her respiration a mournful wheeze. Pav returned to her care, using the sponge to circulate water trickling down her forehead to her eyes, nose, and mouth.

Summoning her strength, the stone being began to speak an ancient tongue only understood in the primordial deep. Her words reverberated in a cacophony of sound that encompassed every language spoken since the beginning of time. To Ernie it felt like a wave of energy brushing against him, until the most extraordinary thing happened. As her words echoed off the canyon walls, suddenly he could understand. She was MotherEarth. He listened in astonishment.

"*Wawaywo*—your return brings hope to the Kingdom." She paused to gather her breath, then spoke again. "Listen close, for there is very little time. The river is dry and my little ones are nearly gone. Only you can save them, only you can bring back the rain."

Pav gave the pole to Cully, then, with a sense of urgency, began to grind colorful minerals from pouches on her belt using a mortar and pestle.

The voice of MotherEarth rumbled through the rocks,

and Ernie could hear her say, "You must make the journey into the Most Dark and plant your Crystal Acorn where the fire burns hot and forever."

Overwhelmed by it all, Ernie murmured, "I don't understand."

"You will."

MotherEarth persisted while she still had the strength. "Go to the place where my little ones are suffering and dying."

A chill ran down Ernie's spine as he remembered the ladder in Holsapple's cellar that led into the oval chamber where he'd found the injured Runnel. He swallowed hard. *I saw a red glow outside the porthole. Was that the fire?* He tried to stop his hands from shaking.

"I can't go there," he pleaded.

MotherEarth insisted, "You must. You were chosen."

"But I'm just a kid. They'll kill me if I go back there," he said, unable to hide his desperation. "I think they already killed my friend."

Pav added a single wheat grain to her ground powder, then caught a water droplet trickling from MotherEarth's chin. She stirred her concoction with a wheat shaft. To Ernie's dismay, she motioned him to bend down. When he did, she took the Crystal Acorn from around his neck. He watched as she pried off its cap, then poured her muddy brown concoction into the hollow.

"*Matuba ka-lo-lo,*" Pav announced as she presented the

potion. Root and Runnel, Buck, Cully, and Chop all pressed eagerly around him.

"Drink and become one of us," said MotherEarth.

"*Matuba ka-lo-lo,*" they repeated, telling Ernie it was time to sip the Acorn so that he would become a Puddlejumper—not only in spirit, but in body, too.

Finally Ernie understood the purpose of his Crystal Acorn. He wanted to help them, he really did, but they were asking the impossible. "I can't," he stammered. "I think I have a dad now. I might have a home."

"This is the way home," she replied softly, her voice weakening.

Runnel tugged on his sleeve with an imploring gaze. He looked at the others impatiently waiting for him to drink. It felt like one of his old crazy dreams, but this time he couldn't wake up. All he could think about was Russ and the farm. He had to find Russ. He needed to explain and make everything right. At last he found his voice, but all he could say was, "I'm sorry."

With an ache in his chest, he set his Crystal Acorn on the platform. He was giving up the treasured totem he'd worn his entire life. The Puddlejumpers murmured, their sadness rippling across the Deep Down like the rustle of dead leaves.

The whole canyon shook as MotherEarth rasped, "*Wawaywo*—only you can bring back the rain." Her energy spent, MotherEarth closed her eyes. Cully dabbed her forehead with the moist sponge. Ernie looked to Runnel and

Root, but they were too disappointed to look back.

"I'm really sorry, but I have to go," he said quietly.

He picked up a lantern and started up the winding stair.

Ernie was trudging across the sand of the grotto, wondering if he could even find his way back to the surface, when a tiny hand slipped inside his own. Chop nodded reassuringly, then led him up the roots of the giant oak. He escorted Ernie past the stone hut to a far knoll where there was an entrance to a tunnel. It was rarely used, and the going was difficult along the eroded floor. When the flame died in the lantern, Chop released a few fireflies, and they went up the steep slope in near darkness. And in silence.

There were so many questions Ernie wanted to ask. *What happened when I was a baby? Why did you choose me? How did I end up in Chicago?* His brain hurt from everything he should have asked when he'd had the chance. Now it was too late because, without MotherEarth's help, he and Chop couldn't understand a word each other said. So he started to think about what would happen when he got back to the farm. He couldn't wait to tell Russ who he really was. Now Russ would have to believe him about the Holsapples. And protect him. Somehow.

He was still daydreaming about it all when the tunnel

ended in a snarl of dried brush. Chop found the opening and they slipped into a cave where a drilling rig for an underground pump station rattled loudly. Chop pointed above to the sunlight, then touched Ernie's heart before disappearing back to the Underneath.

Ernie climbed the rig to the surface. It was twilight now, and he found himself in the middle of the Holsapple waste-land. He clambered out of the pit and took a deep breath. It was bittersweet relief to be in the fresh air again.

He heard the car before he saw it. Ducking behind the derrick, he watched the black Cadillac approach along an access road, then veer across the field until it stopped beside an abandoned mine shaft. Axel popped open the trunk, then Angus reached in to retrieve a sledgehammer, a signpost, and a coil of rope. Ernie watched Axel pound the signpost, DANGER, KEEP OUT, into the ground. Angus tied one end of the rope to the post, then tossed the coil into the hole.

The back doors of the Cadillac swung open and Harvey Holsapple and Dicky Cobb got out. Holsapple supervised as Cobb lifted a lifeless body out of the trunk. He slung it over his shoulder and limped to the mine shaft. Ernie shuddered. Even from a distance there was no doubt it was Joey. Holsapple chortled as Cobb dumped the body down the hole. He said something and they all laughed. They were trying to make it look like Joey had fallen into the mine. Satisfied with their ruse, Holsapple, Cobb, and the twins slunk back to the Cadillac and sped away.

Ernie waited until the car was out of sight before running to the mine. About ten feet down, he saw Joey's crumpled body. He grabbed the rope and slid to the bottom of the shaft. He rolled her over. Her eyes were closed and her skin was pale. He brushed the dirt from her face and the hair from her eyes.

"Please don't be dead, please," he whispered, putting his ear to her heart. He couldn't hear a thing. He covered his face and tried not to cry. His head ached. *It's all my fault.* He wished he could take it all back. He wished he'd never set foot in Holsapple's house. He wished he'd never left Chicago. *Why did this have to happen?*

A tiny finger gently tapped his shoulder. He looked up. It was Runnel, with Root right behind her. Before he could speak, they jumped on top of Joey's chest. Runnel drew back her eyelids to check her pupils. Root put his ear to the girl's nose, listening. They looked to each other, then to the night sky and wailed, *"Hooty-hooooooo!"*

The call rang out across the Warbling River plateau and echoed all the way to Kingdom Come.

CHAPTER THIRTY-SIX

Dearly Departed

A FULL MOON ROSE over the farmhouse as Ernie ran to the porch and looked through the screen door. "Russ? It's me—I'm back!" he called. "Russ? You home?"

When no one answered, Ernie motioned to the field. Buck, Cully, and Chop led a white-tailed deer out of the wheat, hauling the body of Joey Woodruff on a bed of pine boughs. Root and Runnel took turns hopping up and down on Joey's chest while Pav, kneeling on the girl's forehead, squeezed air from a milkweed pod into her nose.

Once they reached the porch, Ernie struggled to lift his blood brother in his arms and carry her inside. The others followed, except Buck and Cully, who hurried back to the field to keep watch for Troggs.

Teetering beneath Joey's weight, Ernie managed to reach the crib room, which was still a disaster from the twins' destruction. He laid her lifeless body on the collapsed bed. He thought she looked sad, her T-shirt torn, her body scratched and bruised.

Pav scooted onto the mattress and began mixing pinches of hornet stingers, moth dust, poison ivy root, and a wolverine's eyetooth from pouches on her belt into a coffee cup. The final ingredient was a dragonfly wing.

Runnel motioned for Ernie's hand and, without warning, stabbed his thumb with a thorn. *Ouch!* She pricked Joey's thumb and pressed the bloody wounds together, then bound them with a shaft of wheat. She met his worried gaze with a reassuring smile, pretending not to notice his trembling hand.

In the kitchen, Root stood atop the stove with a dozen burned matches scattered at his feet. Fire of any kind made Puddlejumpers jittery, and fire from a giant iron contraption, like a stove, made them even more nervous. He struck his last match over the burner, then Chop cranked the gas. The flame surged and both Jumpers vaulted to the top of the fridge for safety. This time the flame held. Chattering excitedly, they jumped onto their jury-rigged ceiling pulley and lowered a kettle onto the burner.

The sheriff's car sped down the dark two-lane state highway. Tom Dashin checked his rearview mirror. In the backseat, Betty huddled against Russ. They'd been back to the Holsapples', over to Gram and Gramp's, the Goetzes', and into the little town of Circle, but no one had seen Joey since the day before yesterday. No sign of Ernie Banks, either.

Dashin flicked a toggle switch and spoke into the handset of his radio. "Wooden Nickel, keep a car near the Holsapples'. We still think the kid could turn up there. Do you roger that?"

A nasal voice rattled from the speaker. "That's a ten-four, One Thin Dime."

Dashin's gaze fixed curiously on the horizon. He turned to Russ. "Ain't that a sight?"

Russ looked out his window. The entire valley was dark, except for his farm, which was aglow with what looked like every light in the house.

"You usually leave your place fired up like a Roman candle when you're not home?" asked the sheriff.

Russ shook his head. *Now what?*

Dashin turned on his strobe and goosed the accelerator, speeding toward the distant farm. With a smug look to Russ in the mirror, he sang quietly to himself, "Turn out the lights, the party's over . . ."

The house was fully lit except for the darkened crib room, where the Snow White lamp, clamped to the headboard, provided a soft glow. Joey's rooster T-shirt was stretched like a canopy above her head. It captured steam misting from a dozen pots and pans laced with Pav's most potent herbs. Ernie, his thumb still bound to Joey's, watched Runnel weave stalks of wheat through Joey's hair while Pav sprinkled hot water over red and yellow autumn leaves covering the girl's chest. The two Puddlejumpers were so intent on their work they almost forgot Ernie was there.

In the kitchen, Root stopped funneling water from the faucet to a kettle on the stove. He thought he heard Buck and Cully hooting from the field, but a whistling teapot made it difficult to hear. By the time he got the pot off the burner, all was quiet. Pav called from the crib room, "*Kadudee-ha!*" and Root leapt onto the pulley rope, hoisting the pot to the ceiling. Boarding from the top of the fridge, Chop maneuvered the teapot onto a taut clothesline, then piloted a perilous ride through the house. Once the water was on its way, Root hurried outside to check on the scouts.

Ernie cringed as Chop steered the kettle down the clothesline to a crashing stop against the headboard. Working quickly, Pav dipped a bottle cap into the kettle, measuring three capfuls into the cup containing her potion. Stirring, she brought the drink to Joey's lips and poured the bitter draft down her throat. Chop shook Shawn's baby rattle over Joey's belly button as the Puddlejumpers chanted, "*Kadudee, mataki, mataki, sadaki.*"

Pav blew into Joey's mouth, filling the girl's lungs with air, until she collapsed in a near faint. The chanting and the rattle stopped. Runnel gripped Joey's and Ernie's bound-together thumbs and snapped the wheat shaft. No one dared take a breath as they waited expectantly. The only sound was the grandfather clock ticking from the hall. A breeze from the window fluttered the T-shirt canopy above Joey's head, but she remained still as death.

Feeling like he was about to break into a million pieces, Ernie prayed with all his might for Joey to move or blink or breathe. He leaned close and whispered in her ear, "C'mon, Rooster—crow."

Suddenly her eyelids fluttered like the wings of a butterfly emerging from its cocoon. She took a deep breath and her chest began to rise and fall in a gentle rhythm. Ernie nearly crushed Runnel and Pav in a joyful hug, while Chop pranced along the headboard.

The sheriff's car sped down the driveway and lurched to a stop by the house, freezing a deer in its headlights. The animal bounded away as the search party hustled onto the porch. When they entered the kitchen, water was boiling on every burner, a milk shake whirred in the blender, the cupboards and fridge were open, and a pulley clothesline dangled from the ceiling.

"Oh my God, Russ. What has that boy done?" said Betty with alarm.

Russ was too shocked to answer, but the sheriff did it for him. "I thought I'd seen everything, but this kid just about beats the band."

They tracked the clothesline and a trail of mud past discarded milk cartons and numerous spills. Two raccoons asleep on the couch startled awake and scurried out the dog door. When the adults reached the closed door at the end of the hall, Russ shoved it open.

They found Ernie standing self-consciously next to Joey asleep beneath Snow White and the T-shirt canopy. Her body was plastered with wet autumn leaves and her hair dreadlocked with wheat. The pots were still steaming, but there wasn't a Puddlejumper in sight.

"Well . . . I found her," was all Ernie could think to say.

Aghast, Betty rushed to her daughter and stripped the leaves from her body and covered her with a blanket. "Oh, my baby. My poor sweet baby."

"And she's gonna be okay," he reassured the adults.

Russ turned to Ernie, his voice grim. "I just hope you didn't do anything you'll regret."

"I saved her! I mean, not by myself . . ."

The sheriff grabbed Ernie by the back of the neck. "If you want to press charges, I'll bust this kid's britches right here and now."

"Just get him out of here," said Betty, trying not to cry.

"But you don't understand . . ."

"Send him back to Chicago or whatever godforsaken place he came from."

"But it was the Holsapples . . ."

"You just shut your mouth, boy," fired the sheriff, then turned to Russ. "Any objection if I zip this kid down to the station?"

Russ shook his head.

"But, Russ, I can explain," Ernie pleaded.

"I'm sorry, Ernie. You need help. More help than I can give."

Dashin squashed the boy with his pudgy arm. "You heard the man—you just got your ticket punched," he said, wrestling him toward the door.

Ernie caught the door frame and gripped it tenaciously. "No! Russ, listen, it's me, Shawn!" cried Ernie. "I'm the Quilt Baby! It was little creatures who took me and the Holsapples are really monsters and they're trying to kill me!"

Russ stared, shaken by the orphan's claims.

Dashin pried Ernie's grip from the door. "You're the only monster around here, and let go of that damn door!"

"Russ! You gotta believe me. Please! Russ!"

Russ listened, transfixed, as Dashin hauled the ranting boy down the hall. Ernie was growing more hysterical. "Let go of me! This is my house! You can't do this!"

Distressed by the boy's fading cries, Russ stared uneasily at Snow White clamped to the headboard, a strange and vivid reminder of his baby kidnapped so long ago. He hadn't seen it since that terrible night. He turned toward the hall, wanting to call the sheriff back.

"We better call Doc Thorpe right away," said Betty as she cradled her daughter. But Russ wasn't listening. His mind was far away, lost in an impossible dream.

"Russ!" said Betty urgently.

"I'm sorry, what?"

Outside, Ernie struggled to break free as Dashin manhandled him into the backseat of the squad car and cuffed his wrist to an overhead bar. "You ain't going nowhere, so stop your blasted squirming."

As soon as the sheriff went back inside, Ernie rolled down his window with his free hand and leaned out to shout at the house. "Russ, don't let him take me! Don't let him take me, Russ!" When Russ didn't come to the door or even to the window, tears leaked from Ernie's eyes but he quickly wiped them away.

Dashin returned with the boy's suitcase, tossed it onto the seat, and rolled up the window. "Now leave it shut, or I'll cuff your other wrist, too," he growled, then slammed the door and got behind the wheel.

Ernie saw the curtains shift in the kitchen window. Russ was watching him with a strange look on his face.

Ernie rolled down his window and leaned out as far as the cuffs would allow and shouted, "Russ, please! I can prove it! I can prove it's all true! I can save the farm! I can make it rain!"

Dashin reached into the back and whacked him, then cuffed his other wrist to the bar. Cursing, he rolled up the window and slammed the transmission into gear. As the sheriff's car sped up the drive, Russ' face in the window got smaller and smaller.

Ernie screamed one last time at the top of his lungs, "I'm Shawn Frazier!"

CHAPTER THIRTY-SEVEN

Between a Buzzard and a Hawk

AT THE TOP OF THE Frazier driveway, Sheriff Dashin slammed on the brakes, barely avoiding a collision with the black Cadillac as it fishtailed off the highway. Dicky Cobb was at the wheel, with Holsapple riding shotgun and the twins hunkered down in back. The sheriff leaned out his window with a frown. "Better slow down there, Dicky—you almost shaved off my front end."

Ernie cringed as Holsapple got out of the car and hobbled around to the sheriff's window. He squinted at the boy handcuffed in the backseat, then, with a forced smile, said, "Evening, Tom—what you got in the backseat?"

"We caught the little bugger," Dashin declared proudly.

Holsapple pressed his face against the back window to get a closer look at the prisoner. "I always said this boy was bound for trouble."

Though trembling inside, Ernie stared evenly at the old man. For once in his life he was glad to be in the back of a cop car.

"Where you taking him, sheriff?" asked Holsapple.

"I got a room with his name on it down at the jail-house."

Holsapple casually opened the back door. "Why go all the way back into town? We'll keep him at our place, least till you find Joey," he proposed.

Dashin turned around in his seat to make eye contact with Holsapple. "Oh, we got Joey. Turns out this kid had her all along," he reported.

"She's alive?"

"Oh, yeah. Devil only knows what all he was up to. Once that little girl comes around, I'm sure she'll have a tale to tell."

Holsapple fell silent. "Where is the poor child now?"

"Don't you worry—she's back with her mother, and I'm sure Doc Thorpe's already on the way."

"Well, that's a comfort," said Holsapple, then leaned into the backseat and thrust his face inches from Ernie's. "I promise you this much, boy—you're gonna get what's coming to you."

Ernie tried to back away but the cuffs wouldn't let him.

Holsapple's stare felt like daggers piercing his skin. Dashin slid out from behind the wheel, put a hand on Holsapple's shoulder, and eased him out of the car. "Look, Harvey, I know how you feel," he said. "But rest assured, this kid's gonna get what's coming and a whole lot more." The sheriff closed the back door. "Well, I'd best be getting on."

For a moment, Holsapple turned his murderous stare to the sheriff, then he smiled. "You take her easy, Tom."

"You know I will," said the sheriff.

Dashin started to get back behind the wheel when a pitiful whimpering sound came from the Caddy. He shined his flashlight into the backseat. Angus and Axel squinted into the bright light. The sheriff noticed a blanketed cage on the seat between them.

"What you got there, boys?" the sheriff asked.

No one said a word until Holsapple replied, "Nothing but a couple of no-good raccoons we trapped."

Ernie watched from the squad car's darkened backseat. He hoped it wasn't Buck and Cully inside the cage, but he had a gut feeling it was.

Dashin flicked off his light. "You got a license for that, Harv?" he joked.

"Yes, sir, I believe I do," said Holsapple as he returned to the Caddy. "If memory serves me right, I picked it up the same day I paid for your election."

The sheriff tried to laugh it off. "Sure enough, Harvey. You all have a good night now."

The Caddy backed onto the highway, then disappeared into the dark.

The humiliated sheriff settled behind the wheel and glared at Ernie in the rearview mirror. "If anything turns up wrong with that little girl, you're gonna wish you never got born."

Spitting gravel, the sedan accelerated onto the highway and sped toward town. The sheriff flicked the toggle on his radio mic. "Wooden Nickel, this is One Thin Dime. Come in, over."

Ernie turned toward a light tapping on the window. Root was clinging to the roof of the cruiser with a frightened look on his face. Up ahead, an eighteen-wheeler was fast approaching. Hoping the noise would distract the sheriff, Ernie waited until the big rig went roaring past to twist like a pretzel and open the window with his foot. Relieved, Root slipped inside and disappeared under the front seat. Dashin reached back to give Ernie a good swat. "I thought I told you to keep that window shut. Oh, you're gonna get it good."

A voice crackled from the radio. "This is Wooden Nickel."

Dashin clicked his mic. "I found Joey Woodruff. The orphan kid had her all along."

The radio squawked. "Yabba-dabba-doo!"

Root peeked up between Dashin's legs and spied the keys dangling from the ignition.

"Ditto, Wooden Nickel," said Dashin. "Get the cell ready. We'll book him for kidnapping, at least for starters. This kid's going away for a very long time."

Suddenly the sheriff hit the brakes hard. The car skidded to a stop in front of a big tree lying across the road. "What the hell?" he grumbled. Ernie watched as he eased his big rear end out of the car and went to investigate. At the side of the road, Dashin stared in disbelief at the trunk of the fallen tree. It looked like a slew of beavers had gnawed right through it. He cursed.

A mysterious *hoot* answered from the pitch black. He swallowed, unnerved, staring into the eerie darkness. Four loud *pop*s broke the quiet, followed by the sound of hissing air. The sheriff hurried back to his car and shined the flashlight. There was a porcupine quill stuck in each of his brand-new Goodyears. He watched helplessly as his car sank slowly to the pavement.

In the backseat, Root found the right key to unlock the cuffs. With a grateful nod, Ernie banged open the door and bolted into the field.

"Get back here, you orphan brat!" shouted the sheriff as he fumbled for the revolver on his belt. He chased a few yards before firing a shot into the air. "Get back here!"

Dashin's stomach flipped upside down when his squad car roared to life with siren blaring and strobe lights flashing. Hustling back, he found the doors locked with the keys still in the ignition. He kicked one of the flattened tires, then winced in pain. "Damn you, Ernie Banks!"

Ernie raced blindly across the dark field, stumbling over the furrows until he fell flat on his face. Spitting dirt, he looked up to see Runnel, Pav, Chop, two beavers, and a porcupine. The animals bristled at the human and scurried off. Motioning for him to follow, the Puddlejumpers scampered through the wheat under a harsh beam of light panning back and forth across the field from the squad car. Every time Dashin's spotlight passed, Ernie dove to the ground, then was up again at full speed. He was a fast runner, but could barely keep up with the Jumpers.

In the next field, they made the rendezvous with Root. Pav went her own way, returning to the Deep Down to tend to MotherEarth. The others continued on as the sheriff's angry rant receded into the distance.

CHAPTER THIRTY-EIGHT

Matuba Ka-lo-lo

ERNIE, ROOT, RUNNEL, and Chop crept to the edge of Black Rock and looked out over the bleak landscape. In the moonlight, the distant derrick pump stations looked like an army of mechanical praying mantises, incessantly thumping and grinding as they sucked the life out of the earth. Below them, the Caddy was parked in the courtyard, and there was a light on in an upstairs room of the manse.

Runnel took the Crystal Acorn from her pouch. She pried off the cap, revealing the muddy potion that Ernie had refused to drink in the Deep Down. She gave it to him. This time no one uttered a word. Ernie held the Acorn in both hands. He was afraid to drink it and even more afraid of the Holsapple monsters. But he remembered what MotherEarth had told him:

"This is the way home."

If he wanted Russ to believe him, he needed to go back inside the house. He needed to go to the Most Dark. *But what is the Most Dark? And how will I make it rain?* His head ached with questions. He looked at Runnel and Root and Chop, all waiting with expectant eyes, then pressed the Acorn to his lips and bravely drank to the last drop. He shuddered.

Then something miraculous happened.

He felt a tingling in his toes, as if thousands of pine needles were softly pricking him. The sensation traveled up his legs, then across his chest and down his arms to his fingertips. His ears got warm and he felt like his body was falling through space as he began to shrink and shrink and shrink . . . until he was only eleven inches tall!

Ernie had become one of them. Ernie had become a Puddlejumper. Climbing out from under his pile of clothes, he rubbed his tiny hands and hopped a few times on his tiny feet. Except for the webbing between his fingers and toes, he was a miniature version of himself. The best thing of all was the feeling of electricity surging through him, as if he could hit a ball out of Wrigley and run to his roof in time to catch it. At the same time, it was unsettling to be so small, and he wondered if Russ would accept a son who was only eleven inches tall.

He put that thought out of his mind because the Puddlejumpers were handing him clothes made from duckweed and ferns, and leggings of yellow foxtail. He dressed quickly, then slipped into mukluks made from water lilies to protect his feet from the fires of the Most Dark. Runnel had even made a Cubs cap from arrowhead leaves and stitched the C with red bog lily. It fit snugly on his head.

Root sprinkled him with fox dander, camouflaging his scent, then strapped a Puddlejumper belt around his waist. Chop double-checked the tools and pouches containing balms, powders, and pods. Runnel gave him a birch-bark quiver holding a cattail plunger filled with water. Ernie slung the weapon onto his back. It reminded him of the Super Soaker water guns he'd seen kids play with back in Chicago. He listened to Runnel's urgent instructions— amazed that he could now understand every single strange word—as she put the Crystal Acorn back around his neck. Now that Ernie was small, it felt almost like a baseball in his hand.

Suddenly he remembered something. Digging into the pile of clothes, he found his pocket watch in his jeans. The Puddlejumpers strapped it to his chest, using the brass chain. The watch was heavy, but it would serve as a shield of golden armor.

Root knotted one end of a long wheat braid to the end

of a stone sickle and asked Ernie to throw it to the Holsapple roof. It was a long way off, but Ernie knew he had a good arm and was willing to try. Gripping the braid in one hand, he bounded to the edge of the cliff and hurled the sickle with a strong overhand throw. It spun through the air until it struck the roof, then clattered down the shingles and locked in the rain gutter. Root and Chop yanked the braid taut, then knotted it around a pine tree. The tightrope of braided wheat now spanned the chasm between cliff and manse.

Root, then Runnel, started across, but Ernie hesitated. He'd been afraid jumping the rooftops in Chicago, and that was nothing compared to this. This was like walking a wire across the Grand Canyon. He tested the rope's give with his foot and felt it wobble. He looked back to Chop, who offered encouragement. With a deep breath, Ernie eased out onto the braid, arms extended for balance. He pretended that he was walking a train track, just inches off the ground, until he looked past his feet at the deep chasm below.

"*Koka lo!*" warned Chop.

Ernie jerked his head up and continued toward the rooftop. He could feel the braid dip when Chop followed behind. Silhouetted by the full moon, the four tiny figures teetered across the braided rope. As their shadows crossed over the manse portico below, the stone Chimeras stirred restlessly.

Ernie again glanced down and froze midstep. The

sentries were glaring up at him like two mutant lions sighting helpless prey. They flexed their monstrous wings, which triggered a violent gust of wind. The high wire vibrated from the sudden gale and the Puddlejumpers dashed pell-mell for the roof. Root, Runnel, and Ernie made it across, but another gust blew Chop off the rope. He lunged for the rain gutter and missed, but Ernie caught his hand and pulled him to safety.

They raced up the steep incline past gabled windows to the crest of the slate roof. In the next instant, the Chimeras, now airborne and breathing fire, rose up above the roofline like a deadly storm. The panicked Jumpers sprinted to the base of the chimney, where they scaled the column of bricks to the summit. Runnel took a cocoon from her pouch and tore it open. A big furry spider emerged and disappeared down the dark chimney.

Root squealed a warning.

The twin Chimeras dove at wicked speed with wings pinned and talons outstretched, knocking them from their perch. One snatched Chop in its claws. Screeching, they swooped around for the next charge. The Jumpers scrambled back, hearing Chop's pained hoots as the Chimeras dove again. Runnel pushed Ernie down the chimney, then jumped right behind. Root dodged the fiery blast from the first attacker, but the second engulfed him in a violent blur.

In the chimney, Ernie and Runnel spun head over heels down the black shaft. They landed in a web spun inches off the stone floor, bouncing on the sticky trampoline. Making room for Root's landing, they peered up the shaft and waited. But he never arrived. Runnel blinked back tears, her wail echoing up the chimney. Ernie put a hand on her shoulder and gently whispered, *"Mataki, mataki lo."* Runnel nodded bravely, then turned to the spider and gratefully scratched its torso. Locking her feet in the web, she swung upside down so she could peek out from the dark fireplace.

The library was quiet. They dropped to the floor and started across the room, but the sound of running dogs drove them back to the hearth. They jumped up the chimney as the wolfhounds bounded into the room, slipping and sliding across the polished floor. Ernie thought they were trapped, until Runnel unexpectedly dropped to the floor. The wolfhounds snapped viciously, but she stood her ground. Ernie watched amazed from the web as Runnel barked and whined and cooed until they let her stroke their big, wet noses with her tiny hand. The dogs whimpered as she whispered in their ears. At her signal, Ernie joined them on the floor. It was scary standing next to a dog as big as an elephant. Ernie scratched behind their ears, which they appreciated after years of abuse. Runnel gripped the studded collar on one of the dogs and climbed onto his neck. Ernie mounted the other dog, then they rode the reformed wolfhounds from the library like two jockeys trotting toward the starting gate.

Suddenly two Troggs came bellowing down the hall-way. Ernie and Runnel swung beneath the dogs and hid in the fur of their underbellies. Upside down, they watched the Troggs stomp into the library. Ernie thought he could see the twins' features buried in their hideous faces. He heard muffled cries of alarm emanating from their fleshy stomach pouches, and knew it was Root and Chop.

The beasts extended their tails high into the chimney, but the only thing they caught was a nostril full of sticky web and soot. Braying angrily, they overturned every piece of furniture and ripped the drapes from the windows. Finding nothing, they stormed away. The dogs, bearing their secret passengers, followed them into the kitchen and down the cellar stairs.

Dicky Cobb, a deep wound from the bear trap scarring his gnarly leg, waited by the open "potato bin." His tail slithered inside one twin's pouch, then the other, checking the new prisoners, wetting them with mucus. Runnel whispered to her wolfhound and the dogs nosed closer to the bin. Despite the fox dander, Cobb caught a whiff of another Jumper. He whipped around and snarled at the dogs. They retreated, whimpering, but Cobb stalked Ernie's wolfhound into the corner. His tail frisked up and down the terrified animal, snorting grotesquely. Ernie felt the nostril sucking on his back like a hairy vacuum.

In a desperate effort to protect her Rainmaker, Runnel scurried into the open, hooting fiercely. Cobb pounced. The twins attacked, too, but Runnel dodged their lunges and wicked tail swipes.

Knowing it was now or never, Ernie dropped off his dog and slipped down the iron ladder.

When the Troggs finally cornered Runnel, Cobb snatched her in a claw, ripped off her Puddlejumper belt, and licked her with a thorny tongue. The twins convulsed with laughter as he stuffed her into his hideous pouch.

Cobb punished the wolfhounds with a tail-whipping before the Troggs pounded down the ladder into the oval chamber. Cully and Buck, scratched and bruised but still alert, watched from a thorny cage as Cobb flipped toggle switches at a control panel that triggered a low hum and flashing red lights. Axel unbuckled latches at the base of the ladder and Angus released a six-foot lever. The ladder retracted into the ceiling.

If Troggs paid attention to detail, they would have noticed that one of the portholes encircling the chamber was ajar. Oblivious, Cobb fired the engines. The Puddlejumpers covered their ears to muffle the deafening roar.

As the vehicle vibrated into motion and began its descent, a tiny hand on the outside slowly pushed the porthole closed.

CHAPTER THIRTY-NINE

The Most Dark

ERNIE CLUNG TO THE outer skin of the oval chamber, a saucer-shaped zeppelin descending through the darkness on rusty cables. It looked like a black blowfish with spikes protruding from its heavy metal skin. Far below, he could see a river of red-hot lava that slithered like a snake through a matrix of pipe and cable, plumes of fire, smokestacks, and a maze of roads, all surrounding a massive furnace embedded in the scorched earth. There were things moving to and fro. It looked as busy as an anthill.

The zeppelin lurched and Ernie lost his grip. He slid down the curved steel plating, desperately grabbing the air until he caught hold of another spike. Dangling precariously, he watched his Cubs cap sail away into the dark. He struggled back up and straddled the spike, hoping he could hold on until the zeppelin touched down.

The Cubs cap landed at the feet of Harvey Holsapple. At the sight of the tiny cap, the old man's eyes began to boil. Black slime seeped from every pore, coarse hair sprouted, his nose grew into a revolting snout, claws shredded his fingertips, and a muscular tail erupted from the bottom of his spine as he mutated into an eight-foot Trogg. Even his ebony cane became a long staff spiked with thorns. Holsapple shredded the cap with his dagger-sharp teeth, then spit it out. Foaming at the mouth, he hammered the ground with his staff, and his screech blew like a hurricane from end to end of the vast cavern.

Covering his ears from the terrible sound, Ernie studied the approaching terrain. Now he could see hundreds of enslaved Puddlejumpers in iron shackles all around the Trogg cavern. *So this is what happened to the others.* His heart sank at the terrible sight. What could he possibly do? Then the words of MotherEarth ran through his mind:

"Plant your Crystal Acorn where the fire burns hot and forever."

It could only mean one thing. *The furnace.* He would

have to sneak past the Troggs and throw his Acorn down the fiery pit. *But how?*

The zeppelin was approaching the noxious smokestacks of an oil refinery, but Ernie couldn't take his eyes off the furnace. There was something strange about it. As he peered closer, his blood ran cold. In the cinders just above the furnace mouth, two encrusted lids cracked open to reveal burned yellow eyes.

It was alive!

Now he could recognize a skeletal female body camouflaged in the rolls and ruts of the charred landscape. The body sloped upward to the head, where the furnace mouth voraciously gulped each load of coal. Soot covered the hilly contour of her knees, hips, and shoulders. The ridges extending from the torso were arms and legs. Two rock monoliths jutting high in the air were feet, with sharp claws protruding at the top. But she wasn't living just on coal. Rusted pipes attached to both arms channeled oil from the refinery directly into the monster's veins.

Ernie stared in horror, his fingers trembling on the Crystal Acorn around his neck, as the zeppelin locked down in the middle of the refinery. Trying to calm himself, he took a deep breath, but the intense heat only made his lungs ache.

The zeppelin portal opened. Holsapple rushed up, bellowing angrily, demanding to know how the Puddlejumper boy had made it into the Most Dark. Cobb and the twins ranted and raved, blaming each other. Shoving them aside, Holsapple began a mad search of the zeppelin while the chastised Troggs shook Cully and Buck out of their cage, then ripped Root, Runnel, and Chop from their stomach pouches.

On the backside of the zeppelin, Ernie swung from spike to spike until he could jump to a ladder attached to a smoking vat. From his tall perch, he could see the soot-covered Puddlejumpers toiling in coal mines around the perimeter of the polluted cavern, digging and tunneling to get the coal to feed the Trogg monster.

Ernie could also see the other creatures that Runnel had warned him about—Red Grunts, cruel three-foot-tall taskmasters with bulbous eyes, needle teeth, and scaly red skin. Shouting and cracking sinewy vines like whips, they forced the Jumpers to push boxcars full of coal along cinder paths that converged onto a main road. The rugged artery followed the river until it veered off between the monster's feet. The route twisted up the buried torso, ending at an iron platform suspended over her mouth, where Puddlejumpers dumped their loads of coal. After each gulp, the insatiable furnace spewed a geyser of flame, which sounded like a wheeze of relief.

When Holsapple didn't find the boy in the zeppelin, the Troggs began to search the refinery. In another minute, they'd reach him. His pulse racing, Ernie scooted down the ladder to the ground. He ran past rows of smelly vats and corroded machinery. Stopping to catch his breath, he noticed a sewer pipe that ran all the way to the lava river, where it emptied its sludge under a trestle bridge. It looked like a good place to hide. He scuttled along the pipe to the river's edge and dropped out of sight beneath the bridge.

Suddenly an earsplitting siren pierced the Most Dark.

Ernie retreated deeper into the shadows under the bridge. He could hear shouting, angry cursing, the clinking of leg irons, and the shuffling of hundreds of little feet. Finally the exhausted miners came into view. Above him, the Grunts marched them across the bridge to a prison on the opposite side. Primitive cells were chiseled out of the sheer rock wall along a narrow ledge high above the river. The workers dropped their tiny pickaxes, shovels, and sledgehammers in a pile. Grunts removed their irons, then locked them inside their cells. Other Grunts shackled the rested Jumpers, equipped them with tools, and herded them back across the bridge.

As the fresh crews crossed above, Ernie spotted the twin Troggs harshly prodding Root and Runnel, Buck, Cully, and Chop to the prison on the far side. They delivered his friends to the chief jailer, a Red Grunt with one good eye and one seared shut. *Just like the one-eyed field worker!* Hissing, One Eye crammed his new prisoners into an open cell, then slammed the door and locked it with a key from the ring on his belt.

The Grunt marched along the ledge past the cells to a

ten-foot water tank at the far end. He climbed a ladder to a platform atop the steel cistern. By cranking a handle mounted on the platform, the jailer could propel a bucket along a wire that ran the length of the ledge to each cell. One Eye filled the bucket, but instead of delivering water to his prisoners, he dumped it on the ground. The thirsty Puddlejumpers moaned as the water trickled down the cliff to the hot lava, where it sizzled away. The sadistic Grunt cackled and jangled his keys, but Ernie felt a glint of hope. The jailer had given him just the idea he needed.

His gaze jumped to the refinery, where the Troggs were still searching for him, then back to the bridge. *Now!* He scrambled onto the support column and started climbing, clambering from rivet to rivet. It was taller than Russ' barn. *Keep going, keep going.* If a Trogg or Grunt looked in his direction, their search would be over.

It felt like forever before he reached the underneath of the bridge. Breathing hard, he slipped one hand through the gap in the boards and got a good grip. Hanging by his fingertips, he reached for the next plank. Board by board, he grappled his way over the river of burning lava. On the far side, he jumped to the cliff, where he caught hold of a notch in the sheer rock.

Ernie poked his head above the ledge. One Eye was stomping past the captives, taunting them. He could see Runnel in the cell closest to the water tank. He took a pebble from a pouch and tossed it into her cell. She looked over and met his gaze. The Jumpers whispered excitedly, but no one looked his way as word of Wawaywo's arrival spread from cell to cell.

Unseen below the ledge, Ernie used niches in the rock to work his way across the face of the cliff to a position just below the cistern. When the jailer went inside a storage cave where the Grunts kept the pickaxes, sledgehammers, and shovels, Ernie hoisted himself onto the ledge, scooted up the cistern ladder, and slipped into the tank. The cool water was a tonic to his overheated body. He resurfaced and peeked over the side.

Runnel and the others were awaiting his command. Ernie put his hands to his throat and stuck out his tongue to show thirst, then pretended to drink. They understood and began calling for water, "*Kadudee! Kadudee!*"

Ignoring their plea, One Eye brought the next pickax to his grindstone and pressed the blade against the spinning wheel, throwing hot sparks. But when all the Puddlejumpers began clamoring for a drink, he stormed out of the cave, snarling and hissing and threatening with his ax. Instead of silencing them, his threats only made them cry louder. The Jumpers became so unruly that the Troggs stopped their search of the refinery. Holsapple's enraged voice boomed across the cavern from the far side of the river, ordering the jailer to silence the prisoners or surrender his keys.

Deathly afraid, One Eye hurried to the cistern and

climbed onto the platform. Ernie took a deep breath and dove underwater. From the bottom of the tank, he could see the Grunt's silhouette cranking the pulley handle. Holding his breath, he waited. When the bucket plunged into the water, Ernie kicked off the side and propelled himself into the bucket, where he curled into a tight ball. He could feel himself being lifted out of the tank and transported along the wire.

The bucket stopped at the first cell, where Ernie surfaced, gasping for breath. Runnel and Root, Buck, Cully, and Chop made a show of drinking water while Ernie urgently whispered his strategy. He'd barely finished when the jailer cranked the handle, sending the bucket to the next cell.

At each water stop, Ernie shared his plan with the prisoners as they drank from the bucket. These Puddlejumpers had lost hope of ever escaping the Most Dark, and now, here inside their own decrepit water bucket, was the Rainmaker. Energized, they pledged their allegiance.

When the bucket was empty, the Puddlejumpers clamored for more. One Eye cranked the handle in the opposite direction and Ernie sailed back along the wire to the cistern. As the bucket dropped into the tank, he dove back into the dark reservoir. One Eye cranked the handle forward again and the refilled bucket shuttled back down the line.

Ernie bobbed to the surface of the cistern. The Grunt

was turned away, watching the bucket. Ernie spit a sprinkle of water onto his shoulder. One Eye brushed it away like a bothersome fly and continued to crank. Ernie refilled his cheeks and powered a gusher that splattered the Grunt's scaly neck, then dove underwater.

Snorting angrily, One Eye peered into the tank. When air bubbles floated to the surface, he growled suspiciously.

Ernie, blowing bubbles from the bottom of the tank, watched as the shadow leaned in to investigate. *Closer . . . closer.* He waited until the grotesque face hovered just above the surface before pushing off the bottom. Shooting out of the water, he grabbed the jailer by the tender flesh between his hairy nostrils, then, leveraging himself against the tank, yanked with all his might. The ambushed Grunt tilted forward and splashed into the cistern. Like all Troggs and Red Grunts, One Eye couldn't swim and thrashed about in a panic. Darting in circles around the Grunt, Ernie poked his one good eye, then snatched the keys from his belt and vaulted out of the tank.

He dashed to the first cell and unlocked the door, but the Jumpers remained inside as if nothing had happened. He raced to unlock the next cell, glancing back as One Eye clambered from the tank, spitting and sputtering and rubbing his eye. Hissing, the Grunt bared his needle teeth and charged along the ledge. But before he could reach Ernie, Cully and Buck shoved open their cell door with perfect timing to whack the Grunt. One Eye tumbled backward off the ledge and somersaulted down the cliff into the boiling river. As the jailer disappeared into his fiery grave, a plume of black smoke sizzled into the air.

Ernie dropped to the ground and peered over the edge. Cobb was policing along the main road, spreading the word to be on high alert. The twins were gathering a knot of Grunts to search the mines. Ernie spotted Holsapple outside the refinery. The Trogg was staring suspiciously at the plume of smoke drifting downstream. He glanced up at the prison and Ernie ducked out of sight. When Ernie peeked again, Holsapple was dispatching two Grunts to inspect the smoke, before tromping off in the direction of the furnace.

Ernie crawled along the ledge and unlocked the remaining cells, but the Puddlejumpers stayed inside, pretending to be locked up. Ernie's heart was beating hard because at any moment a Trogg or Grunt might notice that the jailer wasn't in his usual position patrolling the ledge.

Root and Runnel, Buck, Cully, and Chop slipped from their cell and joined Ernie outside the storage cave. Try as they might, they couldn't budge the heavy iron gate. Working fast, Ernie and Buck burrowed under the gate. The two Jumpers shuttled pickaxes, shovels, and sledgehammers back through the trench, where the others passed them to prisoners in the closest cells. Those Puddlejumpers passed the tools on to the next cell, where eager hands swooped them inside. Before long, the imprisoned

Puddlejumpers were armed and ready.

Leaving Buck and Cully behind to organize the tribe into fighting units, Ernie and the others eased off the ledge, then jumped to the top of the column on the underside of the bridge. They started across, but Chop's arms weren't long enough to reach from plank to plank. Ernie put the littlest Puddlejumper on his back and led them over the burning river. Halfway across, they stopped to rest on a steel girder. If Ernie looked downriver, he could see the refinery. Upriver, he could see the coal mines and the fiery furnace. Getting his Acorn into the monster's mouth seemed more impossible than ever. Maybe some kind of disturbance would distract the Troggs. *There has to be something. . . . But what?* Then he saw it.

"*Rada,*" he whispered, pointing toward the giant pipe that ran from the monster's arm all the way back to the refinery. "If we can shut off the oil," he said, speaking fluent Puddlejumper, "who knows what might happen."

"It might make it worse," said Root.

"Maybe. But we need a diversion," insisted Ernie. "C'mon, let's go." He squatted so Chop could climb onto his back, then they continued across.

Once on the other side, they scuttled down the support column and disappeared into the shadows under the bridge. Ernie pointed to the sewer pipe, the same pipe he'd used to escape the refinery. "That's the way inside," he said. "But we'll have to split up. You guys find the valve that cuts off the oil to that thing's arm, and I'll try to get to its mouth."

"One of us should stay with you," insisted Runnel.

"I will," Chop volunteered.

Ernie shook his head. He didn't want to separate either, but there wasn't a choice. "I was already in there. Those valves are big. We'll be lucky if all three of you can close it." He reached behind to pull the cattail plunger from its quiver and check the water level. It was full and ready to go. Acting as if he knew what he was doing, he started up the embankment.

"Wait," called Runnel. Searching through Ernie's pouches, she found a milkweed pod and squished the milky fluid over his head to protect him from burns. Root squeezed his shoulder and tightened his belt, even though it didn't really need tightening. Chop, smiling nervously, grabbed an acorn cap from one of his pouches. He reminded Ernie how to hold his thumbs in the shape of a V and showed him where to blow.

They all knew that everything that had come before was in preparation for this moment. Ernie, looking each Puddlejumper in the eyes, suddenly realized this was his destiny. He offered a confident nod, but inside he felt only doubt.

CHAPTER FORTY

Hagdemonia

A<small>LONE,</small> E<small>RNIE</small> <small>SCRAMBLED</small> up the steep embankment. At the top of the rise, he looked back and saw three tiny figures running along the sewer pipe into the refinery. He silently wished them well. Waiting until the bridge sentry turned away, he darted across the road and slipped into a shallow ditch. He crawled on his belly through the muck to a giant slagheap. Slipping and sliding in the loose shale, he scurried to its summit and peeked below.

Crews of shackled Puddlejumpers were pushing boxcars along the maze of guarded routes. All the roads led to the main artery that cut between the monster's feet. There, the road forked in two directions. Boxcars heaped with coal went up the right leg, then across the waist and up the chest to the iron platform above the furnace mouth. The adjacent path running down the other side of the body was the return route for the empty boxcars.

Ernie slid down the slagheap to the road and hid behind a full boxcar. He used the pilfered keys to unlock the shackles of a dozen astonished Jumpers. They pressed close as he whispered his plan.

A frail Puddlejumper with a long white beard approached carrying a ladle and bucket. Since he was old and blind, the Troggs allowed him to roam the dusty roads providing water for thirsty prisoners. But he provided much more than water. Greystone was the one who encouraged the Puddlejumpers never to lose hope. He gently laid his hands on Ernie's face. Despite all the years apart, the Ancient Guide knew exactly who he was.

When the furnace belched another blast of flame, it was Greystone who whispered the monster's name, "Hagdemonia," the horrific matriarch of the Most Dark. His hand trembled as he felt for the Acorn under Ernie's shirt. Reassured, Greystone took the jailer's keys from Ernie's hand, dropped them into his bucket, and hurried down the road, where he began to secretly unlock the shackles of the next crew.

The Puddlejumpers boosted Ernie into their boxcar. He crouched in the coal as the inspired crew put shoulders to the car, determined to deliver their Rainmaker. Ernie peeked out from his hideaway. Up ahead, he could see patrolling Grunts and full boxcars moving slowly toward his final destination, the furnace mouth spewing flames. As his car threaded between Hagdemonia's feet, his heart sank. At the fork in the road, Holsapple and Cobb were inspecting each car. Cobb's tail snaked underneath, snuffling, while Holsapple jabbed his thorny staff through the loads of coal.

Ernie burrowed into the coal just before the Troggs stopped his car. He could hear Cobb's gravelly voice demanding to know his whereabouts. The Puddlejumpers were silent. The coal crunched as Holsapple thrust his staff from top to bottom, nearly impaling him. Ernie held his breath as the staff powered past his face. The next thrust cut the skin on his shoulder and he smothered a scream. The one after that would have killed him, but instead only dented the pocket watch strapped to his chest, knocking the wind out of him.

Holsapple was about to thrust again when Hagdemonia's piercing yowl rocked the Most Dark. Even though Ernie could barely breathe and the wound on his shoulder was throbbing, he silently cheered. *They must have shut the valve.*

Aborting their search, the anxious Troggs hurried down the slope to the mammoth pipe feeding oil into her arm. They checked the gauge. The flow had stopped. Hagdemonia wailed again. Alarmed, Holsapple bolted toward the refinery.

Finding themselves unguarded, the Puddlejumpers advanced Ernie's boxcar onto the Hag's ankle. But midway along her rocky shin, the front wheels caught in a rut. The crew frantically pushed and pulled to free the car.

Buried in the coal, Ernie was jostled back and forth until a shrill bark brought everything to a stop. He smelled the stench of an approaching Trogg, then heard Cobb's raspy voice. In the next second he felt a violent jolt as the car was yanked out of the rut. Coal dust shot up his nose. Feeling a terrible itch in both nostrils, he gripped his nose and squeezed tight.

Cobb was walking away when he heard the tiny sneeze. He charged back and toppled the boxcar, spilling the Puddlejumper boy onto the path. Howling, the Trogg swiped his tail, but Ernie jumped it like a rope, then tumbled away. He reached into his belt for the acorn cap and whistled the alarm.

High on the cliff, the prison doors flew open and Puddlejumpers, with Buck and Cully at the lead, flooded across the bridge armed with their tiny sledgehammers, picks, and shovels. Cobb gaped in shocked surprise as hundreds of freed prisoners charged toward him. Dozens more poured from the mines, and unshackled crews rallied up and down the maze of roads.

Ignoring the Puddlejumper attack, Cobb stalked its leader with pounding strides. Ernie crabbed backward just ahead of the Trogg until he could scratch and claw his way up a crevice to the top of the Hag's right foot. Deprived of her oil and coal, Hagdemonia began to shriek and writhe, triggering fiery geysers and violent tremors that rippled along the bedrock. Ernie clung to her toe to keep from falling. Cobb was climbing straight for him.

Ernie thought he was trapped until Root and Runnel led a charge of refinery workers up Cobb's backside. The Jumpers pounded the Trogg with hammers and wrenches. Unprepared for the onslaught, Cobb toppled backward, hitting the ground hard. Seizing the moment, Ernie skidded down the steep incline, bounced off the Trogg's stomach, and darted up the path.

Quicker than a hornet, the Jumper zigged and zagged through a plague of Red Grunts. At the crest of the Hag's knee, the twin Troggs cut him off in a pincer attack from opposite sides. He hit the dirt, avoiding Axel's tail swipe, but Angus pinned him with his heavy claw. Flat on his back, Ernie looked up at the two Troggs sweating and drooling in a swirling cloud of dust. Sure that it was over, he closed his eyes as Axel raised his foot, preparing to bury him with a single stomp, when Buck and Cully shot like two cannonballs into the Trogg's stomach, knocking him off balance. Axel's foot crashed to the ground, just missing Ernie's head. Before either twin could stomp again, the prison brigade swarmed. The Jumpers pelted and picked and smacked and hammered until Ernie could break free.

Hagdemonia wailed and another tremor sent Ernie sprawling. He picked himself up and ran along the crest of her thighbone, never taking his eyes off the goal. He knew if he didn't make it to the furnace mouth, the fight would be lost. *No Russ. No rain. No nothing.*

The Puddlejumpers fought bravely up and down the Hag's body, overwhelming the slow-footed Grunts with a tenacious attack. But the Troggs were too powerful. Swatting Jumpers away like gnats, Cobb and the twins pursued Ernie across the Hag's blistered belly. They were about to catch him from behind when Chop's crew, positioned atop her chest, launched boxcars down her rib cage. Ernie juked left and right as the cars sped past and crashed into the Troggs. One car tripped Axel and the next car smashed his face. Angus toppled into a bin that plowed down the slope into an oil pipe, rupturing it. But Cobb kept charging.

Ernie sprinted toward the Ancient Guide commanding the last Puddlejumper defense. Shouting encouragement, "*Tookla, tookla!*" Greystone climbed into the interlocked hands of two scouts. With others propelling from behind, they launched him into the Trogg's face. Gripping his snout, the old Jumper poked him in both eyes. Howling blindly, Cobb tried to snag him with his tail, but Greystone jammed a hunk of coal into its nostril. The tail ratcheted back and forth, trying to dislodge the embedded coal. Crazed, the Trogg swiped at the Jumper, but Greystone somersaulted to his shoulder, and Cobb clawed his own face. Every time the Trogg tried to squash him, the crafty old Jumper vanished with sleight-of-body to a new hiding place. Cobb swatted himself again and again, spinning madly. Other Jumpers spilled buckets of oil at the Trogg's feet. Cobb slipped and slid in the toxic sludge, finally tumbling into the deep gorge of the Hag's armpit.

For the first time, Ernie could see a clear path to the furnace. *I'm going to make it. I'm almost there!*

The battle-weary Puddlejumpers cheered as he sprinted the last few yards onto the platform above her mouth. Flinching from the intense heat, Ernie ripped the Acorn off his neck and raised his arm to jam the Crystal down the Hag's fiery maw.

But Holsapple, waiting in the shadows behind her ear, was ready, too. He vaulted onto the platform, snatched the Acorn from Ernie's hand, and throttled him like a rag doll. Yawping victoriously, the Trogg held the Crystal in one hand and the Rainmaker in the other.

The Puddlejumpers collectively gasped as Holsapple dangled Ernie over the Hag's snapping jaws. But Ernie's mind was crystal clear, as if he could see all of his thirteen years in the same instant, and something Russ said that first day on the farm came rushing back. *"The bigger they are, the harder they fall."* Reaching back, Ernie yanked the cattail plunger from its quiver and braced it against his shoulder. Knowing he only had one shot, he took aim and pulled the barrel toward him. A burst of water nailed Holsapple right between the eyes.

The Trogg reeled backward to the edge of the furnace, losing his grip on the Crystal Acorn. Ernie watched the Acorn roll across the Hag's cheekbone and down her neck. Tossing the plunger, Ernie yanked the pocket watch off his chest and, swinging it by its chain, smacked the Trogg as hard as he could right on his temple. In that instant, Harvey Holsapple knew he was doomed, but he also knew he was going to take the Puddlejumper boy down with him. Laughing perversely, he toppled into Hagdemonia's mouth with Ernie still in his hand.

The Jumpers fell to their knees as their Rainmaker disappeared into the furnace, not seeing that his belt had caught on one of the Hag's jagged teeth. Ernie dangled, nearly roasting alive. Unbuckling his belt, he scrabbled out of her mouth, burning his hands on a white-hot tooth.

Choking on the swallowed Trogg, Hagdemonia erupted from her rocky bed in a fit of rage, catapulting Ernie, Jumpers, Troggs, and Grunts in every direction. She lurched to her feet, wailing like a banshee and ripping cables from her body. Oil spurted from the broken pipelines, igniting fires throughout the Most Dark.

Caught in the whirlwind, Ernie was thrown all the way to the edge of the lava river. Rising groggily to his knees, he caught a glimpse of something glittering near an overturned boxcar. *My Crystal Acorn.* Shielding his face from the smoke and fire, he slogged up the rise through rubble and ash to recover it.

Armed once again, Ernie turned to confront the monster, but for the first time in the great battle he stood paralyzed, the Acorn forgotten in his hand. Standing before him was a four-story towering inferno. Belching fire, Hagdemonia lurched straight for him, the entire cavern quaking with her every step. As much as he wanted to, he couldn't make himself run. He couldn't do anything.

At that moment a single *Hooty-hoo* cut through the darkness like a peal of thunder. It was Runnel. She hooted again, this time even louder. Root echoed her call, then Greystone, Cully, Buck, and Chop. Soon every Jumper was shouting *Hooty-hoo* until the Most Dark resounded with the deafening tribal cry. *"HOOOOOTY-HOOOOOOO!"*

The Troggs and Grunts covered their ears. It was the first time the Puddlejumper call had ever been heard in the Most Dark, and the sound was so foreign, so completely unexpected, that it froze even the furious Hagdemonia.

Roused by their summons, Ernie found his last ounce of courage. He sighted his target, then reared back, kicked his leg high, pushed hard off his back foot, and hurled the Crystal Acorn straight into her fiery mouth. "Steee-rike!" he shouted at the top of his lungs.

The Hag staggered backward, stunned. For a moment she wavered, then rose again to her full height and spit the Acorn with such force it buried itself in the soot at Ernie's feet. With a terrible shriek, she charged. Ernie's pulse pounded in his ears as he frantically dug to reclaim his Crystal. But before he could wind up and throw again, Hagdemonia snatched him in a claw, lifted him to her mouth, and swallowed him whole.

Horrified, the Puddlejumpers listened to Ernie's defiant *"Hooty-hooooooooo!"* as he toppled down her gullet. The call echoed to silence.

Hagdemonia screeched victoriously, proclaiming the death of the Rainmaker. The battle for the Most Dark had come to its bitter end.

But unbeknownst to Hagdemonia, Troggs, and even Puddlejumpers, Ernie had kept the Crystal Acorn in his grip as he was swallowed alive. Now inside her murky stomach, he felt his chest burning from holding his breath. Struggling to stay conscious, he swam blindly against the turbulent current until he could feel the mushy wall of her stomach. He thrust his fist into the flesh and planted his Acorn just before a surge swept him into the dark recesses.

In the warmth and moisture of the Hag's bowels, the Acorn germinated and began to sprout. Delicate tentacles grew into sturdy vines that shot up, down, and sideways throughout her entire body.

Hagdemonia stared in horror as roots burst through

her feet, anchoring her to the bedrock of the Most Dark. She writhed in agony as branches exploded from her body, then howled with demonic protest as her torso transformed into a trunk. Finally, her hateful face crinkled to bark, silencing her forever.

The Jumpers watched in awe as the great tree surged upward. Water poured from its every blossom and leaf to douse the burning river and extinguish every fire in the Most Dark. The Troggs and Red Grunts howled and cursed and tried to bury themselves in the scorched earth, but the water thundered down and drowned them in a merciless flood.

In the Up Above, the oak smashed through the foundation of the Holsapple manse and water roared through the cellar, corridors, and secret passageways. Titanic branches invaded the kitchen, dining room, and great hall, destroying the posh furniture, antiquities, and stolen loot. The jars of eyeballs from the pantry watched the stuffed buffalo float past, and the mounted animal heads seemed to smile with their final revenge as the current swept them away.

A tidal wave surged up the stairways, and water drowned every story and cascaded from every window. The manse protested with a last shuddering boom as the house imploded in a swirling vortex, and the earth swallowed it whole.

CHAPTER FORTY-ONE

The Return

IF STARS HAD EYES, they might have seen a great horned owl soaring out of a night sky toward a profoundly still turquoise lake. The full moon shimmered on the water like a beacon as the owl circled the giant oak, only its leafy crown visible at the center of the lake. There, in the uppermost branches, the bird settled beside the lifeless body of Ernie Banks.

The lake began to ripple, as if it were raining from below. Tiny hands broke the surface—first Runnel, sputtering and gasping for air, followed by Root and Chop, Cully, and Buck. Soon the whole tribe bobbed to the surface. They swam steadily toward their Rainmaker, buoyed on the oak's lonely pinnacle.

Ernie Banks had fulfilled the ancient prophecy of MotherEarth, but had paid with his life. The Puddlejumpers retrieved the body of their fallen hero from the oak and ferried him to shore.

With Greystone leading the way, Root, Runnel, Cully, and Buck carried Ernie's limp body on their shoulders along the boundary fence. Like a mournful wind, the tribe followed behind.

As the moon dipped below the horizon, the procession crossed into Frazier land. They laid Ernie's body on a bed of wheat. Birds and animals emerged from nearby nests and dens to watch respectfully as Buck and Cully carefully peeled away his burned and tattered clothes. After Greystone washed his body with morning dew, Pav dressed his burns with a balm, then covered him with stalks of wheat.

The tribe chanted a farewell song as each Puddlejumper passed by to touch the heart of their Wawaywo. When the song drifted away with the wind, Root and Runnel knelt next to Ernie. Root steadied his foot as Runnel gently pinched the Spiral Tattoo between her fingers. Whispering farewell, she pulled the thread, unwinding it from his flesh until it stretched between her fingers and his foot.

Runnel held her hand to the east and waited for the sun. As the warm sphere broke the horizon, its golden light surged through her palm, shimmered across the taut thread, and fired into the sole of Ernie Banks. There was a deafening thunderclap and a blinding flash . . . and the Puddlejumpers were gone.

At the Frazier farmhouse, the thunderclap rattled the windows and woke Russ from a fitful night's sleep on the couch. Still dressed in his work clothes, he slipped into his boots and went to the kitchen to make coffee. As he stood at the sink and filled the pot with water, he looked out the window and saw the sun rising over the fields. The eastern sky was a swirl of color, and a gentle breeze swept across the plateau. Something in the air felt different. It smelled like rain, but there wasn't a cloud in the sky.

Russ went down the hall and opened the crib room door. Joey was still asleep cuddled beside her mother, their blanket kicked to the floor. He was retucking it when a staccato rapping startled him.

Russ followed the sound to the kitchen and opened the door. There, as on the day of his son's birth, the elfin mobile dangled from the sill, except now the empty harness cradled a carved figure of Ernie Banks, Cubs cap and all. A gust of wind blew the mobile, and the elves chimed together in a dance around the boy. Feeling faint, Russ braced himself against the door and stared at the carved figure of Ernie. He remembered the last time he'd seen the boy handcuffed in the sheriff's car, driving away. Now Ernie's words echoed in his memory.

"I can make it rain! I'm Shawn Frazier!"

Russ looked beyond the mobile to the deep blue sky streaked with hues of amber and gold. He went outside. A raindrop splashed against his hand. Another landed on his shoulder. From a cloudless sky, the long-awaited rain began to patter down. Russ arched his neck to let the water wash his face.

Before his very eyes, the wheat in his field seemed to revive, as if waking from a deep sleep. For the first time since his baby had been taken away, he dared to believe.

The steady rain woke Ernie Banks from his dead sleep. He sat up and saw that he was naked, his body covered in wheat stalks. He was in a muddy hollow in the upper field, his sneakers, Cubs cap, and clothes in a pile beside him. Even Russ' watch was there, though the lid was dented and its crystal was cracked. *How did I get here? Where are the Puddlejumpers?*

As he stood to get dressed, he realized that the wheat

only came to his waist. He was no longer tiny! He checked the bottom of his foot. The Spiral Tattoo, the tattoo that had been there his entire life, was gone.

Turning in every direction, he called through cupped hands, *"Hooty-hooooo!"* He couldn't believe they would abandon him like this, and he wailed desperately to the rain.

"Hooty-hooooo . . ."

In the farmyard, Russ listened spellbound to the distant cry. It was the same sound he'd heard from the fields the night of Shawn's kidnapping. Suddenly he felt more alert than he'd ever felt in his entire life.

The calls carried down the slope and through the falling rain, *"Hooty-hooooo! Hooty-hooooo!"* Russ stepped to the edge of the wheat. Though his voice was tentative, he tried to imitate the strange sound as he called out, *"Hooty-hoo."*

The voice responded from high up in the field. *"Hooty-hooooo!"*

With growing conviction, Russ hurried through the wheat toward the ridge above. He called again, this time louder, *"Hooty-hooo!"*

In the upper field, Ernie listened, transfixed, to the sound of the distant voice.

"*Hooty-hooooo! Hooty-hooooo!!*"

Then he was running, running as fast as his legs had ever run, running through the wet wheat as the calls echoed closer and closer. He stopped and searched the sloped field, but all he saw was a steady rain. Suddenly a man appeared on the crest of the ridge, calling, "*Hooty-hoooo!*"

Ernie had waited a lifetime for this moment, and now he shouted the one thing that mattered most. "Dad!"

Russ shouted back, "Shawn!"

Father and son sprinted toward each other with all their might until they clung in a tight embrace. All around them the rain pattered the earth in a jubilant song.